LAND OF MY FATHERS

by

P. L. Crompton

A collection of interrelated stories set in a Welsh valley during the 1930s and 40s. Sometimes funny, sometimes sad, a glimpse of life as it may have been then.

Publisher: Crompton Fiction
www.cromptonfiction.com

Copyright: © P. L. Crompton
p.crompton @ nucleus.com

ISBN 978-0-9866701-0-7

Front Cover Photograph:
Felindre, Carmarthenshire, Wales
Taken from Rhiw Cyrff © P L Crompton

Cover Creator: www.inspiredcovers.com

To Lisa and Colton

And to Elizabeth

♥

LAND OF MY FATHERS

CONTENTS

MOELFRE'S FAMILIES

BECKINGHAM	Julius (& wife),
	Church Verger
	Gwyneth, their daughter
BRAITHWAITE	Richard, Major, retired
	Priscilla, his sister
DAVIES	Owen, Vicar
	Margaret, his wife
ELLIS	Morgan (& wife), Farmer
	Luned–m-Tom Jones
	Olwen–m-Emrys Griffiths
	Alun –m- Dilys Jenkins
	Ifor
EVANS	Ianto, Postmaster
	Siona, his wife
EVANS	Tom, Roadman
	Davy, their son
GRIFFITHS	Bogo, Mill Foreman
	Eira, his wife
	Emrys –m- Olwen Ellis
	Idris
GRIFFITHS	Emrys, Mill Worker
	Olwen, his wife
HUGHES	Ned, retired
	Sarah, his daughter

MOELFRE'S Families Cont'd

JENKINS	Mari, widow
	Dilys, her daughter
JONES	Davy-the-coal
	Arianwen, wife
JONES	Gwenna
JONES	Tom, mill worker
	Luned, his wife
	Geraint, son
LEWIS	Rodney
	Twm, his brother
OWENS	Constable
PRITCHARD	Rhys, D.A.I.
RICHARDS	Bronwen
SMITH	Joroway
STOCK	Elias, Red Lion
	Gladys, his wife
	Bethan, daughter
THOMAS	Eirlys, widow
	Davy, son,
	Dewi, Davy's son
THOMAS	Aled, farmer
	Millie, his wife
	Johnny, son
WILLIAMS	Rowlie, grocer
	Bette, his wife
WILLIAMS	William, teacher
	Helen, his wife
	Megan, daughter

♥

Welsh / English Translations

Ach a fi	disgusting
Arswyd	goodness gracious
Bore da	good morning
Calennig	New Year tradition
Cariad	darling, love
Diawl	devil
Duw mawr	good God, great God
Eisteddfod	a contest of the arts
Mamgu	grandmother
Mamgiau	grandmothers
Tocin	bagged lunch
Tylwyth Teg	fairies

ON WELSH NAMES

My grandparents' generation and theirs before them, generation after generation back to the time when the Bible first saw the light of a Welsh day, showed a remarkably restrained quality in their choice of names for their off-springs. Wales abounds with Biblical names, mostly David, which is to be expected in view of the name of our Patron Saint, and for some reason known only to the parents, Thomas is well to the fore, immediately shortened to Twm as though by unwritten law. This meant we had to find ways to differentiate between the men who share the same name. Half the village's male population would descend on you if you shouted "Twm! Come quick!"

It was no good tagging the surname onto the Christian name because the village shares, at the most, only five or six different ones, and thus was born the Welsh people's unique way of explaining to whom they

1

referred. Often picturesque; it is our poetic inheritance from the nomadic bards who once roamed the land in wake of the druids. If a stranger happened to overhear two people discuss one of the Davys, he knew immediately whom they are talking about and he knew where the man lived or knew his occupation. For instance, Davy-the-Coal. If you heard him mentioned in conversation and then saw a man delivering coal, you would know this was Davy-the-Coal. It didn't matter what else he did, even if he was the best pen and pencil artist around as Davy happened to be, he was Davy-the-Coal.

It wasn't always possible to differentiate between the Davys and Twms by tagging occupations onto their names. Davy-the-Fish, Davy-the-Bread, Twm-the-Milk, Twm-the-Organ (so named because he played the organ at evensong)—these are one-man occupations, the difficulty came when a stand of Davys entered the Forestry Commission, and a herd of Twms went to work at the Cow and Gate baby-food factory.

To a certain extent, tagging on house names alleviated the problem. The valley isn't large enough to boast row after row of terraced houses. Even the rank of six down by the bus stop have individual names emblazoned on the stones above their front doors, so none of our Davys and Twms suffered the fate of their city cousins who are often referred to as Davy-Number-Six or Twm-Number-Eleven, like pleasure boats waiting for their numbers to be called. When his day of judgement comes, one can imagine a voice booming from the clouds: "Come in Davy-Number-Six, your time is up!"

Our Davys and Twms were resplendent with names like Davy-Pen-Farm or Twm-Top-of-the-Hill (not to be confused with Twm-Bottom-of-the-Hill), but gradually, as more of the hilly countryside was built on to accommodate new generations of Davys and Twms, some house names, because of the terrain, began to be duplicated.

When such a thing happened and we found ourselves with three or four Twm-Top-of-the-Hills, idiosyncrasies were pounced on with glee and the unfortunates suffered having attention drawn to their shortcomings when their names were mentioned. Davy-the-Belly. Twm-the-Sniff. Even if they outgrew the description, even if Davy went on a diet and Twm stopped sniffing, the names stuck.

The women weren't exempt from this, either, at least not until they reached a certain age when their first names automatically became Miss, and the most memorable is Gwen Flycatcher—named for her habit of going around with her mouth hanging open.

With the advent of greater longevity, the problem became more acute and we'd take up the least little thing. Even a single action could earn a name that stuck for life. An unfortunate Twm acquired such a name after attending Chapel while suffering from a severe case of flatulence. He was fifteen or thereabouts when it happened but they didn't allow him to forget and the four-letter expletive followed him all his life.

We pounced on other things too, sometimes with irony but, more often, the pun was direct, such as the name given to man who lost all his back teeth—Twm-Central-Eating.

Occasionally, a man would forget the name he was born with, as happened at one of our festivals. The Eisteddfod was one of the highlights of our year, one of the few social gatherings not organized by the churches and chapels that abound in the valley. Not truly a festival, it is more of a cultural Olympics where people compete in various musical or recitation categories before a panel of adjudicators. One particular night, after Williams-the-School finished his solo, the call went out for the next competitor, Thomas Evans, to go up on stage. The three tenors sitting nervously in the wings, doubting their ability to equal William's performance, glanced at each other unmoving until the cry went up "Where's Twm-the-Song?" then all three got to their feet.

We viewed births with mixed feelings. We would offer congratulations follow by a tentatively put question: "What are you going to call him, then?" If the proud parents mentioned one of *them fancy names* there was a stunned silence, but if the answer affirmed they'd chosen one of the old names, in particular David or Thomas, the baby was toasted twice as deep, and before the mite was an hour old, we'd be mulling over suitable names to tag on the end.

This searching for names was a kind of national past time. We learned to practice the art at an early age and the playgrounds resounded with our fledgling efforts. No Pulitzer or Nobel could afford the same satisfaction as that of knowing one of our childish taunts would be on everyone's lips for the next seventy-odd years.

Ah, Wales; Land of My Fathers. You can bet there are a few Davys and Twms sprinkled among my ancestors too.

♥

(Previously broadcast on Canadian Broadcasting Corporation Radio, Alberta Anthology.)

P L Crompton

THE VALLEY

Hugged between ridges that extend like sheltering arms from Moelfre, the valley looks as if God came along one day with a spoon to scoop up the earth in search of worms for fishing.

The surrounding hills are steep, as if these imitations of the mountain pay homage by emulation. Topped by trees, the lower slopes bared for crops perhaps by the first people, the gentle Iberians, with no thought for those who would follow. No tractor can stay upright on the slopes, but horses can pull ploughs and men can walk the furrows, as their ancestors did. Now and then, the shallow earth yields arrow tips, mute evidence of the coming of the second race of people—the warring Celts.

From Moelfre's heights, in the early morning there is little to see in the valley except the ghostly shroud of river mist that crowds under the trees and lurks about the hedgerows. Like the mist of time, it could hide a Celtic hall, and at any moment, a druid's song of welcome to the sun might rise from the deepest density around the healing well.

Merlin himself blessed the well they say, and still the back-shivering respect for a magical past runs through the valley like a bogey, albeit tinged with a grin of scepticism. No, they give no credence to the powers of the druids in this modern age, and yet . . .

Old, as old as time it seems for none can mark her birth, the resident druid roams among the people. Mam Derw, a toothless soothsayer, a hobbling harridan, a menacing matron. A woman laughed at—but never to her face for she is a bringer of warts, a blighter of crops and a killer of cattle. A healer of men, she harbours old knowledge with the sadness of one with no disciples.

Defeated, the mist soon loses its fight with the sun and the spire of a more modern religion points a path of dissipation skyward. It marks the centre of the valley, the hub of this small universe where Saint Barnabas Church and the Primary School are at a standoff against the Post Office and the Red Lion Inn. By valley standards, Saint Barnabas is new, a mere hundred years old, and considered inferior to Penboyr, which has stood half way up the mountain like a sentinel for the last five hundred years. The oldest Anglicans hold the belief that Sunday worship is blasphemous unless they sing the opening hymn in the breathless wheeze brought on by the uphill climb, and there are those who believe they are nearer to God at that altitude. There was once a third church now moved to St. Fagan's museum near Cardiff. Built in the twelfth century, it held only twenty people, fifteen if the best trenchermen in the congregation took their constitutional to the same service. There are Baptist and Methodist chapels too, just to keep things balanced.

Time melds in the valley; dimensions traversed as easily as summer meadows. Some see the dead walk and some live in dread of shaming their dead, of committing an act that will damn their descendants for all time. Children have no fear of that horse-headed demonic kidnapper, Ladi Wen, nor do their bedroom wardrobes hide indescribable monsters. To goad them into good behaviour an elder need only mention their great-greats turning mortified cartwheels under their gravestones.

The past was only yesterday, and if Twm-Ty-Gwyn is not to be trusted, it is because his medieval great-great stole a loaf of bread from Davy-the-Bread's great-great. Poor Gwen Flycatcher—three times to church of a Sunday and never out of the house after dark— they brand a scarlet woman because her great-great dallied with Cromwell's soldiers when they came to gunpowder a nearby castle. Bad blood will out, they say.

9

The Reverend Davies, using this concern for those who have gone—and perhaps mindful of the damage to the walls of his churches by the earth-churning cart wheelers—will call to task any who forget their dead. From the height of his pulpit, with an accusing finger he'll thunder: "I see you're growing dandelions on your grandfather's grave, Mrs Evans."

The fir trees rising above the mist mark the banks of the Teifi. Perhaps the second largest river in Wales, it is good for fishing but only an Olympic swimmer or one bent on self-annihilation would dare its treacherous currents.

The trees themselves, the only sizeable stand of firs in a valley that once worshipped the oak, are part of the Plas Gwyn Estate. The first wattle-and-daub manor predates Penboyr. The one now, with its pristine white walls and stone columns, could easily stand centre to a Louisiana cotton plantation, but none considers it an incongruity. The Lord of the Manor was once a rough Norman knight, but the current owner is a retired Indian-Army Major. He lives there with his sister in the midst of elephant-foot tables and tiger skins. He rarely concerns himself with the valley people, except for Davy-Pen-Farm. Davy breeds thoroughbreds, and the Major fancies he is a good judge of horseflesh.

Davy owns the largest farm in the valley, and the last before Moelfre loses patience and towers to full height. The farm harbours one of the valley's peculiarities—a guard cock with a heart as black as his feathers. Even the stalwart, often fumbling Constable Owens takes to his heels if Blackie is about. Davy's dogs are no bother unless a slobbery lick is not to your liking. Most of the time, they lie in the sun like bales of fleece ready for carding and save their strength and their wits for the next sheepdog trials. Even then, they can't hold a whistle to the dogs Toby Rice sends out.

Toby's farm is farther down the hill and incorporates a quarry with walls the colour of Stonehenge. Not worked much any more, the County made him put a fence around the top after Granny Griffiths decided she could fly if she had a high enough place from which to kick off.

Granny Griffiths had been tuppence short of a shilling since the time she tried on Bogo's roller skates in their back garden. Like most of the gardens around the valley, it was on a slope and she started to gather speed, heading for the gate. Instead of leaving the gate shut for her to fetch up against, Bogo opened it and his granny sped through, across the road, through Old Ned's trellis gate and down his path toward the stone wall at the bottom. In danger of collapsing for years, with the arrival of Bogo's granny a whole section gave way. The hole stands, if a hole can be said to stand, as a monument to the old lady. Old Ned hasn't rebuilt it and he spends half his nights sitting up waiting for one of Toby's cows to come to munch on his lettuces, then he chases it off, shouting loud enough to wake the whole valley.

There are no coalmines. When the popular image of Wales is one of columns of coal-blackened men singing as they walk off shift, it isn't easy to convince people this valley, like most of Wales, is the antithesis of the bleak mining valleys to the east and north. The tenors of the valley can sing *Myfanwy* with the best and the choir is the best in the County, but there is one man you will see with his face black from the coal—Davy-the-Coal. He travels the valley with his cart and every day his customers expect to see his half-blind pony drop in its tracks. *Poor dab*, you'll hear them say as they shake their heads and watch the pony plod about. But wait, come the day before Davy makes his rounds there are a lot of black faces if the coal has run out and people resort to mixing water with the dust from their coal-shed floors to make hods. When placed on the fire, they smoke and sizzle like hell in a hailstorm.

Here, they do not mine the stone that burns. If black gold exists, if a plough turns it up or a spring flood sweeps nugget into the valley, it is returned to dark silence for in this valley living is gleaned from that part of the land touched by sunlight. Here are farmers and shepherds, foresters and millers.

The sound rising from the mist is not the song of a druid welcoming the sun, but listen carefully to the clackety-clack and the whoosh of the waterwheels as the woollen mills call to the faithful; is it not a song of welcome?

There are three mills: Drefychan, Cambrian and Dyffryn. All are water driven from the same mill pound drawn from the River Esgair by means of a ditch cut down the mountainside. There's talk of installing that modern magic, electricity, into Cambrian because by the time the pound gets there most of its power is spent, especially on the days the flourmill grinds and dips with vampiric wheels. If Cambrian goes electric, they'll no doubt charge more for the tapestry they weave, then Dyffryn will probably up the price of its blankets, and Drefychan . . . Well, it's doubtful it could increase the price of its tweeds, if you believe the choir members. A trip to London to sing at the Albert Hall, the first time out of Wales for most, and the high point was a group exclamation outside a shop window in Bond Street when they saw the price of a suit made from Drefychan tweed.

Even now, in the Depression that renders the rest of the world to doldrums, the valley seems untouched. It was never wealthy. The byword has always been make-do-and-mend, and what austerity others suffer now has always been a way of life in the valley. The impoverished Welsh. Impoverished by whose standard? Certainly not by theirs for they consider themselves the richest people on God's earth and they live by the adage what you have never had, you will never miss.

The valley has about it a quality of non-change, as though time has chosen this place to rest from the hurry of the world. Changes come, but so slowly, they become incorporated leisurely into a way of life that has existed since well before the Romans came to map the land with stone roads and bridges. Here is the home of the race descended from the ancient Demetae who held fast to their language, culture and religion during centuries of Roman occupation. It is from valleys such as this the Welsh created themselves out of the ragged remnants of Celtic lore.

Nevertheless, change is coming. The world is about to descend on the valley and drag it mumbling and stumbling into step as it faces its greatest onslaught.

♥

ROOTS

The roar of water tumbling down the mountainside grew tranquil when it reached the valley to meander beneath the trees where frogs lay spawn in shady backwaters. The gentle murmur of the river's song soothed the woman working on the bank.

On her knees, Mam Derw dipped and skimmed with the Robertson's jar that once held jam and had a paper golliwog glued to its side. Dip. Skim. Lift. Check. Satisfied, she screwed the lid onto the jar half-filled with frogspawn and dropped it into her pocket before rising to sit on a log.

For more than a decade, her knees ached if she knelt too long in wet grass. In the battered handbag tied to her belt, she rummaged among the vials and packets until she found the one she wanted. Opening the screw of oiled paper, she placed a pinch of its contents under her tongue. In the past year, the dose had doubled in size and, for the first time in summer, she kept the lamb's wool wrapped around her knees.

Mam Derw replaced the packet of herbs and fastened the clasp of the bag. Without looking up, she said, "You come out, Dewi Thomas. I know you're there."

For a moment, Dewi was tempted to stay ducked behind a tree barely wide enough to hide his spindly nine-year-old body. Perhaps she didn't really know he was there and only said what she did on the off chance he was. She couldn't have heard him because he'd left the bike with the squeaky wheel at the gate and tip toed the rest of the way.

In the branches above him a magpie screeched, the cry close enough to make Dewi jump. That's how she knew, he decided. The magpie told her. They said witches had familiars. The magpie must be hers. She had a black cat too, and when he went to her cottage last winter to carry in firewood he'd seen a witch's broom standing in a corner.

"Come on, boy! I need your help here."

Dewi hesitated. What if she needed his help to catch toads for their legs or newts for their eyes? His dat said to be polite to all grown-ups and that included Mam Derw. He stepped away from the tree. Dreading the answer, he asked, "What do you want help with?"

"I want the roots of them marsh golds." Mam Derw pointed to the yellow flowers poking above the water a few steps from the bank. She held out a two-pronged length of iron. "Take off your shoes and socks then you can go into the water and dig them up."

Dewi did as she bade him and stepped into the river. It was cold and mud oozed between his toes. He shivered, not sure if the chill he felt was because of the cold water or the nearness of the old woman. Gulping a breath, as if he could inhale courage, Dewi said: "You promised you'd give me an eagle's egg if I do enough things to help you."

"An eagle's egg is special. It'll take a special favour to earn it."

Mam Derw watched Dewi bend to his task. This wasn't the one, helpful though he was at times; it had to be a girl child. Tradition dictated she pass her skills to a daughter as her Mam had, and Mamgu, and all the Mamgiau of the past stretching back to when the druids first walked the valley.

Some said Merlin himself visited, breaking his journey to Caerfyrddyn, the town named for him. That was more than a thousand years earlier when the place was a Roman fort named Moridunum, but Mam Derw's antecedent, Ceinwen of Moelfre, was there to offer comfort to the powerful wizard.

"Long life," Ceinwen said, and Merlin blessed Ceinwen and her descendants with the same. And a long life it had been, even to this last of Ceinwen's line. Mam Derw couldn't remember the year of her birth, nor could anyone else for she was the valley's oldest inhabitant.

There would be none after her, no wise woman to take her place for she had no daughter. In the old days, they could steal or barter for a daughter not born naturally, but men made laws to end the practice. She had been comely enough before the time when the years forced her to pluck the whiskers from her chin, but no man came near. She had a difference about her that frightened them, and she knew not how to talk to men except to give instructions on the remedies she dispensed.

She never knew her father. The daughters of Merlin lay with men only for the time it took to conceive a daughter. They lived alone, steeped in their art and training their daughters to succeed them, each in her generation. Until now. Her time must end soon, and with her death the magical three of mountain, well and wise woman would end. They would forget her and, without her, they'd forget the well. Only the mountain would endure, the last of the three, as it had been the first of the three.

The world was changing, the old ways faltering. Even she was different from others of her line and, although her pride denied it, Mam Derw knew she was a disgrace to her profession. Over the generations, the skills passed on by word of mouth without written record had declined and she knew only a portion of what her Mamgu had known. These days, people were more prone to laugh at her than stand in awe, but at least none denounced her as a witch for burning.

Dewi climbed onto the bank and held out a bedraggled rope of flowers and roots. "Is this what you wanted?"

Mam Derw snatched the offering and studied the stalks. "You broke one. The root's still back there."

"I'll never find it without the flowers." Dewi dropped the iron tool and reached for his shoes and socks.

"Hmph!" Mam Derw grumbled. She wrapped the stalks around her hand until roots, stalks and flowers formed a clump she could cram into her bag. Pulling hard on the hawthorn stick she used as a cane, she struggled to her feet, pausing until the pain in her knees subsided. Then she bent to pick up the two-pronged iron and hobbled into the trees toward the well.

Tying the last shoelace, Dewi watched her go. He'd given her special help, special because she'd never have gone for the roots herself. Hadn't he read witches were frightened of water and they'd never go into it? Without him, she wouldn't have her marsh-gold roots. However, he could wait for the eagle's egg; more urgent was the need to have an answer about something that had bothered him since he first saw the well. Now might be the time to ask. He ran after her.

At the well, Mam Derw had paused to catch her breath when Dewi reached her. He halted and chewed on his lip when she looked at him. "I've been meaning to ask you . . . The rags . . ."

Around the well, she'd tied strips of cloth to the branches of trees and bushes. Some were faded to a dull grey or frayed where birds had taken threads to line their nests, others were newer, their colours and patterns still bright.

"Why are they here?"

"Have you never heard of a healing well?" When Dewi shook his head, Mam Derw muttered to herself, both angry and sad. Children nowadays knew all about the Greeks and Romans but nothing about the Celts.

In anger, she tugged a rag free of a branch and then reached for others. "This was for your grandfather." She held out a strip of flannel where faint lines of colour wove through the faded scrap.

Dewi hid his hands behind his back, afraid she expected him to take the rag.

"When your grandfather was hurt, your gran came to me." Came in the dead of night, a shawl over her head for fear someone would recognize her going to the witch-woman's door. "This was to heal his leg; to take the badness from him into this rag."

"It didn't work," said Dewi. "He always walked with a limp after that."

"But he walked." Mam Derw bent and, with the same tool Dewi used to dig up the roots, she dug a shallow hole in the moist earth. While she buried the rags, she muttered all the while: "This for Ianto Maesgwyn when he had diphtheria; this for Maggie-Rose-Cottage to bring her a living child; this for Ardwy Bronddu—" It failed to work. Heulwen Bronddu should have come to her sooner, before the modern medicine had done its worst.

A failure. Mamgu wouldn't have failed. If only she'd remembered the right incantation, the right ritual, the right herb, Ardwy would have lived.

She sighed and stamped a mound of earth over the rags, and then Mam Derw climbed onto the path to her cottage.

Dewi looked at the rags still tied to the branches. If the rags she buried were for those now dead, the ones still tied around the well would be for those living. If people didn't believe in witches or in her power, why were there so many rags? And how many rag burials were there beneath his feet? He studied the newest grave and saw the length of iron lying in the grass. He picked it up and called after her. When she didn't respond, he followed her into the sunlight on the path.

"You forgot this." He stood uncertainly, as she drew him into focus.

Mam Derw took the tool without a word then carefully rubbed the dirt from it with her thumb as she studied him. "One day . . ." She looked away, casting her gaze up the valley to the mountain and her eyes grew troubled as she looked into Dewi's future. Sometimes her gift was a curse. "One day you'll go to the mountain. You'll forget to come to me, just like all the others."

Dewi shivered in the heat of the sun and saw the sadness fade from her eyes.

She drew her attention from the mountain and her eyes and voice grew sharp. "What are you waiting for? You haven't earned an eagle's egg!"

Dewi backed away as though struck, not able to understand the change in her.

"Go on!"

Dewi ran. For some time he'd had no fear of her. Different, she was, just an old woman who needed his help to dig roots and carry wood. Not that he was fond of her, as if she'd been his gran or something, but he'd felt comfortable with her. He halted at a turn in the path and looked back.

Mam Derw brandished the hawthorn stick. "Go on! You get away from here!" She watched Dewi run, and then dropped her voice. "Spying on an old woman! Next thing, you'll be like them others, tying me up for a witch and setting fire about me."

But no, that wasn't her, that was another lifetime, another woman; one of the

Mamgiau of the past. Nevertheless, for a moment the flames came close enough to burn her face.

JOROWAY'S ARK

During the early years of the Thirties, social gatherings were restricted to Church- or Chapel-organized events. Fortunately, active amateur dramatic groups blessed the valley. Scarcely a winter month went by without some form of entertainment as spin-offs of the main group vied with each other to enthral their neighbours. The year began with January's bawdy pantomime and ended with December's Christmas play.

Davy Evans was fourteen the winter the Christmas Play Committee decided to do away with the usual offering. The primary-school children were more convincing as the three kings, anyway. They considered replacing it by staging the pantomime before New Year's a blasphemous break with tradition, so they had to devise a new Christmas play.

With that in mind, the drama group held a meeting in early November. Davy's father, Tom, a long-standing member who invariably played the lead male role, went along. At his mother's insistence, Davy accompanied him to make sure the walk home didn't include a detour to the Red Lion.

They held the meeting in the village hall, in the slope-floored auditorium. In what would be the orchestra pit in fancier theatres, several members of the drama group drew their chairs into a circle. Where normally children sat for a worm's-eye view of a performance, there now sat Julius Beckingham, verger of Saint Barnabas, present to ensure they upheld Christian values. Next to Julius, Bronwen-Rose-Cottage overflowed her chair. She would contribute little unless they discussed music. When called upon, Bronwen could be a formidable Valkyrie and they could count on her to end every production with rousing renditions of *Land of My Fathers* and *God Save the King*.

Sitting back from the others was Williams-the- School. William, son of Rowlie who ran the grocery shop, had done well. He went away to college and come back to teach at the village school. Most of the boys hated him. He terrorized them during their last year at Primary, and their parents were forever holding him up as an example of how well a boy could do if he spent more time on his homework.

Huddled close to William, Bogo Griffiths furtively slid up the cuff of his battered trench coat to check his watch as he calculated how many rounds he was missing at the Red Lion. His face brightened when he saw Tom, then he scowled when he saw Davy, knowing why he was there.

"You sit there then, Davy." Tom indicated one of the hard chairs set apart from the group.

Davy sat and took out the comic he'd brought.

"What's that you're so deep into, eh?" a voice asked.

Startled, Davy looked up at the man breezed in late. "It's—"

However, Rodney Lewis didn't expect or want an answer. He never did. Bit of a spiv was Rodney. Black patent shoes, cavalry-twill trousers and black blazer, he bounced up to the group, swung a chair around and straddled it with his forearms resting on the back. "What's to do?" he asked.

Davy returned to his comic while they thrashed out the details of the play. It was to be the story of Noah building the Ark.

"You'll play Noah, of course, Tom," one of them said, and Tom nodded his head in gracious acceptance. Bronwen would play Noah's wife; William, Bogo and Rodney would play Noah's sons. They left out Julius. It not being a production put on by the church, he would take no active part except as a censoring eye for God.

William was to write the play during the coming week. Quickly, he outlined the direction it would take. "We'll have some children to heckle Noah at the beginning," he said. "Later, we can dress them up as animals to enter the Ark."

"We'll have Davy in on that," said Tom, glancing in Davy's direction. If his wife insisted on having Davy accompany him, Tom would make sure he had a valid reason so no one in the village could point a finger and snigger.

The following week they met again with the addition of the three women who were to play Noah's daughters-in-law. William handed out copies of his play and the arguing began over the length of the lines allotted. Once they made the changes, they read the play quickly and to Julius' approval. They settled on the Friday before Christmas as the night of the performance and Rodney set about designing posters to advertise it. Then William raised the question of scenery.

"The play is about the building of the Ark," he said. "The wings can be the forest scene we used last year for Sleeping Beauty, but the backdrop has to be a boat of some kind."

"Never get a whole one on stage," commented Bogo.

"Then we'll have to have just one side of a boat," said Tom.

"Good," said William. "We'll leave it with you then."

"No, no, I didn't mean that," Tom protested. "I'm too busy. Got this part and I'm playing Widow Twankey in the panto in January."

"You've got more time than any of us," said Rodney, and he was right. Tom was a roadman for the County, scything the hedges and verges along the ways in and out of the village. In November, nothing grew and there was little for him to do. In the matter of time, he was in a better situation than any one of them, but Tom was no carpenter. He had only to look at a doorframe for the nails to pop out.

"I can't," he said.

"Get someone to help you," said Bogo. "Joroway's not a bad carpenter, and he's a retired seaman so he'll know about boats."

At the mention of Joroway's name, one of the women gave a little shriek and Bronwen took out a lace handkerchief she held delicately to her nose as though he was already among them.

The man referred to was Joroway Smith. Greased hair and clothes of a steamboat man he moved through the village like a pungent black cloud. Little boys eyed his unwashed state with envy; little girls ran screaming for their mothers' skirts.

Twenty miles from the sea, a lengthy charabanc ride in those days, Joroway could find no steady work. The stream bubbling through the village was too shallow to float even a child's toy boat and the Teifi less than a mile away, bigger, deeper and swift currented, gave little opportunity for boating except in the placid stretches downstream where coracles sometimes floated nets on balmy evenings.

For a living, he did odd jobs: a roof tile replaced here and there; laying scythe to orchard grass; rebuilding a wall. Joroway existed frugally in his small cottage with its weed-strewn vegetable patch. His dwelling boasted no modern plumbing; he carried water up the hill from a well set close to Rose Cottage. Bronwen often spoke of the infrequent visits Joroway paid to the well. In winter, he came not at all, taking for his water the run off gathered from the troughs of his cottage and stored in a wooden barrel. Only in late summer, with the barrel's contents reduced to wormy sludge, did Joroway visit the well. Even then, he carried away no more than a kettleful, enough to quench his thirst.

Elected carpenter for the group, they delegated Davy's father to approach Joroway and enlist his help. Never voluble unless he had an audience, when Tom returned from the visit to Joroway he was deep in thought as he took his usual place before the fire. Chair propped back on two legs, his feet wedged against the brace of the mantelpiece, he mumbled in response to his wife's probing about the interior of Joroway's home. At length, he nodded to himself and said: "He's a good man, is Joroway."

"Is he going to help you, Dat?" Davy asked.

Tom nodded. "Took some persuading, mind."

"What's the house like inside?" Davy's mother demanded to know. "Is it a pigsty?"

"I suppose . . ." said Tom. "Never really noticed."

"Men!" Deprived of a juicy titbit of gossip, Davy's mother walked away in disgust.

Davy, too, was eager for information. They knew little about Joroway even though he'd lived in the village for more than six years. He kept much to himself, but Tom, upon deliberation, decided Joroway was a good man.

In late November, they entered into rehearsals in earnest at the front of the stage while Joroway sawed and hammered behind the scenes. Gravitating to helping him, Davy passed hammer and nails and sawed the odd piece of wood as Joroway raised the side of the half-built Ark against a wooden frame. They'd use it for the first acts and add a top half for the last act, arranged so it could be propped into place.

As he worked, Joroway talked in a voice low enough not to intrude upon the actors, and all the children gathered about him while they waited for their cue to go on stage. He'd been a steamboat man, plying up and down the Mississippi he said was a hundred times bigger than their mighty Teifi. He told them of the gamblers and the dance hall girls and of Indians watching silently from the riverbanks. In addition, he remembered the names of all the riverboats.

"There was the Western Engineer," said Joroway, "the first one up the Mississip. And the New Orleans—the boat, not the city— the Virginia and the Louisiana. Then there was the Natches and the Robert E. Lee. Had a race they did, back in June of 1870."

"Did you see the race, Mr Smith?" one of the younger children asked.

"No," said Joroway, "but I saw the Sprague. Strongest paddle wheeler that ever was, was the Sprague; could pull sixty coal barges and them weighing 67,000 tons. In 1917, that was."

"You remember all those details?" Waiting to go on stage, William eyed Joroway with interest.

"Oh, aye," said Joroway. "Blessed with a good memory, I am."

A born storyteller, and too long without an audience, Joroway seemed a different man when he spoke of his beloved steamboats. Through his eyes, the children saw the paddlewheels churning the water; the hurricane, boiler and Texas decks; the pilothouses; and the tall funnels belching black smoke as they approached a levee. It got so the children felt they knew America and the Americans manning the boats, many of them cabin boys no older than they were. In their minds' eyes, they saw the captain ring the bell and they heard him holler: "All a-b-o-a-a-rd!"

With the sawing and hammering of the lower half of the Ark done, Joroway began to sand it and William ordered the children off the stage except Davy. He had the job of helping Joroway hold the structure steady while Tom, pretending to be Noah, hammered away at imaginary nails.

Joroway was fascinated, eyeing Tom with the same look of rapture Davy saw on his face when he spoke of the paddle steamers. He would stop his work and stand in the wings taking in Tom's every word and gesture. Tom was a ham, overacting to the extent that he overshadowed the rest of the cast, but Joroway couldn't get enough of him.

A week before the performance, and with the top of half of the Ark not done, they rushed Joroway to hospital with pneumonia. The worst of the illness had passed by the time Bronwen noticed the absence of smoke from Joroway's chimney. She summoned Tom and Bogo to investigate, and then Rodney drove the sick man to Carmarthen General.

While he was away, an army of the women involved in the drama group descended on Joroway's cottage with mops and buckets,

Davy's own mother among them. Out of school for the holidays, Davy had to help lift and carry. They hauled out the sacks of potatoes, carrots and turnips, reducing Joroway's hoard as they threw out the rotten ones stinking up the cottage. They scrubbed and disinfected the contents of Joroway's steamer trunk, gave his bedding the same treatment, and threw out the disreputable mattress. Davy helped his father carry a replacement donated from an attic bedroom in the Rectory up the hill.

One task Davy saved for himself. Sneaking it home when his mother wasn't looking, he set about cleaning Joroway's peaked seaman's cap. A bit of Dab-It-Off got rid of the grease stains on the dark cloth, and then a rub of Brasso made the badge above the peak shine like gold.

With everything in the house spick and span, they set traps to catch the mice nesting in the wainscoting and elected Tom to go up every day to empty and reset the mousetraps and to keep the fire going. Davy was with him the day Rodney brought Joroway home.

He scarce recognized Joroway as he stood in the doorway looking around his home as if he'd never seen it before. He was as clean scrubbed as the cottage. Unlike the pleasure Davy expected, the look on Joroway's face made him wonder if they hadn't gone too far, meddling in his life and imposing their own ideas of cleanliness on him. Joroway looked angry, but he said nothing.

"I've been working on the Ark," Davy said, hoping to turn aside Joroway's anger.

Joroway nodded. "There's two days yet. I'll have her finished in time," he said through clenched teeth as he walked past Davy in a cloud of carbolic.

They held their dress rehearsal the night after Joroway came home. He put in a brief appearance to check how much Davy had done on the Ark and then he sat in the empty auditorium to watch the play. When it was over, he rose to leave, promising to have the top part completed before they raised the curtain the following night.

Tom first complained of a sore throat at breakfast the next morning. Davy's mother dosed him with honey and vinegar and wrapped a woollen sock around his neck before he left to spread sand on a slippery patch outside the hall. He was back at lunchtime, still complaining. By teatime, when they left for the hall, his voice had all the sonorous charm of a bullfrog. An hour before the play was to begin and with a few early arrivals picking out their seats, Tom's voice deserted him.

There was panic backstage amid the wood shavings where Joroway finished the Ark that afternoon. They hadn't cast anyone as Tom's understudy because they were all involved with the pantomime. William was busy trying to write himself out as Noah's son so he could play the lead role, when Joroway appeared.

Joroway knew what was wrong the minute Tom mouthed at him like a goldfish. "I'll do Tom's part," he said.

"That's the stupidest thing I've ever heard," snapped Rodney.

"Wait a min—" William began to speak but Bogo interrupted.

"We can't let him do it, not Joroway! He'll ruin the play. They'll all be laughing at us."

"That's right," said Bronwen, on the verge of tears with first-night nerves anyway. "You rewrite it, William, and we'll muddle through."

"Are you sure you can do it, Joroway?" William asked. The resulting volley of protests caused the pianist, engaged to entertain the audience before the curtain rose, to play louder to cover the row.

"Got a good memory," said Joroway. "And I've been watching Tom."

"We don't have time to argue," said William, settling the matter by exerting his authority as playwright and director. Joroway would play Noah while Tom helped Davy steady the Ark.

In Noah's flowing robes that were a bit too short, the curtain rose on Joroway hammering imaginary nails as a group of children heckled him for building a boat so far from the sea. Given his remarkable memory and the times when he'd watched Tom, Joroway knew every line and gesture. Davy was uneasy and remembered Joroway's face when he arrived home to see what they'd done to his cottage. He expected Joroway to get his revenge on the drama group that night, but the first acts when without a hitch. It was in the last act Joroway got back at them.

As they hoisted the upper portion of the Ark into place, Davy saw what Joroway had been busy with that afternoon. When the curtain rose, he peered through a gap in the boards to check the audience's reaction. Sitting in the front row, Julius, the vicar, and all the Church elders were in shock. Mouths agape, they stared in wonder at the two-funnelled steamboat filling the back of the stage. The children, dressed as lions, lambs and chickens, emerged from the wings on cue while, from the other side, Joroway walked to centre stage.

On his head, Joroway wore the cap Davy cleaned, the glittering badge rivalling the star on the Christmas tree at the front of the hall. Imitating Tom's expansive gesture, Joroway threw his arm wide, waving the children toward a doorway in the Ark, and bellowed:

"All a-b-o-a-a-rd!"

♥

P L Crompton

CALL OF THE CURLEW

It was raining. Again. However, to Davy-the-Coal's mind there was nothing like the serenity of fresh-washed countryside. He tried to keep it in mind while the rain tapped drumming fingers into the sack thrown across his shoulders as cushion for the numbing weight of black gold he humped from cart to coal shed.

So many times, he vowed never to make this trek again. It wasn't as if he made a sale, but every week he came, regular as Friday fish, and every week he turned the cart around and headed back. Once, he left a sack of coal without bidding. It stood untouched until the hemp, rotted, vole chewed, fell apart, and the black nuggets burrowed into a pit of their own making. Like as not she'd be at home today, what with the rain and all; and like as not she wouldn't answer the door.

Thirty years without forgiveness. Thirty years of shame, and her father's condemning voice thundering righteously over his bowed head, over the trembling white of her flesh. Elfed was gone now to the Bible-thumping heaven of the Methodists. Did he look down and know the only sin was the sin of his own evil mind? They were without blame. Davy's only crime was the need to put on paper the wonder of the human form, to capture forever with charcoal the vital, glowing ideal that was Heiddwen. He never touched her beyond placing a bough of honeysuckle in her hands, and she— Was there truth in her father's accusations? Was it truth held her face turned away all these years?

How did she live? Some said she walked twenty miles to Cardigan to buy her needs, others said she never ventured beyond the shelter of the forest and lived on what she found there. It would be roots and berries; Heiddwen wouldn't harm a living creature. Once, when a spider crawled from the straw onto a trembling thigh, he reached to brush the blemish away. She caught his hand, dark eyes pleading mercy, and bade him wait. He remembered the twitch of her flesh and the clenching of her fists as she fought the torment the spider crawled across the soft mound of her belly and the rise of her breast. Had she held his hand longer than necessary, closer to her thigh than needed? Was it only Elfed's foul mind that gave birth to those thoughts and caused the shame in her eyes?

Nevertheless, she ran from him, refused to speak to him. Held away from all the backdrops he chose for her beauty. He saw her once, ten years earlier, running across a meadow with a hawk circling overhead. Thin she was; the once rounded flesh lost against the sharp angle of bones in threadbare rags. The life was gone from her, and from him. No more the heart-singing joy as he captured the glow of a sunbeam playing on the curve of her hip. These days the sketches he made were of coal-blackened men who burrowed like moles for the stones that burned. Heavy charcoal. Black drawings of blackness. Dark like shame.

Davy kept a tight grip on the rope as he led the pony and cart onto the slope to the river path. A wall of rain hid the Teifi from view, the tumbling crash of the waterfall muted as if appeased by the offering that swelled its might, then, when the path led him away from the river, the sound was lost beneath the tap of rain.

Beneath the trees, drops clustered on boughs fell like hammering fists. The pathway was awash with peat and pine needles that clung to his boots, and with every step, his heels pitched splatters high as the string tied about each trouser leg beneath his knees. Beside him the pony's hooves slithered over hidden roots, its head bowed as if weighted by the soak of water in its mane and in the blackened-leather blinkers. Davy glanced behind them as the cart creaked and lurched over a root. Thankfully, as always when he made this call there were few full sacks to bog down the wheels, but the dust, swept out each day to make hods for his own use, washed in black rivulets from the tailgate to mingle with the land from which it was wrested.

A rotted branch gave way beneath the pelt of rain and fell with a soft thud onto the battered bluebells. The pony hesitated, mane trembling free of the sheet of rain, but Davy had no word of ease, no touch of comfort beyond a steadying of the leather in his hand. He was as far removed from the pony as he was from his youth's dream of capturing the light of the world with pen and pencil.

The cottage huddled in what was once a sizeable clearing. Now the undergrowth reclaimed its own, blackberry thickets thorning around boarded windows to braid into the mouldy thatch. The witch's house of childhood nightmares. The path through the tangle to the door was barely discernible, hardly more than a rabbit track. Davy raised cold hands to his lips and gave the curlew's cry that had always been their signal.

What did he expect? That she would dance into sunlight, her hair tied with a ribbon she would tear free once she was beyond her mother's eye. Davy raised his face to the rain. "Heiddwen!"

A sheltering crow, startled to anger, stirred and refolded wings the coal black sheen of Heiddwen's hair. Tumbling like a river to the swell of her hip, the remembered contrast of black hair against white skin could still bring an ache to his heart. "Heiddwen."

The rain eased up as Davy retraced his steps. He entered the trees and saw the wall of water over the river had thinned to a damp drizzle, but overhead boughs released a weight of splattering aimed at the back of his neck like accusing blows. From Arianwen.

Did Arianwen know of his weekly visits here? Did she note the pine needles clinging to his trouser legs? Aware this was the only pine forest in the area, did she know where he had been? She questioned him only once, after Eira Griffiths gave vent to her gossipy tongue and told his bride of the scandal. No, he hadn't touched Heiddwen. No, she was not a hussy or a whore. No, she was not as beautiful as Arianwen. No, he had no sketches kept of Heiddwen only those of Arianwen. Arianwen in her apron with the dullness of a kitchen at her back; Arianwen in the dark stable brushing a black pony; Arianwen at a small grave, a thunder sky overhead and a bleak landscape.

Ah, Heiddwen.

Young, he'd been, seventeen to her twenty-five. A scandalous age for a woman to be unwed. His youth brought him forgiveness, and two years spent in Llanelli with his uncle. Two years in the hell of the coal mines where the light of the world died around him, within him. Did she think he had deserted her? Left her to the forbidding silence of sinners glad to cast stones that drew attention from their own misdeeds?

Free of the trees, Davy halted the pony at the foot of the slope and walked to the river. Two thousand years before, the Romans needed three arches to carry the road over the torrent, now only one would have done, for the Teifi that must once have rivalled the Thames in width, had shrunk to one treacherous channel racing beneath a single arch.

Davy clambered across boulders, wet now with rain instead of river, and paused at the edge of the flow. He hunkered and reached into his vest pocket for a Woodbine. He struck a match and held it to the cigarette before flicking the sliver of wood into the river. For a moment, it floated against a rock, and then the narrow torrent swept it out of sight. Beyond the arch, the Teifi had clawed a pool as if it needed a resting place before it continued the headlong rush to the sea. A dark pool under a heavy canopy of branches that, now and then, plopped drops of water onto the surface below. Watching the rings appear, Davy could almost believe the disturbances came from the depths, like hands reaching up from a watery hell. No one knew how deep the pool was. Deep enough to drown. A truth known to many.

A dark place, they said the Romans built the bridge on the bones of Celtic children.

Some said you could hear the children's cries on Midsummer's night if the air was still. And there were newer ghosts, though none joined them for the last dozen years. Two there were then and the vicar's wife praying for forgiveness for not having recognized Meinir's cry for help. And the baby . . .

"Don't you think he looks like a little angel today?" Meinir asked of Margaret Davies, holding Owen to show the white of his clothes, and the vicar's wife agreed, telling her all babies were angels in the eyes of the Lord.

Locked in the crook of her arm and lulled by the dark pool, did the angel demanded entry for his mother when he got to Heaven? Bruised as she was, battered against the Teifi's confines, they knew her for when hadn't she tried to hide her bruises from them. For shame, Tudor, husband of Meinir, for shame, and Tudor sold the farm and went from among them.

For shame. Was his own shame any less when the blows he dealt Arianwen were the blows of omission? *Of course I love you, now leave me be. People of our age don't talk of love all the time.* If their child had lived . . . If there had been other children . . .

Davy sucked the last of the cigarette, felt the glowing tip sting against a fingernail and flicked the butt into the river. He watched it out of sight beneath the arch then he rose and trudged to where the pony waited. He looked back once, thinking he heard a curlew cry, but there was only the river clinging to the narrow channel it had carved for itself.

♥

BY ROMANY LAW

Dewi was racing grass snakes along the top of the pigsty wall. Holding them behind their heads, he dragged two along. "Vroom, vroom!"

In the corner where the wall met the barn, three more snakes untangled and started to slither away. Dewi picked up the two in his hands and grabbed for the others when he heard his gran calling.

"Dewi? Dewi, where are you? Drat the boy; he's never around when I want him. Dewi!"

"I'm here, Gran." Dewi popped up from behind the wall.

"What're you doing there?" Suspicion in her eyes, Eirlys walked toward him and stopped with a shudder when she saw the writhing mass in his hands. "One of these days you'll pick up a viper and it's meeting your Maker you'll be."

"I can tell the difference."

"Never mind that now. Get on your bike and let them know in the village the Gypsies are back on Moelfre." She turned toward the house, saying over her shoulder: "And don't go putting any snakes in your pocket like you did last week. Gave me a turn when I went looking for your handkerchief to wash."

"No, Gran." Reluctantly, Dewi released the tangled mass and the snakes slithered across the garden, anxious to be done with racing. One disappeared into the row of cabbages and Dewi dived after it as it weaved between the leaves. "Not you, Speedy," he said. "You're the fastest one of the lot. I'm going to keep you." He raised the flap of his jacket pocket and dropped the snake inside where he kept all his other treasures: a piece of string, the stub of a pencil, the whistle his dat made him and a handkerchief with a partially sucked bulls-eye mint tied into a corner.

"Hurry up," Eirlys called from the house.

"Yes, Gran." Dewi lifted his bike away from the wall beside the kitchen window. "Just going, Gran."

"Don't waste any time," she called after him as he pedalled across the farmyard and swung onto the road.

A few yards down the hill, Dewi veered into a gateway and pushed the bike into the field. He propped it out of sight behind a bank of blackberry brambles then crept along the hedge until he was adjacent to the barns. He elbowed his way through a gap in the hedge and checked the yard. His gran was nowhere in sight, only the sheepdogs dozing in the sun.

Dewi skittered to the nearest barn. The galvanized ridges pressed against his back as he edged to the door and slipped inside. Groping through the darkness, his fingers found what he was fumbling for—his father's bike. He took a grip of the handlebars and wheeled it toward the door.

One of the sheepdogs raised his head to look at Dewi then thumped a lazy tail as Dewi brought the bike from the barn and dragged it through the hedge. At the gate, he climbed onto a bar and swung his leg over the bike. He pushed off. Wobbling over the rutted entrance to the field, he reached the road and swung onto the downhill slope to the village.

The bike was too big for him but his own bike was too small. If he rode it in the village, the other children laughed at him because he had to pedal with his knees thrust out on either side like jug ears otherwise they hit the handlebars.

Pen Farm was on high ground above the village, the last farm before the mountain proper began. From there it was downhill all the way, so it didn't matter if his feet couldn't reach the pedals, with his legs held out on either side like a water boatman's he could freewheel down the hill. As he gathered speed, his jacket flapped around his skinny ten-year-old body and the pocket with the snake thunk-thunked against his back.

"Where are you off to in such a hurry?" Mari Jenkins called as he zoomed past her gate.

"Gypsies on Moelfre," he shouted, knowing if he looked back, he would see her scurrying up the path to lock herself inside the house.

At the top of Corpse Hill, he skidded to a halt, balanced against the stile with one foot, and studied the slope ahead. Dat said never to ride down Corpse Hill because, if your brakes ever failed, you'd shoot over the hedge at the bottom and end up in the river.

Dewi chewed his lip as he decided what to do. The road surface was rough paving which would skin him if he fell off the bike. Each side of the road, grassed earth banks rose straight as cliffs, the hedges above them prickly with holly and hawthorn. If he went slowly . . . If he braked, every few yards to keep his speed down . . . Dewi aimed the front wheel at the hill.

Half way down, his eyes on the oak overhanging the road where he planned to apply the brakes, Dewi heard shouting. He squeezed the brake levers against the handlebars and drew the bike to a stop, one foot braced against the bank for balance.

"You young varmint! I'll have the police on you!"

The voice was unmistakable. Behind the hedge, old Toby Rice yelled in fury. Miserable, Toby was. He'd sent Constable Owens up to Pen Farm the year before after Dewi and his friends picked plums in the quarry. Toby would rather see the fruit rot on the trees than let the boys have it.

Dewi waited, expecting to see one of his friends scamper over the hedge, but the boy who came was a stranger. Black haired, with skin the colour of a ripe chestnut, he was a year or two older than Dewi. Sack clutched in one hand he looked scared, his eyes wild as he looked up and down the road and Toby's voice drew closer.

Dewi tweaked the bicycle bell to get the boy's attention. "Hop on." He indicated the crossbar. When the boy hesitated, he urged again: "Come on, or he'll catch you."

A holly bush rustled at the top of the hedge and Toby's cursing came from right beside it as the boy ran to Dewi. He hoisted himself side-saddle onto the crossbar, one hand braced on the handlebars, the other clutching the sack. Dewi kicked off and allowed the bike to gain speed as it raced away from Toby toward the sharp corner at the bottom.

Dewi pulled hard on the brakes and felt the bike wobble as it fought against the rubber pads. It veered around the bend out of control and skidded onto the grass verge outside the

Vicarage, depositing the boys in a tangled heap beneath a clump of rhododendrons.

"Are you hurt?" Dewi asked and examined his skinned knee.

"'Course not," the boy said. "Whatcha 'elp me for?"

Dewi shrugged. "Don't like Toby Rice, is all. Why's he chasing you?"

"These." The boy held up the sack. "Been snarin' rabbits from around the quarry."

"Poaching?"

"Never!" The boy's black eyes widened with innocence. "Chased the rabbits all the way down from the top of the mountain, didn't I? Is it my fault I didn't catch 'em 'til they got to Rice's fields?"

Dewi considered that while he applied a gob of spittle to his knee. "I suppose it isn't poaching then . . ."

"'Course it's not." The boy leapt to his feet, sack slung casually over one shoulder.

"What's your name?" Dewi squinted up at him.

"Seth. What's yours?"

"Dewi. How old are you?"

Seth hiked a shoulder. "Thirteen, mebbe."

"Don't you know when you were born?"

"'Course I know. It was the same year Leah was made *phuri dai*."

The words were neither Welsh nor English and Dewi was at a loss. "What's that mean?"

"*Phuri dai*—Headwoman. I was dropped the same year."

"Dropped?"

"Yeah! Borned! Don'tcha know nothin'?" Seth rubbed a sleeve across his nose. "Havta go." He limped across the grass, and then he stopped and glanced back. "Thanks for whatcha did. I'm beholden to ya."

Beholden? Dewi giggled, got to his feet and righted the bike. Only the vicar used words like that.

Seth eyed Dewi's antics as he tried to push off and mount the bike. "Whatcha doin' ridin' a bike too big for ya?"

"It's my father's," Dewi explained.

"Ain'tcha got yar own bike?"

"It's too small."

Seth walked back to Dewi. "'Ere, reckon as I c'n 'elp ya on." He put the sack down and balanced the bike while Dewi clambered on.

"If you'll give me a bit of a push . . ."

"Yeah. But this don't mean I paid me debt."

"You don't owe me a debt," Dewi said.

"By Romany law, 'tis so."

"Romany?"

"Gypsies, you calls us, but 'tis Romanies is what we are." Seth moved his legs out of reach of the pedals and gave Dewi a push toward the gradient leading down to the village. "Wherja live, Dewi?"

"Pen Farm. Up on the mountain," Dewi shouted as the bike carried him toward the next slope.

Dewi tweaked the bell at Bronwen-Rose-Cottage puffing up the hill with a basket of groceries. "Gypsies on Moelfre!" he shouted.

As he passed Rowlie's shop, two women ran out. "What's that?" one of them cried.

"Gypsies on Moelfre!" he shouted again, at the same time informing Old Ned who came to the cobbler's doorway. Looking over his shoulder, Dewi saw the women scatter.

He juddered the bike to a halt by the bridge and used the low stone wall as a step to get off. As he wheeled the bike off the road, one of the women ran past with an empty shopping basket and a panicky look on her face.

Dewi propped the bike against the bridge and clambered down the slope to the river's edge. The snake stirred when he fumbled in his pocket for his handkerchief. The bull's-eye was stuck to the cloth. He held it in the flow of water to soften it, and then he pulled the linen away, popped the sweet into his mouth, and dabbed the wet cloth on the beads of blood on his knee.

He'd never before thought about the Gypsies and the way Gran sent him to tell the villagers they were on the mountain. The

Gypsies came to the mountain every year, camping on the common beneath Moelfre. From his bedroom window, he would see their fires sparking into the night. After they moved on, he'd go up and examine the charred circles in the grass, which looked like the black eye he'd given Ifor Ellis the summer before when he said Dewi had a sweetheart.

Dewi didn't know why he had to warn people about the Gypsies. He didn't know much about them, only what people said. *Dirty as a Gypsy*. At ten, he didn't know much about clean and dirty. He knew Joroway Smith smelled funny, and Gran dragged out the galvanized tub every Saturday night, dumping him in it as she said: "Must to be clean for church tomorrow."

Ragged as a Gypsy was another saying. True, Seth's jersey had a few tears in it, but he'd been after rabbits and anybody could tear their clothes, Dewi decided. Gypsy was the worst name one person could call another. It condemned as dirty, ragged and— What? Seth had been all right, but Seth said he was Romany not a Gypsy.

"Dewi Thomas fell off his bike. Dewi Thomas fell off his bike," Gwyneth Beckingham sang from the top of the bridge.

Dewi looked up. Gwyneth had a smaller girl with her—Molly Griffiths. With his tongue, he shoved the bull's-eye to one side to bulge his cheek. "Shut up, Gwyneth."

"Been riding his father's bike. Been riding his father's bike," Molly taunted.

"Mind your own business," muttered Dewi, getting to his feet.

"Riding his father's bike and fell off it." Still taunting him, the two girls crossed the bridge, pushing a doll's pram. They stopped at the top of the bank.

"Bugger off!" said Dewi.

"Ooh! Dewi Thomas said a bad word!" Gwyneth lifted her doll from the pram and clamped both hands over its ears. "Mustn't listen, Dolly."

The girls moved down to the river's edge. They took off the doll's knitted bootees and stood it in the water. "Dolly's going paddling," they informed Dewi.

Dewi ignored them and climbed the slope, his knee stiff and stinging with every step.

"Going to tell your father," Gwyneth sang. "Going to tell your father."

Dewi rammed the wet handkerchief into his pocket and felt the coils shudder. When the girl's weren't looking, he took the snake from his pocket and slid it under the blankets in the doll's pram. "Goodbye, Speedy," he whispered.

It was after supper Dewi's sins found him out. He was sitting at one end of the kitchen table with three old wireless sets and a jumble of valves and wires he'd gathered from the rubbish tips all over the valley. "I found a good one, Dat," he said, inserting a four-pronged valve and watching it light up.

"Mmph," Davy grunted, nose buried in a stack of horse magazines he'd brought down from the attic. "Look at this picture, Dewi. That's Pete Knight. Best rodeo rider there ever was. That man could ride."

"Yes, Dat." Dewi rummaged through his box of valves in search of a three-prong.

"Lucky for them I shut Blackie in for the night," Eirlys said from where she sat beside the window darning socks in the last of the light. "I wonder what they want."

"Who's that?" Davy asked.

"Julius Beckingham and Bogo Griffiths."

"We'll soon find out." Davy crossed to open the door. "'Evening, gents. What brings you up here?"

"This isn't a social visit, Mr Thomas. It's about Dewi. May we come in?"

"What have you done now!" Eirlys whispered, and to Dewi her voice held a warning of coming punishment.

"There's the culprit!" Bogo pointed at Dewi. "Scared my little girl half to death, and Mr Beckingham's Gwyneth, too."

"Oh?" Davy waited to hear more.

"Put a snake in their dolly's pram, he did," said Bogo.

"And used bad language," said Julius Beckingham. "As verger of Saint Barnabas, I insist he be punished."

"He will be," Davy said.

"And another thing, he was seen talking to a Gypsy boy."

"And as good Christians, we can't have that, can we. He'll be punished for what he did wrong."

"Good." Julius and Bogo waited expectantly.

"I said I'd deal with it," said Davy. "The days of public whippings are past."

"He was riding your bike," said Bogo.

"What!" Davy's voice rattled the brass plaques on the wall above the mantelpiece and Dewi cringed. "Riding my bike!" He rounded on Dewi. "After I told you not to?"

Dewi hung his head and sidestepped behind his grandmother.

"We'll leave it with you, then."

Davy waited until the two men had crossed the yard, then he turned to Dewi. Without a word, he hooked his thumb toward the door. Eyes downcast, Dewi passed his father and headed for the back of the house. "Don't be too hard on him, Davy," he heard Gran say.

Behind him, his father's heels dug angrily into the ground. Dewi heard him snap a branch from the hedge and, when he faced him, he saw his father strip the leaves off the stick.

"Dat . . ."

"I don't want to hear it. Over!"

Dewi bent over the sawhorse.

"For frightening little girls . . ." Whack!

"For saying bad words . . ." Whack!

"For taking my bike . . ." Whack! Whack! Whack!

"Take my bike again and I'll take the skin off your backside!"

His father's footsteps moved back toward the house and Dewi glanced up in time to see him throw the stick over the hedge. Gingerly, he straightened, his buttocks smarting.

"Psst! Dewi!"

Dewi looked around.

"Over 'ere! Behind the raspberries."

"Seth?" Dewi spotted the swarthy face and glanced anxiously toward the house to see if his father had gone.

"Whatcha do ta fright the hinnies?"

"What?"

"The girls. Howja fright 'em?"

"Put a snake in their doll's pram," Dewi owned and heard Seth smother a laugh.

"Dewi?" Eirlys came around the corner of the house. "Who're you talking to?"

"Nobody." Awkwardly, holding the serge of his trousers away from his stinging buttocks, Dewi walked toward his grandmother.

She put a hand under his chin, tilting his head as she studied his face. "Does it hurt bad?"

Dewi swallowed back the tears her sympathy threatened to drag from him. "It's all right."

"I don't know why you do these things." With an arm around his shoulders, she led him toward the house.

"Gran? Why don't people like the Gypsies? Why do you send me to warn them in the village when the Gypsies are on the mountain?"

"They steal," she answered. "If people know they're here, they can keep a look out for their things, can't they."

"Dat didn't smack me for talking to the Gypsy boy . . ."

"They don't steal from us, except once when they took one of the ponies your father was running up on the common."

"Did they give it back?"

"Your father went up there and got into a fight with their *voivode*, their chieftain. Since then, they've left us alone."

"Dat was in a fight?"

"Yes." Eirlys pushed him toward the door. "And you're growing too much like him."

Dewi next saw Seth when he rode his bike across the square with a crowd of children in his wake.

"Time you gave up that baby bike," one boy called.

"My baby brother's got a tricycle bigger than that," a girl called.

"Ought to join the circus as a clown," one of the others shouted.

"Bugger off!" shouted Dewi as he skirted the churchyard wall, half-blinded by scalding tears. To add to his humiliation, he saw Seth sitting on top of the wall. "And you bugger off and all," Dewi shouted as he pedalled past.

The next time he went to the village, Dewi hid his bike in the rhododendrons outside the Vicarage and walked the rest of the way, collecting his bike on the way home. The second time, when he went to collect it, the bike was missing. He heaved a sigh of relief and went home to tell his father.

". . . so you see, I'll have to use your bike from now on."

Davy eyed him suspiciously. "We'll see if Constable Owens can find it."

A week passed without a sign of Dewi's bike. When his gran sent him to the village on an errand, he had permission to ride his father's bike. "Only until your own bike turns up, mind," said his father.

Dewi rode all the way into the village, ringing the bell at every bend. Balanced against the bridge wall he dismounted and pushed the bike to the shop next to the bus stop.

With the knitting wool for his gran tied to the handlebars, Dewi was standing on the bridge wall ready to mount the bike when he saw the Gypsy caravans wending their way down the road. They were brightly painted, pots and pans rattling to the rhythm of the horses' hooves. On the seat before the open door of the lead caravan sat the headwoman, Leah, a clay pipe firmly clamped between her toothless jaws. Beside her, Seth handled the reins, his head held proudly. He gave Dewi a sly wink before returning his attention to the road ahead.

From his vantage point on the wall, Dewi could see through the open door to the jumble of paraphernalia inside the caravan. There, resting on the high, padded bed amid a collection of baskets was his lost bike.

Dewi grinned as he waited until the last caravan passed, then he mounted his father's bike and gave the bell a trilling tweak.

♥

THE GHOST ON THE HILL

There's a ghost on Corpse Hill, the cry went up. The village had more than its fair share of ghosts, none of them particularly welcome, so they held an emergency meeting in the village hall to decide what to do about the new one.

"I tell you," said Bogo Griffiths, standing to face his neighbours that Saturday afternoon, "there's a ghost up there. I saw it Monday night."

"You're daft man," said Elias Stock, remembering Bogo's two-steps-forward-one-step-back gait when he left the pub. "It's drunk you were then you left my place."

"I'll admit I was a couple of sheets to the wind but I know what I saw."

"Something you saw from the corner of your eye, perhaps?" Williams-the-School was sceptical.

"*Diawl*, no," said Bogo. "Stopped to have a leak—oh, sorry ladies." Bogo reddened under Bronwen's glare. "Looked up the hill, I did, and there it was sitting looking down at me."

"Did it speak to you, Bogo?" Elias asked.

"Don't be daft!" answered Bogo. "Ghosts don't speak."

"Oh? Met a lot of them, have you, Bogo?" William asked.

Bogo snorted and sat down, grumbling to himself. "Why don't you speak up, Eirlys Thomas? Tell them what you saw."

Eirlys rose self-consciously. "I can't be sure what I saw. I was walking up the hill, Wednesday night it was, after choir practice, and I saw something ahead of me."

"What did it look like?" asked Elias.

"Well . . . It was like a column of white, about as tall as a man, standing on top of the hill waiting for me."

"So far it's been seen sitting and standing." Elias grinned. "Has anybody seen it doing a jig?"

"No need to be flippant," said Ianto. "Everybody living on our side of the valley has seen it up there."

"And is everybody here this afternoon?" asked William, looking around. "Including Old Ned?"

"Here I be." Old Ned, ninety-six if he was a day, waved his walking stick.

Ned's daughter caught at his arm with a warning: "Doctor said to be careful, Dat. You shouldn't have come, so just sit quiet."

"I don't care what anybody says," Eirlys said, "from now on I'm taking the forest road home."

"And me," chorused a few others who lived on the high land beyond Corpse Hill.

"That's dangerous," said Tom Evans, the valley roadman. "With the warmer weather coming, there'll be vipers along the forest road. I kill them every year. Somebody could get bitten."

"Then we've got to do something," said William. "Let's examine this logically, shall we? There are no such things as ghosts." A gabble of voices raised a protest and drowned his words. Some agreed, some didn't, and arguments broke out. When it died down and they were back to giving him their attention, William continued: "Everything I've heard so far points to this thing on Corpse Hill having the appearance and actions of a man. Have you considered the possibility of it being a man dressed up to put a scare into us?"

There was another argument. A few concurred with William but others were convinced the hill was haunted.

"That's no man up there, William Williams." A voice cut cleanly through the tumult and a hush fell on the hall as they looked toward the door where Mam Derw stood. "Thought you'd have the meeting without me, did you?" she cackled.

Only the Good Lord knew how old Mam Derw was. The elders of the village said she'd lived in her cottage by the well when they were children and her appearance hadn't changed in all those years. As a boy, Elias and a couple of others climbed into her cottage through a window. The place was full of pickling jars, he said. He opened one and a dead frog fell out. Ever after, he'd been cursed with warts on his hands.

Black straw hat flat as a burnt pancake on top of her head and held on by two bulbous pearl hatpins, Mam Derw leaned heavily upon a gnarled hawthorn stick and hobbled into the hall. On her feet, she wore leather boots with a row of winking black buttons, which marched up her frail ankles to disappear under the hem of a coat rescued from an earlier era.

"Looks like a bloody ghost herself, doesn't she?" Elias whispered.

"Quiet man or she'll put the evil eye on you." William grinned at Elias.

There was silence as Mam Derw limped to where they were gathered. Tom Evans, who could hold the stage and render them all to tears or laughter with his monologues, squirmed in his chair. Bronwen, whose contralto could rattle the rafters, found a lot of threads to pick from her sleeve. Only William had the courage to speak.

"Now don't start spreading superstitious nonsense," he said while Mam Derw lowered herself onto a chair.

She eyed the teacher who had been away to college. "I remember you when you were in short trousers scrumping apples. You haven't grown any wiser."

"What do you think is up there on the hill?" Bogo asked.

"It's a spirit." She threw a hard look at Elias when he sniggered. "And not the type of spirit you sell, either."

"What's it doing up there?" Tom asked.

"It's come for one of you," she answered, and Old Ned's daughter clenched her fists in her lap.

William leaned forward, forearms resting on his knees. "What do you mean *it's come for one of us*?"

"Come to guide the way, it has. Someone is going to die and it's come to show the new spirit the way."

"It's come for me, hasn't it?" Eirlys started to cry. "It was waiting for me on Wednesday night."

"No, not you gel, not yet."

"Me then," said Bogo in a small voice. "I was the first to see it."

"The one as comes for you, Bogo Griffiths, will have horns and a tail," she said sharply. "And the same goes for one or two of you others."

"Are you saying, when we die, a spirit or a demon comes to show our spirits the way to heaven or hell?" asked William.

"Not all," she said. "There's some not wanted up above or down below, have to find their own way, they have. Some of them never do and they stay around the places where they used to live, hoping to follow when another spirit goes."

William smiled and sat back. "That's an interesting theory."

"Don't go making fun of what you don't understand." Mam Derw rose to her feet. "Believe what you will but that's no man dressed up to frighten you. And before this week is out, someone in the village will die."

"The week is out tonight!" said Tom.

Mam Derw cackled. "That's right."

Her words hung on the air, holding everyone silent as she gimped to the door. It had been closed on her for several minutes before William broke into the silence.

"Who's coming up with me to catch this man who's putting a fright into us?" he asked, as though Mam Derw had never been.

"I will," said Elias without hesitation, then he looked around. "Anyone else? Bogo?"

"Not me," Bogo said firmly.

"Whoever goes up there with William and me will share the bottle I'm taking. Best brandy it'll be and all."

"Well . . ." said Bogo. "All right, I'll go. But I'm not happy about it, I'm telling you."

"I'll go," said Tom Evans. "When do we leave?"

"It'll be pitch dark by eleven," said William. "We'll meet at the bottom of Corpse Hill then."

Later, as the four started up the hill with William and Elias in the lead, Bogo asked: "Why do they call it *Rhiw Cyrff* - Corpse Hill anyway?"

"Years ago," said William, considered an authority on the history of the valley, "before they built Saint Barnabas in the village, all the church people were carried up to Penboyr for burial. The pallbearers carried the coffin up this hill on their shoulders. When they reached the top, they set the coffin on the wall beside the stile and took a rest."

"I always wondered why that bit of wall was there," said Bogo.

"No wonder it's bloody haunted," said Tom.

"Quiet now," Elias cautioned. "We don't want to scare off whoever it is." He took a flask from his pocket and removed the stopper. "This will give us a bit of courage, boys." He took a swig and passed the flask around.

"It's turned cold all of a sudden." Bogo passed the flask on to Tom.

"What do you expect?" asked William. "It's May, the middle of the night, and we're on high ground. It's bound to be colder."

"No more talking now," said Elias, "or the bugger will know were coming."

"Always supposing he doesn't already know," said William. "He might have been at the meeting."

"Then what the hell are we doing up here?" asked Tom.

"Drinking Elias' best brandy." Bogo nudged Tom in the ribs.

They moved on in silence. At the top of the hill, the road levelled out as it moved around the bend and prepared for the next slope. Tall hedges grew up from the steep earth banks bordering the road. The four crouched a few steps from the stile to listen but heard only the hoot of an owl in the trees.

"I'll get a bit closer and take a look," whispered William. "Wait here."

"It's getting cold again," Bogo grumbled as William disappeared into the darkness.

"Shut up!" snarled Elias, keeping his voice low.

Minutes passed before William came hurrying back. He hunkered beside them. "He's up there."

"The ghost?" Bogo couldn't keep his teeth from chattering.

"Don't be daft!" hissed Elias. "Let's get closer."

They crept to the stile and crouched next to the wall.

"Near as I can make out, he's off to the right behind that hedge," whispered William. "I heard him breathing."

"Ghosts don't breathe." As Elias spoke, there came the gushing sound of water. "And they don't take a leak, either!"

"Quiet now," said William. "We'll have to go about this the right way if we're going to catch him. I'll go to the right of the hedge, just in case he cuts through it, and you—Elias and Bogo—go to the left of it where he's hiding. You stay here, Tom, in case he gets past us and comes over the stile."

As William sought for toeholds in the bank, Elias and Bogo climbed over the stile. Keeping close to the bank, they edged forward with Elias in the lead.

"I can hear him," Elias breathed in Bogo's ear. "Watch out for that clump of nettles, he's behind them."

As they took another step, William appeared at the top of the bank and jumped into the field. At the same time, a white shape leapt away from the hedge, horned face turned to Elias and Bogo.

"Oh, *diawl*!" shouted Bogo. "It's the Horned One! He's come for me!" With that, he took off down the field.

"Bogo! Come back!" yelled William.

71

"Like bloody hell!" shouted Bogo, still running.

William and Elias sank onto the grass, laughing helplessly, as Tom peered over the stile.

"Did you catch him?" Tom asked.

"Her," said Elias. "We caught her all right—Toby Rice's cow. But there's nothing in this world going to catch Bogo tonight."

"A cow?" Tom climbed over the stile and sat next to Elias.

"One of Toby's white cows," said William.

"*Damn!* Gave me a start it did when it jumped away from the hedge." Elias took out the flask. "Let's have another drink, boys, and then we'll go home."

In the moonlight, Tom's hands trembled when he reached for the flask and took a sip. "It wasn't a cow those other times," he said quietly.

"Come on, man! I didn't think you believed that nonsense," said William.

Tom lifted the flask a second time and gulped at the contents. "I was up here at noon on Thursday, scything the hedges, and I stopped here to eat my *tocin*. It came over cold and the tea I'd just poured steaming from my flask turned to ice."

"Need a new flask is all," said Elias.

"I'm not so sure," said Tom. "What's that over there on the other side of the valley?"

William and Elias looked to where Tom pointed with a trembling finger. On the opposite hill, a white shape was moving up the field toward a row of cottages.

"You mean—while we've been buggering about up here that thing was working its way across the valley?" Elias grabbed for the flask.

"It's a cow. That's all," said William. "Seen from this angle, it looks like a column of white as it moves up the hill. If it starts grazing side on to us, you'll see it's a cow."

They watched the moon-shimmered shape move through a wall on the far slope. "I've never seen a cow that could walk through walls," said Tom. "Mam Derw said the spirit had come for one of us. It looks as if it's going into one of those cottages." Tom leapt to his feet. "Hey up! It's coming back!"

"Bloody hell! It's moving fast," said Elias. "Let's get out of here."

"I'm for that," shouted William and all three ran, fighting to be the first over the stile.

Across the valley, Old Ned brandished his stick at the cow that had been munching on the lettuce seedlings and was now running off down the hill. "If I've told Joroway to mend that wall once, I've told him a dozen times. Stay out of here, you great big lummox!"

He dropped the stick and clutched at the sudden pain in his chest. The doctor had warned him about getting worked up, and now—

♥

WHEN THE HAREBELLS CHIME

When she was six, Gwenna Jones spent three days sitting in the snow under the apple tree, her attention on the small hole in the wall next to the water barrel as she watched for the fairies.

It was no good her mam scolding and saying rats made the tracks, to Gwenna the dainty footprints were human-shaped and she continued her vigil.

On the fourth day, the snow melted and froze, and the scattering of earth and sand beneath the wall was too hard-surfaced to hold the imprint of fairy feet. Gwenna gave up and went inside to nurse the cold she'd caught. Even then, when she heard her mam busy in the kitchen, Gwenna crept to the window to peep out, certain that from the corner of her eye she had seen a dainty creature in a yellow gossamer gown ducking behind the water barrel.

Gwenna's mam fed her chicken soup, insisting it she made from mushrooms because Gwenna restricted her diet to things that didn't have to die to give her nourishment. She'd consume cake because Gwenna's mam was careful not to let her know she used embryo hens in its making, but she was at a loss to explain why Gwenna was often ill after eating a cake made with eggs. Eggs were taboo and she wouldn't touch meat or fish. It was bad enough someone slaughtered the animal, in Gwenna's eyes, but it didn't mean she had to hurt it further by chewing on it.

At school dinners, Gwenna would eat the vegetables, and then she'd sit before her plate of meat while the other children at the table told her she was being cruel not to eat of the animal after they sacrificed it for her. Gwenna wanted to say but she didn't know how to put her feelings into words they would understand even if they'd listen--*if none of you ate meat, none of the cows and sheeps and piggies would have to die*--so she sat in silence with tears washing down her face to tickle her chin. Gwenna often had raw patches under her chin where she'd rubbed the tickles away with the ribbed cuff of her cardigan sleeve.

The other children rarely allowed Gwenna to join in their games. If they took her fishing: once the stormy defence of innocent worms was over, if anyone was lucky enough to catch a fish Gwenna would carry on until they *threw the fishy back*. Girls arranged flower-picking excursions with the stealth of mini Mata Haris because, if Gwenna came upon them with posies in their hands, she'd make a fuss about how the poor flowers were hurt and crying where they'd snapped and crushed the stalks. Even in church, faced with the vases of flowers on the altar Gwenna would cry as much for them as for the terrible things done to the Son of God bleeding on His cross. She liked going to church during Lent best of all because there were no flowers decorating the altar.

Gwenna didn't particularly mind if the children left her out of their games. Although she didn't think of applying the word *barbarians* to them, she had a very good idea what she thought of them. She had gentler friends who showed her where the robins nested, where the grass snakes knotted for the winter, and where the frogs laid spawn she could watch while tadpoles wriggled from the jellied beads. Every Saturday, well before breakfast, Gwenna left the house to roam the woods and fields with her friends. She was always home before dark and, at first, she shared her day's discoveries with her parents:

"Rosy showed me a baby owl today."

"Daisy took me to watch the newts dance."

"Marigold let me listen to the harebells chime."

At first, Gwenna's mam asked about the new friends and Gwenna would reply casually: "Oh, they're the Blossoms. They live at the edge of the wood, close to Mam Derw's cottage."

Gwenna's mam knew everybody in the valley and there was no family called Blossom. "Such an imagination!" she said to Gwenna's father. "I don't know where she gets it from." Then, when she thought of the wizened old crone, concern creased her brow. "You don't think she's been talking to that old witch, Mam Derw, do you?"

For a while, Gwenna's mam worried about Mam Derw filling Gwenna's head with fancies, but gradually she paid less heed to her daughter's tales:

"These are the first snowdrops in the valley, Mam. Marigold showed me where they grew. She said I could pick them because the flowers' feet were getting frozen."

"Marigold talked to the black eels today and told them not to bite my toes when I go paddling."

Sometimes guilt overcame Gwenna's mam for not listening to her daughter and she'd ask: "How were the Blossoms today?"

"They're fine," was Gwenna's usual answer but occasionally she added snippets of information. "I helped them chose new harebell bonnets today" or "Marigold was chased by a wasp but I shooed it away" or "Mrs Blossom was baking stuffed wild strawberries."

Once, after Gwenna's mam scolded her for getting grass stains on her dress, Gwenna said: "Mrs Blossom wants me to go to live with them."

After a while, Gwenna's mam forgot to ask about Gwenna's imaginary friends unless something happened to jog her memory, and she noticed Gwenna herself spoke of them less often. "Growing out of it, I expect," she confided to Gwenna's father and heaved a sigh of relief.

Once, after weeks of silence on the subject of the Blossoms, Gwenna volunteered: "Marigold's got a new dress. Bright yellow it is and thin like a spider's web."

Gwenna's mam frowned at learning the Blossoms hadn't shrivelled out of Gwenna's life, and because it was Christmas she gave Gwenna a doll with a bright yellow dress.

Gwenna untied the parcel carefully on Christmas morning and folded the wrapping paper neatly before lifting the doll out of the box.

"Are you going to give her a flower's name?" Gwenna's mam asked. "Snowdrop or Violet?"

Gwenna gave her mam a withering look. "Julie," she said firmly and sat the new doll with the china face on top of the dresser beside her raggedy doll with the painted face.

Months passed. By day, the doll sat on Gwenna's dresser, by night Gwenna's mam tucked it into bed with Gwenna. Yet, by the end of May, it looked as untouched as the day Gwenna unpacked it. "She never plays with it,"

Gwenna's mam complained to Gwenna's father.

At the beginning of June, a week before Gwenna's birthday, a measles epidemic splotched its way through the valley and she was one of the first struck by the virus. Gwenna's father brought her bed down to the parlour next to the wireless and she took to the sheets without a murmur of protest. After a day, the constant chatter of the wireless palled and her mam spent time reading to her from one of her fairy-tale books. Even that failed to draw a response and Gwenna's mam said to Gwenna's father: "There's something funny about her eyes."

They called in the doctor. With her mam hovering at his back, Gwenna allowed him to examine her. He put his stethoscope away, took the doll with the china face from the dresser and held it up. "What's the name of this dolly, Gwenna?"

Gwenna's mam bit back a cry when Gwenna reached out a fraction to the left of where the doctor held the doll. Quickly, he placed it in Gwenna's hands.

Gwenna touched her fingers to the cold china face. "That's Julie."

"A temporary blindness that often accompanies measles," the doctor said after they'd left the parlour. "Keep the curtains closed. She'll be better in a few days."

However, Gwenna didn't get better. Her fever rose and they called the doctor back on the morning Gwenna was seven. "Pneumonia," he pronounced, in the tones of a death knell. "Both lungs." He produced a bottle of medicine. "By the way, who's this Marigold she keeps talking about in her coma?"

"Oh, no!" Gwenna's mam came close to fainting. "It must be the fever. It's got her imagining things again."

Mam Derw was on her knees in the tall grass beside the druid's well. With the breast feathers of a robin, she brushed dew from the grass and transferred it carefully to the silver-topped vial.

"Dew that is drawn when the sun is high fights all evil drawing nigh.

"Grass and willow shed their tears to save mankind when evil nears.

"Scarlet feather of a robin's breast, take the good and leave the rest."

It took a year to fill the vial with the dew that lingered to midday in the shade of the trees around the well. It was tiring work and, of late, it made her back and knees ache. She stoppered the vial and dropped it into the bag tied to the belt of her coat. With the help of the hawthorn stick, she clambered to her feet and went to sit at the edge of the glade on a rock warmed by the sun.

As the sun dried the dampness clinging to her face and hair, Mam Derw closed her eyes on the golden wheat field stretched before her and on the echoing gold of honeysuckle braided into the mottled green of willow, holly and hawthorn bordering the river. Here and there, a bank of yellow celandines put the wheat to shame and, in defiance, the field threw scarlet poppies at the sun. She felt their battle wash over her and sensed the distress of the aspen trembling at her side. In the distance a dog barked to warn a hedgehog away, the sound carried on the gentle breeze that played around the valley, truant from the family of winds gathered on the mountain.

Then another sound. Closer, faint, and barely caught on the breeze. She raised her head and listened.

Bells.

Tiny, tinkling, fairy chimes.

And voices. Hushed and whispering.

Agitated.

Angry.

Threatening!

And one name heard clearly from the tumult: Gwenna.

The *Tylwyth Teg*!

Mam Derw sprang to her feet, one hand clutching the amulet about her neck. The *Tylwyth Teg*. More frightening than Merlin's curse, they were all the more deadly because of their beauty. Dainty, gossamer gowned gnats of evil that beguiled men and little children.

She hobbled under the trees. On her knees beside the well, she reached into the water and withdrew a corked bottle. Once, the bottle held medicines dispensed by fools who knew no more of healing than a moithered hornet, but the wax and wane of seven moons purified it and the water it held was sacred. She wiped the bottle on the hem of her coat then put it still damp into her pocket before leaving the well.

Gwenna's mam answered the door, her eyes red from weeping.

"The little gel." Mam Derw pushed into the house.

Gwenna's father confronted her in the hallway, his face black with anger. "You and your potions are not wanted here. Get out!"

It didn't seem as if Mam Derw heard him. Surrounded by doors and a stairway, she couldn't be sure which one would lead to Gwenna. She tilted her head to listen and heard the faint chimes of bells. She turned toward the parlour door and Gwenna's father stepped into her path.

"Get out!"

Gwenna's father wasn't a tall man, even in his studded work boots he barely passed the five-foot mark, but many found to their error that he was a scrapper, like a yapping terrier that won't let go when it's got its teeth into something. His eyes met those of the bent old woman, and what he saw there—a veiled hint of dark knowledge—made him shrink. His shoulders sagged, folding in upon his chest and the bluster went out of him. He stepped to one side.

The parlour was dim with heavy chenille curtains closed against the sun, and even the light of the solitary candle paled behind the sheet of oiled paper propped in front of it.

Gwenna's mam clung to Gwenna's dat as they watched the old crone move toward their daughter. Mam Derw sat on the edge of the bed; scarce denting the mattress, so small and fragile was she. She took a vial from her bag, wet her fingers with the contents, and then leaned forward to touch Gwenna's brow and lips. The child stirred and mumbled.

About them bells began to chime, discordant and wild, then a cutting draft slammed the door shut and the wind whistled in the chimney, its breath dousing the candle.

Through the darkness, Mam Derw's voice filled the room, the chant in a half-forgotten tongue low and persistent at first, then louder and louder until it rang clear above the din. And the bells clanged, deafening Gwenna's mother and father.

Then, all of a sudden, the bells were hushed and there was only the monotone chanting, soft, coaxing, and persistent, changing into a language they knew.

On the dresser beside the bed, a yellow glow hovered. The doll's dress, Gwenna's mam thought, as she remembered the painstaking stitches that went into its making at night when Gwenna was in bed. Then the glow moved; leaving only a reflected light that was the doll's dress.

The pinpoint of light hovered above Gwenna's bed like a moth agitated by a flame, and in the eerie radiance they saw Mam Derw with a bottle in one hand and knot of red feathers in the other. She flicked water over Gwenna and the bed, spattering dark splotches onto the ivy trails of the wallpaper, and Mam Derw was calling Gwenna, her voice soft and relentless.

Gwenna's mam shrank against Gwenna's father as the wisp of light sped about the room. Dashing itself into the walls and against the framed photographs on the mantelpiece, it even half opened the curtains in its panic to find an escape. Finally, it found the keyhole of the parlour door and was gone, one shred of a gossamer gown clinging to a sliver of wood.

In the glimmer of light from the window, Gwenna's parents clung to each other in silence and watched Mam Derw put the bottle and the knot of red feathers into the battered handbag tied to her belt. Still in shock, they weren't aware of her question.

"How old is Gwenna?"

When they didn't answer, Mam Derw twisted around to look at them and the shaft of sunlight fell on her face. For a moment, she had the appearance of a young woman dressed in a white robe, her hair black and wild about an unlined face. Then she spoke and the wizened old woman with the bent frame was back. "How old is Gwenna?"

"S–seven today," Gwenna's mam whispered.

"And the hour of her birth?"

"Two o'clock," Gwenna's father answered, wondering why it was important. "The children were running to Sunday school when she arrived."

"Then she's safe. Once past seven, they won't come after her again." Mam Derw rose and walked from the room. Outside, she paused on the doorstep and lifted her face to the sun for a heartbeat before setting off down the path. She was close to the gate when Gwenna's father came running out.

"She's better! Gwenna's better. The fever's gone and she can see again. She's asking for food. Poached eggs, she wants."

Mam Derw nodded.

"What happened in there? What were those bells? And that light?" Gwenna's father braced himself as Mam Derw lifted her eyes to his. Meeting them, he heard an echo of chanting and remembered the glimpse of the young woman she'd been. "What was it you did in there?"

Mam Derw looked away, studying the hazelnut tree growing in the hedge on the other side of the road, seeing how the lower leaves lifted in the breeze to show the paler surface underneath. "We're in for rain tonight."

She stepped away from the gate and hobbled off down the road, muttering to herself. After the rain, it would be days before she could be sure the pearls of water on the grass beside the well were pure dew, and it would take months to replace the contents of the vial.

♥

.

CURSES

Bored with the BBC news that seemed to have nothing but talk about some man called Hitler, Olwen tuned the wireless to the Welsh program broadcasting the National Eisteddfod from Llangollen. Humming along with the male-voice choir, she picked up a knife to continue peeling the potatoes for the evening meal and a knock came at the door.

Olwen put the knife down and wiped her hands on her apron as she crossed the kitchen. Opening the door, she stepped back with a gasp of dismay. A Gypsy!

Unlike any of the village women, she was black haired and swarthy, dressed in a long black skirt and an embroidered blouse, with a brightly patterned, long-fringed shawl thrown around her shoulders and knotted at her breast. In her hand, she held a basket filled with wooden clothes pegs. She raised the basket like an offering. With the movement a waft of sandalwood and rosemary, and something Olwen couldn't identify, enveloped the woman in an exotic cloud. "Pegs, lady?"

Olwen shook her head and reached for the door intending to close it in the woman's face. She tried to take a step back, but her knees shook. Gypsies were bad luck. They put curses on people. Gypsies stole anything not nailed down. They said Gypsies were—

"Only a shilling." The woman held the basket higher, so Olwen could reach out and take it.

"No." Olwen didn't recognize the squeak as her own voice, but it came from her own lips and with the same ring to it as the voice that said *I do* the year before when she'd stood with Emrys before Reverend Davies in Saint Barnabas. Her knees trembled then, too. She cleared her throat. "I don't need pegs."

"I will tell your fortune if you cross my palm with silver."

"No, I—I don't have any money."

There was a mocking glint in the black eyes as they glanced past Olwen to the interior of the cottage then swept over the outside whitewashed walls and the lace-curtained windows. "To live in a nice place like this, you must have money, pretty lady."

Yes, Olwen wanted to say, but I'm not a very good housekeeper yet. The money Emrys gave her every Friday for housekeeping never seemed to last beyond Wednesday, and this was Thursday.

She was extravagant. That was the word her sister, Luned, used. Perhaps it was extravagant to buy sweet-scented freesias from the shop in Newcastle Emlyn when she had flowers growing in her own garden, and perhaps she should have bought cheaper lace for the windows instead of the Nottingham, but Emrys never took her to task for it. Only Luned. The last time, when Olwen failed to resist the brass umbrella stand, Luned threw a fit. Perhaps she was right because the mill was working only part time now and Emrys' pay packet would be less. He'd said not to worry because, if the trouble in Europe turned into full-scale war, the mill would be working day and night to make blankets for the army.

The Gypsy was watching her, as though she could read Olwen's mind. They could do that, some people said. Could read your mind and tell you what you were thinking. "I don't have any money, only ten shillings to pay the coal man."

Now why had she said that! The Gypsy wouldn't leave now she knew there was money in the house. She saw the woman look past her at the Toby Jug on the mantelpiece as if she knew where Emrys put the coal money.

"Only a shilling. To help a poor Gypsy."

"I can't. The money is for coal." Emrys had been firm about that. Without coal, they'd be forced to rely on wood for the fire. The last time, a spark burned a hole in the half-moon rug placed against the brass fender. And without coal, Olwen would have to cook the Sunday roast in the oil-fired oven that stank up the cottage and made her curtains yellow.

"Bad things happen when you turn a Gypsy away. A pretty lady like you doesn't want bad luck."

Olwen sucked in her breath. The Gypsy was going to curse her. She knew it! In the eternity before she breathed out, she glanced behind her at the Toby Jug.

"Only a shilling," the Gypsy coaxed, as if sensing Olwen was weakening.

"All right!" Olwen cried in desperation. Anything. She'd do anything to get this woman off her doorstep and avoid being cursed.

Olwen left the door ajar, crossed to the mantelpiece and took down the Toby Jug. Mr Pickwick, Emrys called the jug with its smiling red-cheeked face and black, brimmed hat. It was the name of a man in one of the books he'd read. Always reading, Emrys was, and the shelf in their bedroom so filled with books some had to be stacked on the dresser. He was going to put up another shelf one of these weekends. Not this coming weekend because he was going away to train for the Army Reserve.

"Got to be ready to defend ourselves. If Hitler thinks he's walking into Wales without a fight, he's in for a bloody shock," he'd said.

"If there's a war, Emrys can't go because he'll be needed at the mill," Olwen repeated to Luned the words which comforted her for weeks, and then gone into a fit of depression at her sister's reply.

"All the men will go. They'll have us women running the mills, you'll see."

Olwen upturned Mr Pickwick and the coins fell into her hand. She put the jug back and walked toward the door, counting the money: two florins, a half-crown, two shilling pieces and three sixpences.

At the door, she looked up and met the Gypsy's gaze. There was greed in the black eyes, the same greed as the man running the bran tub at the annual fair in Newcastle Emlyn. Once, when she was six, she'd handed over her fairing—a silver threepence—dug deep into the sawdust and come up with a plastic whistle like the one she'd bought for a farthing at Woolworth's in Carmarthen. She'd cried, but the fair man wouldn't give her back her silver threepence. Eyes hard as the slate of her doorstep, he'd waved her away. The eyes facing her now bore the same black-slate look. Olwen's fingers curled around the coins. "I can't spend any of this on pegs," she said, as much to herself as to the Gypsy.

"Bad luck, lady. Bad luck comes to this house." The woman uttered strange-sounding words and then stepped back. Basket hooked over one arm, she raised her hands and made several passes that encompassed the cottage and Olwen, accompanying the movements with a string of words that, for all she couldn't understand them, put a fright into Olwen. Finally, the woman shot Olwen a venomous look and spat on the ground before flouncing down the path.

Close to tears, Olwen closed the door and stood with her back against it, breathing deeply. Emrys said it was silly to be afraid of Gypsies, except when they stole things. He said it wasn't possible for them to put a curse on you and only silly people believed they could. Bronwen wasn't silly but when she'd refused to buy pegs the year before the big cedar at the back of Rose Cottage came down and flattened their outhouse. Emrys pooh-poohed that, saying if it had fallen because of the curse Bronwen or her father would have been using the outhouse at the time.

With a calming breath, Olwen stepped away from the door. Dropping the coins into her apron pocket, she went back to the potatoes.

As she peeled the last potato, the knife slipped and sliced her thumb, spattering blood. With an oath, she dropped the knife and wrapped her thumb in the hem of her apron. The Gypsy's curse was starting to happen. It didn't matter what Emrys might say, she'd never before cut herself while doing the potatoes.

Blood dripped into the pan of water, staining it red, and the floating potatoes looked like dead white faces staring up at her. Olwen clamped a hand to her mouth to smother a cry, lifting the hem of her apron in the process so the coins fell from the pocket to scatter across the floor. Dumbly, she watched a shilling piece roll across the kitchen, flip onto its side and slide under the skirting board.

Olwen dropped to her knees and gathered the coins, all but the shilling that had disappeared. She took the knife she'd used for the potatoes and slid the blade under the skirting board, probing for the coin. Finally, she gave up. The shilling was lost—the shilling the Gypsy wanted— and her coal money was still as short as it would have been if she'd bought the pegs.

With the same impulsive gesture that had led her to buy the brass umbrella stand, Olwen decided to buy pegs from the Gypsy before something worse happened. She ran to the door and along the path.

To her right the road through the village rose at a gentle incline, an easy climb, a pale shadow of the steep rise leading from the edge of the village up to the mountain, a warning to the unfit if they huffed and puffed on this stretch they'd collapse gasping when the rise grew to full gallop. "Worse than bloody Everest," Emrys often said after they'd been up on Moelfre gathering whinberries. Not that he'd ever seen a mountain higher than Snowdon, but even Snowdon made Moelfre look like a molehill.

There was no sign of the Gypsy; the road deserted in the afternoon sun. Drawn against the heat, the blind on Rowlie's shop window had caught up on a corner of a Peak Frean's biscuit tin glinting like dulled silver. The village looked peaceful, even sleepy, but Olwen knew that behind the laced windows of every house the women were busy preparing the evening meal.

To Olwen's left, the road flowed over the humpbacked bridge and spread like a concrete lake into the village square. That, too, was deserted; dead as the churchyard behind the high stone wall, and the school playground was empty, the children held silent inside the grey building like chicks inside an egg waiting for birth with the three-thirty bell. Only the ten-past-three bus to Carmarthen moved, rounding the Post Office toward the bus stop beyond Olwen's sight. She saw the driver lean forward, his arm moving to the gear stick as he began to slow the bus for the stop. Two seats behind him, nose pressed to the window, a little girl stared out and across the bridge to where Olwen stood.

Olwen felt a hand on her shoulder and gave a shriek as she spun around.

Unprepared for Olwen's reaction, Gladys took a step back. "Whatever's the matter, girl?"

Olwen relaxed at the sight of the older woman. "You haven't seen a Gypsy, have you?"

"Old Leah?" Landlady of the Red Lion, little in life could perturb Gladys, but the Gypsy headwoman always could.

"No, not Leah; a younger woman not much older than me."

"I've been clonking with Mari Jenkins and Rowlie for the past half an hour and I didn't see anybody go past the shop."

"The blind is drawn," Olwen pointed out. "She could pass without you knowing."

Gladys shrugged. "Why are you looking for her, anyway?"

"I wouldn't buy pegs," Olwen explained, "and she put a curse on me. I was looking for her to buy pegs so she'd lift it."

"What sort of curse, gel?" a voice asked from behind Olwen.

Olwen whirled around, hands clasped to her breast in fright. Her fear didn't lessen when she saw it wasn't the Gypsy who stood there but Mam Derw. Nearly as bad as the Gypsies she was, in Olwen's eyes.

With a face as shrivelled and leathery as one of the dried figs Olwen's mother always bought at Christmas, despite the heat Mam Derw wore the long black coat and high-buttoned boots she wore all year. As a concession to summer, she abandoned her fusty Melusine cloche for the wide-brimmed black straw hat perched on her head like a burnt pancake. From beneath its dusty brim, eyes black as currants peered at Olwen. "Nervous, aren't you."

97

"Had a fright, she did." Gladys put an arm around Olwen's shoulder. "Come on inside and I'll make a cup of tea to calm you down."

"Thass right," said Mam Derw, following them up the path. "And we'll have some of that seedy cake you've got in your basket, Gladys."

"Oh, no!" Olwen groaned and felt Gladys' hand tighten on her shoulder. She didn't want Mam Derw in her cottage. Not that she stole, but as bad as the Gypsies the old crone was and she could put curses on you, too, if you offended her. "There's no harm in her," Emrys said. "Just a silly old woman gone senile." Well, Emrys wasn't the one whose brother fell off his bike and broke his ankle not ten minutes after making fun of Mam Derw. And she knew things, like the time Olwen and Emrys went up the mountain and did things before they were married.

"Sit down, girl." Gladys sat Olwen in a chair beside the kitchen table and bustled about filling the kettle.

Olwen kept her eyes on Gladys, afraid to look at the dark mass of the woman sitting on the other side of the table like a wizened gnome.

"What sort of curse did she put on you?" the gnome asked.

"Nothing in particular," Olwen answered. "Just bad luck."

"Oh," said Mam Derw, "one of them all-contingency curses." She cackled like a broody hen.

"Now don't go laughing at the girl," said Gladys, taking a knife to the seedy cake she'd unwrapped. "Had a bad fright, she did."

"So you said, and I can see she did." Mam Derw smacked her lips at the sight of the cake Gladys was arranging on a plate. She glanced sideways at Olwen. "I can lift the curse."

"Would you?" Olwen looked at her with gratitude until she saw the crafty look in the woman's eyes. Mam Derw wasn't in the habit of doing anything for anyone unless she saw gain in it for herself. "I don't have any money to pay you," she warned.

"Got some tomatoes coming ripe, haven't you?" said Mam Derw. "A pound or two of them will do."

Olwen avoided looking at Gladys who was shaking her head. "When can you do it?"

"Right now." Mam Derw clambered to her feet. Fumbling in the battered handbag tied to her belt, she hobbled over to the fireplace. Muttering under her breath, she took a pinch of something from the bag and cast it into the flames. There was a bright blue flash and a cloud of ash drifted onto Olwen's brass fender.

In her anxiety, Olwen failed to notice the mess. "Is it done?"

"The curse is lifted." Mam Derw hobbled back to the table just as the door burst open and Luned rushed in.

Luned halted, mouth open in a silent *Oh!* when she saw Mam Derw.

"Looks like another one had a curse put on her," Mam Derw commented dryly.

"How did you know?" Luned asked.

"Magic," Mam Derw sniggered.

"Did the Gypsy come to your house?" Olwen asked Luned.

"Wanted me to buy pegs," Luned took a cup from the dresser and joined the others around the table. "I told her I didn't have any money because Tom won't get paid until tomorrow, and do you know what she did? She looked straight at the jug on the mantelpiece, the one we got in Weston-Super-Mare on our honeymoon, and said I had money in it. I did too, the money for Davy-the-Coal, but how did she know about it?"

"Magic," said Mam Derw.

"There's no magic in it," said Gladys. "The Gypsies know Davy-the-Coal comes this afternoon. They know we'll have the money ready and they know we all keep the coal money in a jug on the mantelpiece."

Mam Derw ignored Gladys. "Put a curse on you, did she, gel?" she asked Luned.

"Said I'd have bad luck, and I did. Dropped a full bottle of milk. It just slipped out of my hands and smashed on my new carpet.

Terrible mess I've got; milk everywhere. And I didn't stop to clean it up."

"Got chickens ready for the chop, haven't you? Fancy a nice bit of chicken, I do," said Mam Derw. "I'll lift the curse for the price of a chicken."

"When can you do it?" asked Luned.

"Right now." Mam Derw crossed to the fireplace and repeated her earlier action.

"Don't know which is worst," Olwen confided to Luned and Gladys as she studied the mess on the fender, "the Gypsy laying the curse or Mam Derw lifting it."

Luned closed her eyes against the blue flash that filled the room. "Will it work from here?" she asked.

"Trust me, gel. The curse is lifted."

"You should have come earlier, Luned," said Gladys. "Could have had two for the price of one."

"We're not out of trouble yet," said Luned. "As I came in, I saw your gatepost's marked like mine with those symbols the Gypsies use. We'll have Old Leah with us in a day or two with her basket of pegs, and there's no getting away from her."

"Oh, no!" Olwen buried her face in her hands. "I wish I'd bought the pegs. I forgot Leah goes to whoever doesn't buy from the other women. I can't stand it if she comes. Got five shillings out of me last time and nothing to show for it but a dozen pegs I didn't need and a fortune that said I'd come into money the next day."

"And did you?" Gladys asked.

"Yes. Emrys brought the Christmas Club money home," said Olwen. "What're we going to do?"

"We can hope for Constable Owens to move them on," said Luned. "It's not safe when they're up there on the mountain. You never know what they'll steal next."

"I don't know why they keep coming back year after year. Nobody wants them or their pegs, and if we wanted our fortunes told we could always go to old Mam—" Olwen bit back the rest of her words and glanced nervously at Mam Derw.

"Whether the police move them on or not, you'll be all right until Monday," said Gladys. "Old Leah won't come when the men are at home."

"But they won't be!" wailed Luned. "Half the men in the village, including my Tom and Olwen's Emrys, will be away at the Army Reserve camp from Saturday morning until Sunday night."

"Then she'll come on Saturday," said Gladys. "Won't be tomorrow, 'cos the men won't bring home their pay packets until tomorrow night."

"And it'll have to be Saturday afternoon because many of us go to the market in Newcastle Emlyn in the morning," said

Olwen. "Do you think we should stay at the market all day?"

"Why put it off?" said Gladys. "We'll just have to think of something to do by Saturday."

"I might be able to stop Leah," said Mam Derw. "But then—spells don't come cheap."

"No, cost a lot they do." Gladys winked at Olwen and Luned. "These girls don't have the money to pay you; not with their husbands on short time at the mill."

"I've got a pig fattening up for Christmas." Luned ignored the frantic gesturing Gladys was doing behind Mam Derw's back. "Bit of pork would be nice with my apple sauce."

Mam Derw smacked her lips. "An old woman like me might not live to see Christmas."

"Well . . . There's rhubarb wine set up since last year . . ."

"Partial to a drop of rhubarb wine, I am." Mam Derw looked expectantly at Olwen.

Olwen blushed at having to be reminded payment was due. "I've got strawberries coming ripe, and I'll make tomato chutney next week."

"That'll go well with the chicken I'm getting." Mam Derw turned her eyes on Gladys.

"Don't look at me," said Gladys. "I wasn't home when the Gypsy came. Now I know they're about, I won't answer my door."

"Why didn't Eirlys send Dewi down to warn us as she usually does," asked Olwen. "I suppose he was at school."

"No," said Luned. "My Geraint came home for lunch and said Dewi wasn't in class."

"It's an ill wind . . ." Mam Derw struggled to her feet. "I'll take those tomatoes now, Olwen."

Olwen took a paper bag from a drawer and went out. Mam Derw hobbled outside to wait for her with Gladys and Luned on her heels.

As they emerged from the gate, Luned shouted. "Watch out!" and dragged Gladys and Mam Derw back as a boy hurtled down the road on a bicycle much too big for him.

"Gypsies on Moelfre!" he shouted.

"You're too bloody late with your warning," shouted Gladys. "And why aren't you at school?"

"Could've picked up a viper instead of a grass snake and been bitten," Luned volunteered. "Eirlys told me three times this month, when she went through his pockets looking for handkerchiefs to wash, she found a snake."

Gladys shuddered as Olwen hurried around the side of the cottage with a bag of tomatoes in her hand. She thrust it at Mam Derw. "I'll bring the chutney when it's made."

Mam Derw scarcely heard her. Snatching the bag out of Olwen's hand, she pushed past Luned and Gladys. Out on the road, with a voice surprisingly strong for so bent a frame, she shouted after the boy. "Wait up there! I want a word with you."

As Mam Derw hobbled toward where he'd just dismounted using the low wall of the hump-backed bridge as a step, Dewi was sure everyone could see his knees knocking. Still infant enough at eleven to remember the tale of the wicked witch who poisoned Snow White, there was a time when, after his gran read him the story of Hansel and Gretel, Dewi wouldn't venture into the forest surrounding the village. Had nightmares, he had, and now here was Mam Derw coming toward him, as frightening as any witch he'd read about. He was tempted to run, just throw down the bike and run, but he was eleven and he'd be going to Grammar School in September. He was too big to run from an old woman. He waited as she came closer.

She was shorter than he was! Up close, the bogey-woman the younger children scared each other with was shorter than he was.

"Well, Dewi Thomas, there's something you can help me with on Saturday."

Shortly after noon on Saturday, Gladys, Olwen and Luned got off the bus in the square and saw Leah climb down from the seat of her cart. She tied the horse to the churchyard gates and went to the back of the cart.

"She's even older than Mam Derw, don't you think?" said Luned.

"Dress Mam Derw in shawls and beads and you couldn't tell them apart," said Olwen.

"Aye, sisters under the skin, they are," commented Gladys.

"What's she doing?" asked Olwen, watching Leah rummage about in the back of the cart.

"Getting her basket of pegs, I expect," said Gladys. "But I'd rather know what Mam Derw's doing in the churchyard."

"Where?" asked Olwen, "I can't see her."

"There, by the gate," said Gladys. "She's feeding something to Leah's horse."

"If Leah sees her, there'll be hell to play," said Olwen.

"Do you think we can run past Leah and go home?" asked Luned.

"Mam Derw's coming out of the gates; let's wait and see what she's up to." Gladys put down her shopping basket.

"I don't know which of those two old biddies I'm more frightened of." Olwen shrank closer to her sister when Mam Derw moved to stand between the horse and Leah.

"Hey, you!" Mam Derw shouted at the Gypsy woman crossing the square. "I want a word with you. What do you mean by coming into the village every year and frightening the women?"

Leah halted and turned slowly to see who challenged her. In fifteen years as *Phuri Dai*, none of the *Gajos* had dared do more than shrink away from her in mortal fear. In fifteen years, the growing wealth of her tribe made her the envy of the other headwomen and the daughters of her tribe eagerly sought as wives. To be thus revered but challenged by a village woman was not to be borne. "What is it to you, old woman?" Leah shouted across the distance separating them.

"Old woman!" shrieked Mam Derw. "Old woman! Who're you calling an old woman? I got most of my teeth. I'm not like you; I don't have to go gumming my food to death."

"Have a care, old woman," Leah warned.

"Or what?" challenged Mam Derw.

"Evil comes to those who interfere with a Romany."

"Evil comes every year when you camp on the mountain. You're not wanted here, nor your pegs. They're well made, I'll grant you, but you've been frightening the women into buying them for years and we don't need any more. You be off and don't come back!"

107

"I'm warning you!" shouted Leah. "Stay out of this or I'll put a curse on you."

"I've got spells and curses will outdo yours any day of the week," Mam Derw countered.

"You've asked for it!" shouted Leah. She put down her basket of pegs and raised her fists to the heavens, screaming in the Romany tongue, and then she lowered one arm, two fingers of her hand extended and pointing at Mam Derw. "Death, old woman. I curse you with death!"

"Ooh!" Olwen shrank behind Luned and Gladys.

"Hush up, girl," said Gladys. "We've all got to go sometime."

Mam Derw cackled and a rooster up the hill crowed in response. "You're getting too old, Leah," she shouted. "Can't even cast a curse any more. Your eyes must be bad too because look—you've put the curse on the horse, not me." She stood to one side so Leah could see the horse. It sagged at the shoulder then flopped to the ground between the traces.

Leah's mouth dropped open in disbelief and she started forward, but Mam Derw stopped her with a shout.

"No closer! You've done enough harm to this innocent animal." Mam Derw dropped awkwardly to her knees beside the horse. "I'll reverse that curse, you poor thing. Struck down in the prime of life by that wicked woman . . . Come now . . . Come on, boyo, up you get."

She laid her hands to the horse's head, her back to Leah.

"Did she feed it something?" Luned whispered.

"I'm not sure," said Olwen.

"Hush up," said Gladys. "It's getting back to its feet."

Mam Derw rose stiffly and faced Leah. "I've undone your curse, Gypsy, now I'll lay one of my own. And it won't be one of them all-contingency curses you people use, either. This one will be particular so every time it happens you'll know why it's happening."

"You don't frighten me, old woman," Leah screamed.

Mam Derw continued as if she hadn't heard Leah. "From now on, every time you come into the village—you or your people—one of them dear to you will die. Your family tree will wither. One by one, the branches will fall dead—dead like the branch of that oak behind you that I shall smite." Mam Derw moved forward until she was only a few feet from Leah and clapped her hands twice. From inside the leaves of the tree beside the square, a dead branch snapped free and sailed out to drop at Leah's feet.

Leah leapt back, eyes and mouth wide as she looked from the dead branch to Mam Derw.

"Let that be a warning to you," shouted Mam Derw. "One by one, I said, until you're left all alone with no chick to comfort you. Now go!"

For an old woman, Leah ran remarkably fast. She threw the basket of pegs into the cart and tore the tether free of the churchyard gates before scrambling onto the seat. Gathering up the reins, she slapped the horse into a gallop and sped out of the square.

Olwen and Luned were laughing, tears running down their faces. "That got rid of her," said Olwen.

"Aye, but we're left with that old witch," said Gladys, inclining her head toward Mam Derw. "What's she up to now?"

Mam Derw fumbled under her coat and brought out a small box as Dewi climbed down from the tree. "There you go, Dewi. As I promised—an eagle's egg." Mam Derw handed him the box.

Dewi opened the box and unfolded the tissue paper. He had the egg in his hand when Olwen, Gladys and Luned reached him. "This isn't an eagle's egg," he said. "It's a duck's egg you've painted. I can see where the paint's run onto the paper."

"It's an eagle's egg if I say it is," said Mam Derw.

"That's cheating!" protested Dewi.

"I'd be careful what you say," said Mam Derw, "or the grass snake in your pocket will turn into a viper and bite you." She hobbled away.

"How did she know I had a snake in my pocket?" Dewi asked the three women edging away nervously.

Mam Derw stopped and glanced over her shoulder. "Magic," she said.

♥

SUNDAY SCHOOL TRIP

For as long as Dilys could remember, every summer she'd gone on the annual Sunday school trip to the seaside. This might be the last time. Next year, she and Alun would be married, and after that . . . Once they opened the shoe shop, they'd be too busy to take a Saturday off. He'd tell her to go on her own, but she wouldn't. The trip had special meaning for them.

They shared a seat on the coach for the first time when they were six. Scrunched next to her father they learned how to play noughts and crosses, which Alun always won. She got back at him by splashing him when they were on the beach and he chased her the length of it while her father laughed. When they were eight, her father died and she cried on Alun's shoulder.

They celebrated passing the Eleven-Plus with ice-cream cones, watched the Punch and Judy show, and then went on the bumpers where they rammed each other's cars until the concerned owner threw them off.

She was fourteen when Alun first kissed her. She had thought the steady rain would ruin their special day together. The sea was in turmoil and the beach deserted, but they'd huddled in a sheltered corner under the cliffs, knees to their chins under raincoats. Then Alun put his arms around her and kissed her. His lips were cold and tasted of the sea, but she glowed in his arms.

Two years later, he led her to a quiet spot under the castle tower and asked her to marry him. They chose the ring that day. She wore it on a length of ribbon under her dress for another two years before she plucked up the courage to tell her mother, show her the ring and say she was getting married.

"Not until you're twenty-one, my girl," her mother said.

Alun comforted her and said they would use the time to save for the shop he wanted to open. He'd taken a job at Oliver's Shoes in Newcastle Emlyn to learn the trade. Dilys worked at the bank there, but they rarely travelled to and from work together because the shop stayed open longer hours than the bank. They had Sundays and summer holidays together, which they arranged to coincide with the trip. Five more months . . .

They planned the shop down to the smallest detail. Alun's elderly Aunty Ellen had a house close to the village square and she was willing to give up her front room and one of the bedrooms for rent to help with her pension. The front room would be a shop; they'd sleep upstairs and share the kitchen. They'd paint the shop white and have a white curtain to section off part of it as a stockroom. "Shelves filled with white boxes," Alun said. "And we'll have to stock wellies big enough for Joroway's feet."

"Leather chairs for customers to sit on while they try on shoes," she suggested.

"Not leather," he said. "We won't be able to afford that at first. Plain wooden chairs."

"And I'll make cushions to go on them." She'd watched him smile and happiness warmed her when he said: "Yes. You're good with the needle and you know about colours."

Dilys could never remember a time when they'd quarrelled. It was important not to hurt Alun and he clearly felt the same way about offending her. Some people said they were like two halves of a coin, but Alun said some of his friends asked him how he could stand her temper that matched her fiery hair. She'd never been angry with Alun, although they wouldn't believe it.

She shivered. The sun was barely up, but it was their habit to get to the square in good time to catch the coach. Despite the giggles from some of the children milling around, Dilys smiled and snuggled into the warmth of the arm Alun placed around her.

"Won't be long now," he said, tightening his hold.

"I should have worn a thicker cardigan."

"No, no, you look lovely." He touched his lips to her cheek. "You always do."

She smiled her thanks for the compliment. Five months was a long time to wait, but they'd agreed on a Christmas wedding.

"Aunty Ellen said I could go in at the beginning of next month to work on the front room. Joroway will help me move the furniture out and we could start painting any time after that."

"We need to put up the stockroom shelves first or there'll be sawdust stuck in the paint."

"I talked to Joroway and he'll give me a hand as soon as we get the wood. I'll bring a shoebox from work to use as a measure."

"I can't wait."

"She says we can have the back parlour for ourselves, if we want."

"Really?" Dilys knew her eyes were shining at the thought. "Would she let us put up new wallpaper? The one now is . . ."

Alun laughed. "I think it was put on in the last century. We'll talk her into letting us change it."

"If it's to be our parlour, where will she sit of an evening?"

"I think she'll be making a place in the back bedroom. She mentioned taking her rocking chair up there, anyway."

"Your aunty is being so good to us. We're very lucky."

"I am anyway." He glanced sideways at her and smiled.

Dilys giggled. There wasn't one girl in the world as happy or as lucky.

"Hello, here they come."

In a flurry of skirts and sunhats, shopping baskets laden with their food for the day, a group of women descended upon the square. Behind them strode the tall figure of Williams-the-School and the children formed nervous, quiet groups.

"Aunty BBC says it's going to be a nice day," Gwen Flycatcher said and the other women murmured their agreements.

"He's coming! He's coming!" one of the girls shouted.

The children forgot the headmaster's presence and broke into a dancing, hopping, leaping mass of pigtails, cowlicks, and brown-paper bags of sandwiches as the coach rounded the corner at the far end of the village.

"Now then! Now then!" Williams-the-School herded them from the middle of the square and tried to organize them into a line as the bus with Edwards Luxury Coaches painted on the side eased level with the churchyard wall.

The children scrambled on, pushed and shoved as if it would take off and leave half of them behind. Williams-the-School followed and called them to order. With the voice of authority, he assigned them seats to separate the troublemakers. That done, he emerged and indicated it was safe for the adults to board.

Dilys and Alun chose a seat half way along the aisle. They'd migrated from the back where courting couples sat but they weren't staid enough to sit in front where their elders always sat and fell asleep on the return journey.

Alun took her hand and held it so the diamond shone in the sunlight. "I never get tired of looking at it."

Nor could she. At work, she was the envy of the ringless clerks. They'd picked out the gold band to join it and Alun said he'd buy her an eternity ring as a first-anniversary gift. She sighed and laid her head on his shoulder. No one could be happier.

There was only one empty seat left when a cry came from Dewi Thomas sitting at the front. "Here she comes!"

"Thar she blows," Alun whispered in her ear.

Dilys punched him playfully and grinned as she watched Bronwen make her way down to the square, legs pumping and everything jiggling inside the flowing summer-print dress. Sunhat askew, she clambered onto the bus in a flurry of sunglasses and a straw bag crammed with knitting wool and needles, sandwiches and a Thermos flask.

"Not late am I, Mr Williams?"

"No, no, plenty of time, Miss Richards."

The engine throbbed to life but the driver waited for Bronwen to settle herself next to skinny Gwen Flycatcher then, when Williams-the-School took his own seat, Edwards-the-Coach let out the clutch and they were off.

"Might be the last time for a while," Alun said quietly.

Dilys refused to let the thought make her sad. What took the place of the Sunday-school trip would be far more wonderful. She looked out of the window without seeing the countryside flashing past. In her mind, she was picking out the new wallpaper for the parlour. Alun wouldn't want flowers. Leaves perhaps. Autumn leaves. If Aunty Ellen left the sofa in the parlour, she could make a loose cover and curtains to match. Something in off-white. By the time the coach topped the hill leading down to Aberystwyth Bay, Dilys knew exactly how the parlour would look down to the geranium on the windowsill.

The coach crawled through the narrow streets to pull up alongside other day-trip coaches in the seafront car park. The children stood trembling in the aisle, eager to be out where the blue water beckoned but held prisoner as Williams-the-School rose to bar their way. Careful not to let his eyes stray in the direction of the ever-late Bronwen, he gave them the time of departure. "Six o'clock sharp!" He repeated it several times before jumping to one side to avoid being trampled as the children fought their way from the bus as eagerly as they had fought to get on.

Alun helped Dilys from the bus and then gave a hand to the other women. On her own for a moment, she took her first gulping breath of diesel fumes and stale beer, and the unappetizing aroma of a bag of chips discarded the night before and now picked over by a flock of garrulous seagulls. Alun took her hand and they walked out of the car park. Now Dilys could smell the mixed savour of steamed cockles raked from the sand, cod in batter, and fresh chips with rissoles. A step farther were the ice-cream stands and the toffee apples, a Punch and Judy show, and a hurdy-gurdy with a monkey shivering on its master's shoulder as it peed down his back.

She nudged Alun to draw his attention and they both laughed as they followed the children to the beach. Throughout the day, they'd see the others: the men would be lolling about the pubs while they sampled the local beer, the women flitting from shop to shop to compare the prices with those at Rowlie's shop in the village. At any given time, they could find Bronwen firmly wedged in a deckchair close to the bandstand, her hands busy with the steel knitting needles clicking in and out of the woollen whatever she was making.

But that was for later, for now they had to renew their acquaintance with the Atlantic, homing to it as if with half-forgotten primal memory. Releasing Alun's arm, Dilys removed her sandals and ran to join the children.

Across the warm sand they hopped, Dilys gaining the lead because they stopped to discard shoes and socks. She was standing in the foam when they caught up to her and squealed at the cold. Heedless of the splashes staining their clothes, they left her to race up and down the golden arm of beach curving to embrace the white horses speeding landward with the fresh-caught-mackerel whiff from the fishing boats trawling out in the bay.

A yearly treat, never doubting the following year would bring the same joy, Dilys laughed with them as they wriggled their toes in the sand unaware that soon the bay would be a mooring place for mines and the beach stretched its length with rolls of wire barbed against an invader.

♥

BIG BERTHA

War came to the valley on a Wednesday. Trundled in on a two-wheeled carriage towed behind a khaki-coloured truck, it came to a halt in the square.

The Vickers anti-aircraft gun, misnamed Big Bertha, nosed from beneath the camouflage net draping her like a bridal veil, surveyed the fragile foot-thick walls of the churchyard and settled down to wait.

Sergeant Holloway grunted at the private to stay where he was and leapt heavy-booted onto the pavement outside the post office, a clipboard in his hand.

"Hoi!" shouted Ianto Maesgwyn from the post-office doorway. "You can't leave that thing there."

"Are you Major Braithwaite?" the sergeant asked. "I'm supposed to meet a Major Braithwaite at eleven o'clock."

"I'm the postmaster. And he isn't here, is he?" shouted Ianto. "Move that thing. The ten-past-eleven bus will be along any minute and it can't get past."

"Where should I put it?"

"You didn't ought to ask a man questions like that," said Ianto, backing inside and closing the door firmly.

From the number-three bedroom at the Red Lion where she was changing the sheets, Gladys looked out and saw the army man give what she thought was the Victory sign at the post office. He looked around the square and she ducked out of sight when he turned toward the pub. He clumped his way to it as Gladys ran down the stairs.

Elias stood in the pub doorway, drawn there by Ianto's shouting. Above his head, the Lion Rampant sign swung in time with the sergeant's boots.

"Is that one of them guns like you went for training on?" Gladys asked as she joined her husband on the doorstep.

"It's one like that knocked the wind out of Bogo." Elias stepped away from the door to meet the sergeant. "What can I do for you?"

"I'm supposed to meet a Major Braithwaite," said the sergeant. "Have you seen him?"

"Not this morning," Elias said. "It's market day in Carmarthen and he's probably gone there. Are you sure you've got the right day?"

Sergeant Holloway consulted his clipboard. "Right day; right time; right place.

He was supposed to direct me to the gun's position and sign these papers."

"Anyone can show you the way to Moelfre, but the major is the only one with the authority to sign anything," said Elias. "Come inside while I telephone Plas Gwyn to see if he's there."

Gladys stood to one side to allow the sergeant to enter and she grimaced as he clumped his way through the public, his boots leaving white scratches on the blue slate of her newly washed floor.

"Hoi! You in there!" Knuckles rapped on the window of the truck. "Get this thing moved."

Private Nicholas B. Flynn, barely eighteen and in uniform, had the night before been introduced to the dubious joys of a pub-crawl. He had no recollection of anything after nine-thirty until roll call that morning when he found a pair of ladies' knickers bulging his pocket. Slumped in his seat, desperately trying to remember if he had or he hadn't, the rap on the window came as a rude awakening.

He squinted at the window. Above the khaki paintwork where his head rested, a blue peaked cap with the words Western Welsh on the front came into view. Private Flynn slid his shoulder up the paintwork until his sore and burning eyes came level with the glass and a pair of startled eyes on the other side.

With an oath and a look of horror, the bus conductor leapt backwards off the truck step. Ready to run for the safety of his bus, he studied the window and decided the white-faced apparition with the bloodshot eyes was harmless. "Move it!" he shouted.

Private Flynn, his head wobbly and not quite belonging to him, rolled down the window. "I can't," he said. "I don't have the authority."

"You're blocking the road and I've got a busload of passengers and a schedule to keep," the conductor informed him. "Get this thing out of here."

"But—"

"Where's your driver gone?"

"Don't know, sir." Flynn was too relieved at the ending of the nightmare noises of crashing gears and rumblings from the gun carriage to notice where the sergeant went.

"What's the problem?" One of the passengers joined the conductor.

"This one won't move the truck."

"I can't move it without orders, sir," Flynn explained.

"You didn't salute," said the passenger, "so it's obvious you don't recognize me in civvies. I'm on my way to an important meeting at the War Office and you're going to make me late. I order you to move this contraption away from the bus route, Private. On the double!"

The private came to attention, winced, and saluted. "Where shall I put it, sir?"

The passenger looked around, and then pointed to the open space between the humpbacked bridge and the privet hedge around the pub orchard. "That looks a likely spot."

"Yes, sir." Private Flynn slid onto the driver's seat and Ianto came out of the post office to watch.

Flynn studied the gear-lever knob, memorized First and started the engine, grimacing when he grated the lever into gear. He eased the truck forward a few paces to line it up, then he checked the knob again. Marking Reverse, he changed gears with a squeal, and then stuck his head out of the window to check where the gun carriage was heading.

The bus driver came out to give him a guiding hand as the truck pushed the carriage on a wavering course toward the clearing. "Hard right!" The nose of the gun swung into view. "Left!" The gun and carriage disappeared behind the tarpaulin sides of the truck. "Straight back now."

The bus driver, the conductor, the passenger and Ianto watched the carriage wheels speed toward the edge of the tarmac where it met the sandy stone-and-gravel slope down to the shallow river.

"Stop!" shouted the bus driver.

Private Flynn thought he'd found the brake pedal and he hit it with a heavy foot. With the truck in Neutral, the gun carriage pulled the truck behind it and the edge of the tarmac crumpled under its weight. It rolled onto the slope, stopping when the truck's wheels sank and Flynn found the brake pedal.

"Come on," said the passenger, heading back to the bus.

"Shouldn't you stay to help him?" the driver asked.

"What's your rank, anyway?" asked the conductor. "Are you a General?"

The passenger eyed him. "I sell insurance. Now let's get out of here."

Ianto took the pipe from his mouth when the three ran back to the bus. "Could've told you the surface was breaking away over there," he said. He watched Flynn emerge from the truck and grinned as he went back into the post office to watch from the window.

Camouflage net trailing like a weed, Big Bertha nuzzled the water as if with an unquenchable thirst. Private Flynn studied her, then he looked at the carriage wheels buried to the axle in soft mud and the back wheels of the truck buried to their rims. He groaned.

Sergeant Holloway emerged from the Red Lion. He strode to the corner where he'd left the truck and halted open mouthed when he saw the vacant space. A sixth sense made him turn around. "Private Flynn!"

Flynn cowered beside the truck, focussed on the church across the square and said a quick prayer.

"Who told you to move the bleedin' truck?" Sergeant Holloway clumped down on him in quick-march time.

"An officer on the bus—" Flynn realized he hadn't asked for the man's identification.

Sergeant Holloway marched down one side of the truck and carriage, leapt the shallow river in both directions, and walked back up the other side and around the front to where the private stood. "Bleedin' idiot," he commented, climbing into the truck.

The engine started and the wheels spun, showering Big Bertha with gravel confetti as they dug deeper.

Sergeant Holloway got out and went to see if he'd made any progress. He turned to the private. "Take your puttees off and put them under the wheels. At the double!"

Flynn bent to his ankles and his head threatened to explode. Blindly, he unstrapped the puttees and placed one under each wheel. He stood back as the sergeant revved the engine and then watched the khaki webbing disappear into the mud.

"I'd better go and give them a hand," said Elias to Gladys, "otherwise he'll have the private stripped to his underwear."

Big Bertha had settled deeper by the time Elias arrived. "I'll see if the miller's got any chains." Elias set off across the bridge.

"Go with him, Private." Sergeant Holloway climbed back into the truck. He settled down to wait, his back against the door as he tried to ignore the mothers gathering on the bridge to wait for the children due out of school at noon.

"Why did you back up so close to the edge?" one of the women called.

The sergeant pretended not to hear and spent five minutes studying his clipboard until Elias and the private came back. He jumped out of the truck to supervise chaining the wheels.

"Try it now." Elias stood to one side.

As the sergeant climbed back into the truck, he saw the crowd on the bridge had grown. He put the truck into First and heard the wheels spin. He stamped on the accelerator in a burst of anger and a chain broke loose to form a necklace around Big Bertha.

"It won't work." Elias came to the truck window. "If you uncouple the gun carriage and get the truck onto firm ground . . ."

Used to taking orders, Sergeant Holloway acted on Elias' suggestion and the army men freed Big Bertha from her marriage with the truck. The sergeant swung into the cab and tried to ignore the crowd on the bridge that now included primary-school children. He let out the clutch and heard the wheels spin as Elias came to the window.

"The wheels can't climb over the edge of the tarmac," he said. "I've got some planks in my shed. If we put them under the wheels to form a ramp . . ." Elias disappeared behind the privet hedge.

"Private!" Sergeant Holloway shouted grim-faced and Flynn hopped smartly to attention. "For this, I'll have you scrubbing every bleedin' latrine on camp. With your toothbrush!"

Elias came back with four planks and they wedged two under each wheel. Then Sergeant Holloway started the engine. The truck edged forward and the crowd on the bridge cheered. Then the wood splintered.

"It's no good," said Elias. "The rise is too steep. We'll have to dig a trench behind the wheels then you can take a longer run at it. I think you'd better lighten the load at the back while I go for my spade."

"On the double, Private!" the Sergeant ordered. "Get those boxes of ammo out of there."

As Private Flynn let down the tailgate and started hauling out the crates of shells, one of the women called out: "Why don't you help him, you big bully?"

"Bully!" the children chorused. "Bully! Bully!"

Red faced, Sergeant Holloway went to help the private. "I'll have you digging the compound with a bleedin' mess fork!" he muttered.

Elias returned with the garden spade and more planks, and waited until they finished hauling out and stacking the crates beside the hedge. He passed the spade to Sergeant Holloway who passed it to Flynn.

Private Flynn dug two shallow trenches behind the wheels then stood to one side as the sergeant got into the cab and allowed the truck to roll back.

"Far enough!" shouted Elias, and then he and the Flynn placed the planks in front of the wheels. "Now try it."

The truck eased forward, splintered the planks, and settled into its original grooves.

"I don't know what else to suggest," said Elias. "I don't think even Morgan Ellis' tractor could tow the truck over that ridge."

"Isn't there another truck in the village?" Sergeant Holloway asked.

"Not big enough. You'll have to call your depot and have them send something out."

In twenty years as landlord of the Red Lion, Elias had never heard some of the words Sergeant Holloway threw at Private Flynn before he marched to the pub and clumped to the telephone.

Private Flynn sank onto the tarmac, his back against a front wheel of the truck and a murmur of sympathy came from the crowd.

"Do you think he hit him?"

"No, only shouted, I think."

"Mam? What does *X!!?!X!!* mean?"

"You don't look well." Elias studied the private. "Come inside and have a drink and something to eat."

Private Flynn decided he would never again see the inside of a pub. He thanked Elias, declined, and leapt to his feet as the sergeant came back.

"Every truck is out. They're not due back until six, and then it'll take an hour and a half for them to get here."

"You're in for a long wait, then." Elias addressed to the crowd on the bridge. "You can go home. Nothing's going to happen until after six o'clock." He turned back to the sergeant as the crowd dispersed. "We don't often put up a midday meal, but Gladys can do you sandwiches."

Private Flynn watched the two men disappear inside the Red Lion, sank next to a wheel and closed his eyes.

He slept a troubled sleep. He didn't see Ianto Maesgwyn come out and lock up the post office for the lunch hour. Nor did he see him hobble across the square pushing his bike, or how he rested the bike against the bridge and took a closer look at the truck. He certainly didn't see Ianto go back to the post office, running faster than he had in sixty years, and he didn't question the bucket Ianto brought to place under the truck's fuel tank. The steady drip, drip into the galvanized bucket became part of Private Flynn's nightmare of tom-toms and garish faces with ladies' knickers draped about them.

The children gathering for afternoon school woke Private Flynn. Bleary eyed, he watched them clamber over the boxes of ammunition, then a hand bell summoned from somewhere beyond the bridge and they swarmed out of sight. He rose like a deep-sea diver, in halting movements as the world swayed around him, then made his way down to the river to dip his handkerchief into the water. Leaning against Big Bertha, he mopped his face and the back of his neck.

"Private!" Sergeant Holloway barked.

Private Flynn tried to turn and jump to attention. He lost his footing in the mud and sat down more hurriedly than he intended.

"On your feet!" the sergeant ordered from the edge of the tarmac beside the truck. He sniffed. He bent over and sniffed again. "Either we've struck oil or the bleedin' fuel tank's bleedin' leaking."

"Was it leaking before?" Elias asked. "Or did a piece of gravel do the damage?"

The sergeant shook his head to indicate he didn't know, and then he crawled under the truck to investigate.

"Here—drink this." Elias held out a glass of mud-coloured liquid he brought for the private.

"What is it?" Flynn asked suspiciously.

"If I told you, you wouldn't drink it," said Elias. "Made a night of it last night, didn't you? This'll cure it."

Flynn gagged on the first tentative sip and then he drank the lot in two gulps at Elias' urging.

Sergeant Holloway emerged from under the truck. "By the size of the hole, I'd say it was hit by a stone when we tried to get the truck out of here. There was nearly a tankful of petrol, but it's not even dripping now."

Elias shrugged. "Better not let anybody smoke around here or the truck and that lot over there," he inclined his head toward the ammunition crates "will go up and take us all with it." He went back to the pub and left the army men on guard.

"There they are." Davy slowed the Morris when they approached Henllan Bridge where his son and two other children waited. "I told Dewi I'd take him to see the prisoner-of-war camp they're building if he got off the bus and waited here. Shall I drop you off at Plas Gwyn first, Major?"

"I'd like to see for myself how they're progressing." Major Braithwaite eyed the children. "That's Elias Stock's girl, isn't it? Who's the other boy?"

"Edwin. He and his mother just moved into Ridge House, up by Cartref." Davy

135

stopped alongside the three teenagers and rolled down the window. "I'm going to park here and we'll walk up." He eased the car off the road and under the pine trees.

"You'll stop in at Plas Gwyn for a drink, won't you?" Major Braithwaite asked, puffing as they left the level of the bridge and started up the hill.

"Not today," Davy said. "I have to get back and I expect Dewi's got homework to do."

The three youngsters raced ahead. They reached the top of the hill and came upon the camp at the first bend in the road. Dewi was disappointed. "I thought it would be built of stone like our houses, or concrete like the pillbox at the bottom of Corpse Hill."

"It's what they call prefabs," explained the major, out of breath after his climb. "The pieces are made in a factory and brought here to be put together."

"It looks like a feather," said Bethan, pressing against the wire fence while she studied the layout of the camp, "with that road going straight up the middle and the paths coming off it like that. Will they put huts on all those squares of concrete?"

"Just like the two they've finished." Davy glanced at Edwin. The newcomer to the village hadn't spoken since they met at the bridge. "What do you think?"

Edwin shrugged. "I think those guns the guards are carrying are very small."

"They're smaller than your double-barrel, Dat," said Dewi.

"But they hold more than two shells." The major pointed to the towers at the four corners of the camp. "They'll have machine guns up there."

Beside him, Davy felt Dewi shiver. "Are you cold?" he asked.

Dewi shook his head. "I don't think I could shoot a man."

"If you were under orders, you'd have to," said the major. "Don't worry. You're only fourteen; by the time you're old enough to fight, the war will be over."

"Even if it isn't, as a farmer you'll be spared," Davy pointed out. "The country needs its farmers."

"I suppose . . ." said Dewi, as they returned to the bridge. "But I wouldn't mind going as a wireless operator, though."

Priscilla Braithwaite was watching for them. When Davy pulled up outside Plas Gwyn, she ran out. "Dickie! You were supposed to take delivery of the gun today. Hello, David." She bent to peer into the car. "Hello, children."

"I didn't think it was today." Major Braithwaite stepped out of the car. "Where is it now?"

"Mr Stock telephoned to say the gun is in the river by the bridge."

"They're supposed to put it on the mountain, not in the river!"

"Yes, Dickie dear, but it seems the truck ran off the road."

"We'd better get up there." Major Braithwaite climbed back into the Morris. "David can drop me off."

Major Braithwaite arrived at his assignation four and a half hours late. He pushed his way through the crowd and halted when he saw the truck and the gun. Then he saw the crates of ammunition stacked against the hedge. "Who was the damned fool who put those there?" he bellowed.

Private Flynn emerged from his hiding place in the cab of the truck and cowered against it when the major turned to him.

"Who ordered the ammo stacked there?"

"The—the sergeant, sir," Private Flynn stammered.

"Good God!" Major Braithwaite looked around and spotted Constable Owens. "Owens! Get these people out of here. If that lot goes up, it'll take half the village with it."

As Constable Owens shooed the crowd away, the Major questioned the private. "Where's the sergeant?"

Flynn glanced toward the Red Lion. "He's—er—he's having a cup of tea, sir."

"Go and get him," the major ordered. To Davy, he said: "Those crates have to be moved, and fast. Is there anyone with a lorry to haul them out of here?"

"There's the coalman's horse and cart." Davy tapped Dewi on the shoulder. "Go and fetch Davy-the-Coal."

Major Braithwaite climbed down the bank with Davy on his heels. "This is sacrilege," he muttered. "A gun should not suffer this indignity." He patted Big Bertha's flank and checked under the camouflage net. "Those bolts won't hold her much longer," he informed Davy. "We must pull her out of here."

"I could go for my shire," Davy suggested."

"We'll need two horses to get her and the truck out of this mud," said the major. "I'll send somebody to get mine."

"I'll go," volunteered Bethan.

"Fine," said Major Braithwaite. He called for Constable Owens as Davy left and Bethan went for her bike. "Evacuate everybody from the houses lining the road from here to Moelfre, especially around Corpse Hill. If any of those crates fall off the cart it'll be the end of the village." He eyed the sergeant emerging from the Red Lion. "This is gross negligence!" He bent and sniffed. "Do I smell petrol?"

"The—the tank—a stone put a hole in it when we tried to get the truck out."

"What!" Major Braithwaite stared at him, speechless.

"If you'd been here at eleven . . ." Sergeant Holloway mumbled reproachfully, but Major Braithwaite had gone to meet the coalman and his horse and cart.

"We need your help." Major Braithwaite stood beside the pony, one hand patting its shoulder. "Those crates must be carried up to Moelfre."

"What's in them?" Davy-the-Coal asked.

"Shells for the anti-aircraft gun."

Davy-the-Coal shrugged. "I'll draw the cart closer."

"And the army men can to the loading, what?" The major beamed as he barked the order and added: "You go with the ammo, Private."

With the crates moving slowly through the village on Davy's cart, the crowd returned to the square. Major Braithwaite set the men and a few of the older children to gathering willow branches from the banks along the river and then he and Sergeant Holloway laid the branches under the wheels of the truck and gun carriage. "Used this trick in India," he said. "A green branch is more resilient than the dry planks you used." He left the sergeant on guard and went into the Red Lion to wait for the shire horses.

Half way down Corpse Hill with his shire, Davy came across the coalman's cart with the private slumped dejectedly on the seat. "Where's Davy–the-Coal?" he asked.

Private Flynn gestured toward the bottom of the hill. "I told him the shells might explode if a crate fell off the cart and he ran away."

"Well, you'd better move or we can't pass up the hill with the gun."

A city boy, Private Flynn studied the rear end of the pony. "I've never driven one of these, and I don't know which way I'm to go."

"If you follow the road you'll end up on Moelfre," said Davy. "Try slapping the reins."

He did as Davy suggested and the pony turned its head to look at him.

"Harder!"

Private Flynn slapped harder. The pony leapt forward a few feet then halted when the crates slid down the cart to rest against the tailgate.

Davy shook his head. "You lead Boyo into the village and I'll take the cart up to Moelfre."

"Does he bite?" Private Flynn asked eyeing the shire as Davy put the lead rope into his hand.

"Go!" said Davy, climbing onto the cart.

Ianto closed the post office for the day and pushed his bike across the square to join the crowd gathered about Major Braithwaite and the shire Bethan brought from Plas Gwyn.

"I wonder where David is?" The Major eyed the road through the village. "Briggie can't pull the truck or the gun out on his own."

"Boyo might be out in the high pasture," Dewi suggested.

Major Braithwaite eyed the boy. "Go and look if you can see him." To the sergeant, he said, "We can't wait much longer. There's rain promised for tonight, and if the bank gets any muddier we'll never drag the truck or the gun out."

"What if we harnessed the tractor with the shire?" Elias wondered aloud.

"That would work," said the major. "Bethan? Where are you? Go to Plas Gwyn and ask someone to bring the tractor up."

"It'll take a while," said Bethan. "I'll have to walk because I left my bike down there so I could lead Briggie back."

"Does anyone have a bike?" The major's eyes fell on Ianto. "Lend the girl your bike."

"No fear," said Ianto. "This is government property."

"We're doing work for the government," said Elias. "The least you can do is lend my daughter your bike."

"Better still, lend it to the sergeant and he can drive the tractor back," said Major Braithwaite.

"What happens if he damages it?" asked Ianto.

Sergeant Holloway muttered under his breath and reach for the bike. "I'm commandeering it, Postmaster!"

"No, you aren't," said Ianto, keeping a firm grip on the handlebars.

"Gentlemen!" The major stepped between them. "If there's any damage to the bicycle, the War Office will compensate you, Mr Evans."

Reluctantly, Ianto gave up his bike; waiting in silence while the major gave Sergeant Holloway directions to Plas Gwyn. Then he muttered: "Going on his past record, I don't think that bloke could find the river if he was drowning in it."

Forty minutes later, Sergeant Holloway arrived in the square at the wheel of Major Braithwaite's tractor. With chains borrowed from the miller, they harnessed the shire and the tractor. Elias urged the shire forward and the tractor crept alongside with the Sergeant at the wheel.

The truck came onto firm ground but Big Bertha was reluctant to leave her watering hole where she could see her gleaming reflection in the water. On either side, men laid hands to the carriage wheels and Major Braithwaite coaxed: "Come on, girl. Come on, my beauty."

Unwillingly, she mounted the willows spread before her wheels like an offering while the crowd cheered her on. Straddling the tarmac, she viewed the houses lining the road on the far side of the bridge. Fragile stone and mortar, they wouldn't stand against her anger for a minute, but beyond them, rising to the south in full sunshine, towered a might she could never hope to dominate. Nosing upward, she eyed Moelfre.

Major Braithwaite and Elias both leapt forward as the gun tilted on the carriage. "It's the forward bolts," the major said. "I didn't think they'd hold much longer."

"Are the other bolts strong enough to hold her for Corpse Hill?" Elias asked.

The major nodded and ordered the horse and tractor to tow Big Bertha out into the square so they could turn her around. Slowly, the shire straining, they climbed the humpbacked bridge. When they reached the bottom of the slope on the far side, the tractor sputtered and gave an oily cough.

"Didn't you check the petrol?" Major Braithwaite asked a red-faced Sergeant Holloway.

"Where's the nearest petrol station?" the sergeant asked.

"Two miles away in Newcastle Emlyn," one of the crowd answered.

Elias spotted Bette Williams in the crowd. "Mrs Williams! Does Rowlie have any spare petrol?"

"Yes," said Bette. "But it's Wednesday and he'll be out making deliveries until eight. He has the spare can with him."

"I have some," said Major Braithwaite, "but a five-gallon container can't be carried on a bicycle. It means a long walk for somebody." He looked around for volunteers and was surprised when Ianto hobbled forward.

"I've got a couple of gallons," said Ianto. "What is the army paying for petrol these days?"

"Well, Sergeant?" Major Braithwaite said. "Either you pay this man or we wait for another hour while somebody goes to Plas Gwyn."

"The War Office will pay the going rate," said Sergeant Holloway.

Ianto shook his head. "It'll be months before I see my money. If ever. Cash on the nail, Sergeant, or I don't part with my petrol."

"What are you waiting for?" Major Braithwaite urged. "Pay the man."

Reluctantly, Sergeant Holloway dug into his pocket and came up with a handful of coins. He handed three to Ianto.

"Is this the going rate for petrol?" Ianto showed the coins to Elias.

"You must know what you paid," said Elias. "Take it and shut up."

Ianto pocketed the money and hobbled to the post office. A minute later, he was back with his bucket. They gleaned a length of hose from the miller, siphoned the petrol into the tractor, and they were off through the village.

On a level stretch close to the newly built pillbox, they heard shouting coming from behind the eight-foot-high walls of the vicarage garden. Then the vicar's wife came running out.

"Major! Oh, Major! Do something!" she cried when the procession drew to a halt.

"What's the problem, Mrs Davies?" Major Braithwaite asked.

"Just come quickly. Please!" She tugged at his sleeve.

The major handed Briggie's lead to Bethan then he, Elias and Sergeant Holloway followed Margaret Davies through the heavy gate into the garden.

The vicar's normally placid and compassionate face was purple with rage. "Hellfire and damnation!" he shouted, brandishing a stick as he rounded the end of a tall row of runner beans. "What will he be into next? My apples?"

"Ooh!" Margaret cowered behind the major when Davy's shire horse pushed through the middle of the row of beans.

The major ran forward and caught Boyo's lead rope, but the shire resisted, lowering its mouth to the row of tasty cabbages. "No!" Major Braithwaite rapped

Boyo on the nose. Boyo tossed his head, eyes rolling white, and half-lifted Major Braithwaite off his feet as Elias ran forward to help. They calmed Boyo and heard the vicar shouting from the orchard.

"Come down out of there. Come down, I say!" The vicar saw Sergeant Holloway and called to him. "This is one of your men. He's responsible for the destruction to my garden."

Sergeant Holloway trudged to the orchard and peered up through the leaves of the apple tree to where Private Flynn cowered on a branch. "Get down here on the double!"

"Where's Davy Thomas?" asked Elias. "This is his horse."

"He isn't here," said the vicar, "you can depend on that. Davy would never allow Boyo anywhere near my garden. But this man . . . This man can't even control the most docile of God's creatures."

Private Flynn reached the ground and stood with downcast eyes.

"Where's the man who owns the horse?" Elias asked.

The private told them how Davy had taken the cart up to Moelfre and given him Boyo.

"And you led him into my garden!" the Vicar accused.

"Where's the coalman?" Elias asked.

Private Flynn shook his head. "Don't know, sir. He got frightened and ran off."

"What are you going to do about this destruction?" the vicar asked.

Sergeant Holloway threw Private Flynn a baleful look. "If you'll make out a list of the damage, and the cost . . ."

"I will certainly do that," Reverend Davies snapped. "As for this man . . ."

"The horse pulled me in here!" Private Flynn protested.

Sergeant Holloway laid a heavy hand on the private's shoulder and propelled him from the garden. "When the bill comes in for all this, you'll spend the duration spud bashing!"

They harnessed Boyo alongside Briggie, in place of the tractor, and Big Bertha began her ponderous climb up Corpse Hill.

"It's just like the old days," said Major Braithwaite to no one in particular. "We always used horses to pull the gun carriages."

Davy left the cart outside Pen Farm. By the time Big Bertha reached there, he and Dewi had the milking done and the churns set out ready for collection beside the gate. "What took you so long?" he asked.

"It's a long story, David," the major answered wearily as he climbed onto the coalman's cart and ordered the sergeant up beside him.

The climb up the mountain road gave Big Bertha ample opportunity to study the valley, and now the distant haze of coastline came into view, spreading to the west and south. Others of her ilk waited there, lying in ambush for invaders droning for the land. She was the rear-guard, the valley's sentinel, and the ghosts of other sentinels hovered around her. But this time the threat was not from dark-skinned Romans but from a blonde race. She would hold safe the trees and the hills, and the nestled homes of those who had brought her. Surveying her domain, she swung around, nudging Moelfre's granite hardness with her nose.

"Hold her firm!" Major Braithwaite shouted to Private Flynn. "Another swing like that and she'll be making her way back down the hill."

It took six of them to bolt Big Bertha onto her cradle. Then they locked the crates of ammunition inside the concrete hold built against Moelfre's side. The sun was already setting and a fine rain began to fall as the men moved away, climbing onto the coalman's cart for the ride back to the village.

Slumped against the tailgate, Private Flynn studied the mountain through the grey drizzle; eyed the sharp-thorned gorse bushes; and sniffed the pungent bouquets one of the shires left to mark their passing. He decided digging a compound with a mess fork would be easy after this.

♥

A GIFT OF TEARS

Dilys waited until her mother was asleep, then she went down to the kitchen and dressed by the glow of the fire banked for the night. Tucking cigarettes and lighter into the pocket of her slacks, she let herself out of the front door and closed it quietly.

Ahead, moonlight bathed the garden path, and beyond it was the gate that squeaked. Dilys bent low. Running the length of the path, she vaulted over the gate and collapsed breathlessly on the far side, listening for her mother's cry of alarm.

It was too soon. They all told her that, but she couldn't stay cooped up in her room a minute longer. It was ten days and the bleeding had stopped. What did it matter if walking about meant she could never have a child? Without Alun, it didn't matter.

She had to get away, if only for an hour. Sneaking a cigarette at an open window, blowing the smoke outside as she listened for her mother's step on the stairs, was nerve wracking. She had to be away; to be free and without the feeling of panic at what would happen if her mother caught her smoking.

It was silly to feel that way, she kept telling herself. She was a grown woman. A widow who just lost a baby, she was twenty-two and old enough to do as she liked.

She peered at the house through the bars of the gate, watching for a movement behind the curtains of her mother's bedroom. When she saw none, she got to her feet, ducked below the height of the hedge, and ran up the road until she was around the bend and out of sight.

She lit a cigarette and inhaled slowly, exhaling with a sigh of relief. To be out of the house was like having a weight lifted from her shoulders. If she'd had to contend with her mother's solicitous questions an hour longer, she'd have gone mad.

She walked slowly, feeling the blood begin to sing through her limbs after the days of lying in bed. In some countries, women were up and about an hour after giving birth. "But not after a miscarriage," her mother said. And Millie Thomas said. And Bette Williams said. All the old biddies with no medical training were certain and united in their prescription. Bed rest. And Mam Derw! To think her mother had allowed the old crone into the house! God! What was in the mixture she gave Dilys to drink? Musty it was, like water after soaking sweaty socks, but it didn't seem to have done any harm to the flowers beneath her bedroom window.

Dilys halted, aware of voices ahead in the darkness. Dammit! She'd forgotten the Home Guard. These would be the two gunners coming off shift after their stint with Big Bertha up on Moelfre. If they saw her out here at this time of night, it would be all around the village tomorrow and her mother would hear about it.

Quickly, she ground the cigarette under her heel and leapt for the bank, cursing under her breath when her hand brushed against a nettle. She eased over the wall of woven branches and slithered down into the field, her back pressed against the bank.

"What the bloody hell was that?" Bogo Griffiths' voice came over the hedge.

"Damned if I know." Tom Evans answered. "It could have been one of Davy's dogs out hunting."

"Or it could have been a German spy," said Bogo.

"Don't be daft, man. How could a German spy get here without being caught?"

"Could have parachuted in," said Bogo.

"What the hell for?" asked Tom. "What's he going to do—steal Mam Derw's secret cure for warts or check how much water Elias puts in his beer? Come on. It was

probably a dog or a fox. Davy said he'd seen a
fox after the chickens."

"I still think we should take a look,"
Bogo suggested.

"Then you look on your own. I'm home
to my bed."

Dilys heard Tom move off down the
road, but Bogo was still on the other side of the
hedge. She pressed back, ducking deeper
beneath the new growth spreading untrimmed
like an umbrella at the top of the hedge. Under
her right heel, a dry twig snapped like the
ricochet of a bullet.

"Hang on, Tom!" shouted Bogo. "I'm
coming."

Bogo ran after Tom and Dilys relaxed.
She scratched at the white lumps raised on her
hand by the nettle and lowered herself onto a
root bole sticking out from the bank.

From the blackness of the hedge, Dilys
watched the moon shadows play across the
stubbled field, then all turned darker and
clouds raced from the north to gather over
Moelfre. From her window, she'd seen it
happen two weeks earlier, on the night after the
news came about Alun.

Damn Ianto Maesgwyn! He could have
shown a bit more feeling; a bit more
understanding. Had there been any need to
come running up the path, hobbling as fast as
his bent old legs would carry him and waving
the yellow envelope with the black border as if
he was bringing an invitation to Buckingham

Palace? Alun told her in his last letter he was going for special training and wouldn't be allowed to write for about a month. That was three days before Ianto ran in his excitement, unable to wait a second longer to bring her the bad news. "Damn him!" she muttered. "Damn all postmen to hell!"

It rained buckets the next day after the clouds gathered like that, and she'd gone out in it without her coat, down to the Vicarage to shout her anger at Reverend Davies. But he hadn't been there. She found him in Saint Barnabas, him and Margaret, changing the cloth on the altar to purple for Lent. Eira Griffiths was there as well, taking away the flowers. She tried to stop Dilys, and Dilys pushed her into one of the pews, scattering flowers and water and crystal shards all over the place. Damn Eira Griffiths, the sanctimonious old witch. Went to church three times on Sundays to beg forgiveness for the venom her wicked tongue spread the rest of the week. By God, didn't her eyes widen when Dilys said that to her!

And damn the bloody vicar, too, spouting about God being good. Huddled in the discomfort of the hedge, Dilys gave free rein to her anger. What God would take Alun away before he knew about the child she carried? Didn't have an answer, did the holy vicar. Standing there like a stick of wood while she pummelled the hell out of him. Was there any call for Margaret to slap her face and then hug her tight the way she did? And who the hell asked Bette and Gladys and Tom Evans and Williams-the-School to come crowding into the church to stare at her?

In the darkness to her left, a twig snapped. Dilys froze as stealthy movements made soft sounds in the long grass beside the bank. The bull? No, Davy wouldn't leave the bull out at night, and never in a field of stubble. Whoever—whatever—it was, moved closer and stopped. A shotgun barrel snapped into place, breaking the silence.

"Who's there?" Dilys asked; her voice shrill.

"Dilys? Dear God!" Davy Thomas moved out of the darkness to stand in front of her. "I nearly shot you, girl. I thought you were a fox."

"You've called me a red-haired hoyden in the past, Mr Thomas, but I never thought you'd take me for a fox."

"What're you doing up here in the dark?" He cracked the shotgun and lowered himself onto his haunches.

"I had to get out of the house for a bit." She felt no need to explain why because her mother's ways were well known.

"Does your mother know?"

"What do you think?" Her laugh sounded brittle to her ears.

"I suppose not."

Dilys heard him chuckle and saw the white flash of teeth when he grinned. That was one thing everybody envied Davy—his white and even teeth. Although she recognized he was good looking, she always thought of him as an old fuddy-duddy, stodgy and dull as dishwater, but both Olwen and Luned made a play for him a few years back when his wife died.

Eldest son of old Dot-Down-Carry-One, as Dewi called his grandfather, Davy inherited the biggest farm in the valley. Who'd have thought he'd come back from Canada with a wife and son? It must have been one in the eye for the old biddies. Davy would have been a catch in those days. Still was, for he never remarried.

"It's going to rain soon." Davy looked up toward Moelfre. "You shouldn't be out here."

"Don't you start telling me what to do, Mr Thomas!" she snapped. "Everybody's telling me what to do."

"And you're too old for that now, aren't you? Do you think you're old enough to call me by my first name?" When she didn't respond, he said: "I don't suppose you saw a fox on your way up here?"

"Only two old guzzlers—Bogo and Tom Evans."

"That's another reason why you shouldn't be out here. Bogo's carrying a rifle these days and he's jumpy enough to shoot first and ask about it later."

"Like you nearly did?"

"You're a country girl. You know better than to skulk around hedges in the dark."

"I wasn't skulking!" she protested loudly.

"Stop shouting or you'll frighten the fox away."

"Why isn't Dewi out here helping you look for it?" she asked.

"I suppose you haven't heard, you being ill and all. Dewi went and signed up for the Navy."

"What! But he can't! He's only—" Dilys mentally deducted the years between herself and Dewi. "He's only sixteen!"

"And barely that. He altered his birth certificate. They didn't even look at it long enough to see he was born in Canada."

"And you let him go? You should have stopped him."

"I wanted to, but—Gran's right. If I'd stopped him, I would have lost him for sure. By letting him go there's a chance he'll come back."

"Not in this war. None of them are going to come back. Somebody should put bloody Hitler and Mussolini and Churchill in a room and drop a bomb on them. You don't see them fighting, do you? They're good at sending men out to be killed, but they sit in their bomb shelters and make speeches."

"I'm not sure what I'll do if Dewi doesn't come back. I had high hopes for him. First one of us Thomas's ever to go to grammar school, Dewi was, and he could have made the Olympic team as a runner. He could have been anything he wanted."

"He still can. Alun was told he could go to college after the war."

"What man would want to be a schoolboy after he's spent years killing other men?"

"You're doing Dewi's thinking for him."

"He's sixteen! I counted on doing his thinking for him until he was twenty-one."

"Is that what your mother and father did?"

"Me?" His chuckle was low, almost a growl. "When I was sixteen, I took the bit of money Grandfather Thomas left me and booked passage to Canada."

"And met Meg."

"Aye, met her at a box social."

"What's that?"

"Sort of an auction, you might say. They were raising money to get a horse for the schoolteacher so she wouldn't have to walk five miles through the snow to get to school. What happens is the girls pack boxes with picnic lunches and the men bid on them. The highest bidder shares the picnic with the girl who brought the box."

"And you picked Meg's."

"Three dollars it cost me but, see, I knew whose box it was. Didn't know her, not then, but I'd seen her come in with the box.

Lovely, she was. And delicate looking, like a doll among the big-boned farm women."

"I remember her a bit. Mam brought me up to see the baby," Dilys' voice faltered, "after you came back." She wrenched her thoughts away from her lost baby. "So you fell in love over the picnic and got married."

"I was twenty. Meg was three years older, but I'd grown up fast in the four years of herding cattle into the railway station in Calgary. From up Caernarfon way her family was originally and it didn't take much persuading for them to let her come back with me."

"And you had Dewi." Firmly, she pushed aside the ghost of her own tragedy.

"Born in the middle of a blizzard he was, two years after we were wed. I'd gone to help bring in a herd from Water Valley. They sent to fetch me, but it was morning before the snow stopped and I could get through the drifts to her father's place where I'd left her. Well, it was all over by the time I got there. I had a son and a wife lying close to death. She was never strong after that and the sawbones warned me another child could kill her. I was ready to bring her back here when the letter came about my father being hurt in a fall. In Canada, Meg wouldn't have lived through the next winter so we came here, and two years later we had the hardest winter in history."

"You still miss her."

"Sometimes I see her in Dewi. Taken after my side of the family, he has, but, once in a while, he'll turn his head a certain way and I see Meg. The pain never really goes away, Dilys, but you can learn to live with it. Alun will always be a part of you."

"I don't need you to tell me that!" she snapped, as if anger would push the pain away.

"Let it out, Dilys. If you hold it inside, it'll destroy you."

"You talk as if I haven't lost anyone before. You forget my father died when I was eight."

"That was different. He belonged to your mother, not to you. Do you want to end up as bitter as—"

"As my mother? Are you starting into her now?"

"Mari was never the way she is now, not when Tom was alive. Full of fun she was then. Remember the singsongs we used to have around the piano in your parlour? It all ended when your father went, and your mother— She never cried, Dilys. Not once."

"How would you know? You don't live in her pocket, do you?" Her voice rose shrilly. "How would you know if she cried or not?"

"I know. And I know you haven't cried."

"It's none of your business anyway, Mr Thomas!"

"It is my business, Dilys Ellis. I owe that much to you."

"You don't owe me anything!"

"Don't I? Don't I remember you taking Dewi by the hand to school his first day? And don't I remember you coming to fetch him to go singing for *calennig* on New Year's morning when I was too lost in grief to take him and Gran too feeble for all the walking? You were always a good neighbour, Dilys, and now it's my turn."

"What can you do? Can you bring Alun back? Or the baby?"

"Nothing can bring them back, but dealing with their loss is easier than dealing with the lost dreams. That's what hurts the longest; losing the hopes and dreams you shared. We were going to buy a cottage by the beach at Llangrannog. Meg was going to spend the summers there with Dewi and I was going to get Aled to keep an eye on the farm and go out there every weekend. To this day, I can't go near Llangrannog for the memories it brings."

"We were ready to open a shoe shop in the village but the war started. Before he was called up, Alun worked at Oliver's in Newcastle Emlyn to learn the trade. Stout brogues for winter, he used to say, and white daps for summer, and wellies big enough for Joroway's feet. I could still do it. Still open the shop."

"That was a dream you borrowed from Alun. There'll be no shop, and all of us will have to catch the bus to Newcastle Emlyn to buy our shoes. It's gone, Dilys. The dream is gone."

Dilys gulped back a sob as the half-seen shop with its shelves of white shoeboxes tumbled around her. Without knowing how it happened, she was crying quietly with her head on Davy's shoulder. Then she was sobbing, deep shuddering sobs and Davy was holding her. He thrust a handkerchief into her hands as the sobbing subsided, and then he released her. In the darkness, she saw the flare of a match as he lit two cigarettes, then he held one out to her.

"Go on. I know you smoke. I've seen you at your window when I've been out in the fields at night."

Dilys took the cigarette and inhaled with shuddering breaths. "How can you bear it? You never married again."

"It would take a special girl to replace Meg. And it would take a special girl to put up with Gran. Bad tempered she can be at times."

Dilys said nothing for a while, her shame at breaking down in front of him holding her silent. Her father used to say a woman who burst into tears was the worst thing a man had to deal with. Then her shame got too much for her. "I'm sorry . . ."

Silence followed, as if he hadn't heard her, then: "Do you remember when you came scrumping apples on your way home from Sunday school at Penboyr?"

Unwillingly letting go of the present, she searched her memory. "When your mother threw a pot of water over me?"

"And your mother came up screaming about how your best dress was ruined."

"It was crepe-de-chine. Every time she washed it, it took hours to iron. I hardly ever got to wear that dress, except on Sundays."

"And now you wear trousers, like a man."

"It's better than drawing seams down the backs of my legs with eyebrow pencil because there aren't any nylons to be had!" she retorted. "I smoke. And I've been known to go into the Masons Arms in Newcastle Emlyn with Alun and drink a pint. So there!" She heard him chuckle. "What're you laughing at?"

"Nothing."

"It had to be something."

"I was just thinking of something Meg did once," he answered quietly. Again, silence hung between them until Davy broke it. "Ianto Maesgwyn is retiring next month. It wouldn't be a bad job for you, running the post office. After all, you've worked in the bank in Newcastle Emlyn and working in a post office can't be much different."

"Now you're back to telling me what to do! Keeping me busy, are you? Don't you know I'm too weak to work after losing the baby and all?"

"There's nothing weak about you, girl. Never has been."

"Well, I'm not working in the post office. If I do anything at all, I'll join the Land Army and get away from this place where everybody keeps telling me what to do."

"That'd be a pity. If you worked in the post office, I think I'd send myself a letter just for the pleasure of seeing you puff up the hill with your bike."

"I wouldn't put it past you." She flicked the stub of her cigarette out into the stubble. "But you'd have to keep Blackie under lock and key. I swear if that damned cockerel of yours comes after me again I'll wring his neck."

"Does that mean you'll take the job?" He went to heel the glowing stub she'd thrown.

"It's the Land Army for me. In with a crowd of women all wearing trousers and smoking and mucking out barns." She watched him heel his own cigarette, guarding against a fire in the stubble. Stodgy. Careful. Dull.

He eyed the deeper dark hovering over Moelfre and hefted the breeched shotgun. "Well, it's bed for me."

"You're not going after the fox?" She rose from her perch in the hedge.

"Any fox with half a brain will be home in bed by now." He looked at her. "If it wasn't for you getting mad at me, I'd be telling you to get home to your bed too."

"Or what? You'll sue me for trespassing on your land?"

"I could tell Mari you're up here . . ."

"*Arswyd!* You wouldn't do that, would you?" She stood in front of him, her head barely level with his shoulder. "You won't tell her, will you?"

"Not if you use the gate this time." He led the way along the hedge to the gate.

"You saw me coming over the hedge earlier?"

"I didn't know what it was for sure. All I saw was a flash of red that could have been a fox." He held the gate open for her to pass through and then he followed, closing it at his back. "Do you want me to walk down with you?" he asked when they both stood on the road.

"With Bogo and his rifle safe in bed, I'll be all right."

Against the dim light of the sky, she saw him nod. "Yes, you'll be all right now."

"Goodnight and—thank you." On an impulse, she reached up and touched her lips to his cheek and then she ran down the hill, slowing only when she turned the corner and was out of his sight.

What had possessed her to do that? What ever would he think! And what, she wondered, was her mother going to think when she found a man's handkerchief in the wash? Knowing Davy Thomas, he'd have initials in the corner of it.

And what if somebody had seen them in the field! What if they'd seen her kissing him!

They'd think the worst and she'd be blamed because dull, stodgy Davy Thomas wouldn't initiate a thing like that with any woman, least of all one widowed only two weeks.

Oh, dammit, what did it matter what people thought. Her conscience was clear.

She pushed the garden gate wide, heedless of its squeak and creak. It closed behind her with a bang when she was half way up the path. As she threw Davy's handkerchief into the hedge the curtain twitched at her mother's window.

"Mam!" she called. "I've decided to take over Ianto's job, as you wanted. If somebody has to deliver black-bordered telegrams, it might as well be me."

♥

DISTANT THUNDER

A cocoon of uneasiness surrounded Helen as she went about her morning tasks, chilling her in spite of the August heat. Even Megan's artless five-year-old chatter failed to dispel her apprehension as they walked to the village with the basket of eggs.

The shop window blinds were drawn caught up on a corner of a Peak Frean's biscuit tin, and the interior was dim and cool. Rowlie was behind the counter clipping coupons from a ration book and commiserating with Mari Jenkins on the shortage of sugar.

"There's Black Market for them with money," Mari complained and looked to see who had entered the shop. "Any news of William?"

Helen shook her head, but Mari's question showed her the foreboding had to do with William. He needn't have joined up. A teacher, he could have claimed exemption, but even men with families were going now. If the war went on much longer, how soon would it be before they ordered women and children to the front line, she wondered bitterly.

Rowlie scooped up Megan. "How's my big girl?" he asked, laughing when she hugged her arms around his neck. "Gram's been waiting for you to help her with the baking." He put Megan down and watched her run along the hallway to the kitchen. He sighed. "It's a sad day when a man can't even give his only grandchild a sweetie because of rationing."

"Don't worry." Helen handed him the basket of eggs. "There are raspberries to pick when we get home, thanks to the canes you planted last year."

"Even so . . ." Rowlie studied her. "Are you feeling all right?"

Helen nodded, not trusting herself to respond verbally to the concern of a man who looked so much like William.

"Go through to Bette then. I'll finish with Mrs Jenkins then I'll come back for a cuppa."

Bette's ample arms were white with flour to the elbows. Beside her at the scoured table, Megan was modelling a lump of dough. "See, Mam?" she said when she saw Helen. "I'm making a pussycat and Gram's going to bake it. Aren't you, Gram?"

"That's right, *cariad.*" Bette glanced at Helen. "Haven't had bad news, have you?"

Helen shook her head. It was two months since William's last letter. In it, he told her he was starting a new training course and wouldn't be able to write for several weeks. It was a sure sign he was going into action. Everyone knew that. Despite censorship, one could read between the lines. Dilys' husband had written more or less the same thing two years earlier. When next she heard, it was a black-bordered telegram from the War Office.

"Helen?" Bette eyed her questioningly. "What's the matter?"

"I'm worried, that's all." She took the kettle from the Aga and filled it at the tap. "Rowlie said he'd be in for tea soon. I'll get it ready."

Helen put the kettle on the burner and sat down. Bette's rhythmic working of the dough was comforting; the mesmeric folding, kneading and dredging somehow holding her uneasiness at bay. Megan chattered, sometimes talking about the cat she was making, sometimes about starting school the following week.

Helen would be going to school, too, using the teacher's certificate gathering dust in the attic. She'd be taking over William's work while he—

No. She must not speculate on what William would be doing. After all, he might not have passed as a navigator on a bomber crew. Better to hope he'd failed and was sitting safely behind a desk somewhere. Better still to put her mind to what she and Megan would be doing.

They'd be coming to Bette's and Rowlie's for lunch during the week and Joroway would be going up to the farm to see to the heavy work. She'd still have to gather the eggs and milk the goat. Her! Milking a goat! Almost, Helen laughed. She was a city girl. How had she ended up in a rural backwater with a small farm on her hands?

She knew the answer, just as she knew the answers to the soul-searching, long-ago questions of adolescence that demanded a purpose to her life, a reason for her existence—William. William of the laughing dark eyes in a mud-spattered jersey waving to her from the rugby field before he shouldered into a scrum. She'd known him since they met in college eight years earlier, and she'd been his wife for seven of those years but, whenever she thought of him, she pictured him as he looked the first day. William, the rugger player who quoted Keats and Wordsworth at the drop of a hat, and read aloud the Shakespearian sonnets.

There was never any question of William taking a post in the city after he left college. For two years, he'd seen the rush and squalor of Cardiff and it was enough.

"But the culture!" she protested when he spoke of going back to the village where he was born.

"Culture?" he said. "When you've seen Tom Evans and Bogo Griffiths as Athos and Porthos prancing across the stage in their tights, or had your ears blasted by Bronwen Richards' Brunhilda, nothing here will satisfy you. And our choirs! Best in Wales. Our male-voice choir took the cup at the Eisteddfod in Cardigan two years ago."

But the narrowness of small communities . . . The suspicion. It was there, but hidden. On the surface, they accepted her because she was William's wife and her in-laws ran the village shop. But without Bette and Rowlie . . . And if William didn't— She mustn't think of that. William would come back.

But without him, what was there to hold her in the village? Who? There was Dilys. And Joroway. Joroway didn't belong here any more than she did and a natural affinity had grown between her and the old man. She could not explain her friendship with Dilys as easily. Dilys was of the village, born and educated here with no knowledge of the outside world beyond a week spent in London on her honeymoon. Dilys was an anomaly. Dilys wore slacks. Dilys drank beer. Dilys hid in odd corners with a cigarette in her mouth. If Mari Jenkins knew her daughter smoked she'd have her chained to a pew in Saint Barnabas.

A cigarette started their friendship. Helen had been sitting on the step outside the house watching Megan make mud pies when Dilys came around the corner with the post. Knowing the name the villagers called women who smoked, Helen hid the cigarette and waited for Dilys to hand her the letters and leave. But Dilys flopped onto the step next to her and pulled out a packet of Woodbines. It became a regular thing, with Dilys dropping in for a cigarette and a cup of tea during her twice-daily rounds with the post.

"The worst part of this job is telling people their husbands or sons have been killed," Dilys said once. "I go to see them every day, them with men away in the war, that way they won't suspect until the last minute I've got a telegram from the War Office for them."

Dilys told her that before William went to the recruiting office and signed up. Dilys came to see Helen every day whether there was post for her or not. With William away, each day when Dilys arrived, Helen's heart went into an agonizing spasm until she saw Dilys hang the postbag on the handlebars of the bike she always left propped against the gate.

Helen rose when Rowlie rushed in from the shop with Dilys on his heels. "Where's my tea?" he asked as he untied the white apron and hung it from a hook behind the door.

"Just making it," Helen said her eyes on Dilys. Dilys shook her head to indicate she had no post and Helen busied herself making the tea while Bette cleared a corner of the table.

"The news is on." Rowlie fiddled with the wireless knobs as Helen carried the teapot to the table and poured with a trembling hand.

She sat down, hiding her clenched hands in the folds of her skirt, and listened. The allies had taken Sicily, the Americans had attacked Japanese bases in the Pacific, and then—slipped quietly among the list of victories—bombers continued their night raids on Hamburg . . .

Helen's gasp drew Rowlie to her side. "What's wrong, *cariad?*"

"Nothing. I can't explain it." Before her, Megan stood close to tears. She drew the child onto her lap and rocked her. "It's all right, pet."

"Did you bring Helen any news today?" Bette asked Dilys.

"No." Dilys lit a cigarette and placed it between Helen's fingers.

Helen drew on the cigarette, avoiding Bette's eyes. Bette disapproved of her smoking and Helen rarely did so in front of her mother-in-law. "I'm all right," she said, at a loss to explain her overwhelming sense of something unpleasant about to happen.

"But you're shaking like a leaf." Rowlie pushed her cup closer. "Have a drink of tea to calm you down."

"No. I must go." Helen put Megan down and rose to her feet. "I must get home."

175

Home where William's books were around her. Home where his photograph smiled down from the piano.

"Leave Megan here," Bette suggested. "I'll bring her up after supper."

"Helen needs Megan with her today," Rowlie said, his eyes meeting Helen's over the child's head. "We'll come up after supper tonight."

"And I'll be up on my regular round about four-thirty," Dilys reminded her.

Helen handed the cigarette to Dilys and hustled Megan out, ignoring the child's protests and the worried faces of Rowlie and Bette. Only Dilys seemed to understand. Dilys whose own husband— "You wouldn't keep anything from me, would you?" she asked, and Dilys shook her head.

Helen came close to running the mile back to the farm; carrying Megan when the child complained at the pace she set. She couldn't explain her need to be home, or her anger as the steepness of the hill slowed her pace.

"We'll get Megan a bike when she starts school," William had said.

"Why bother?" she argued. "All it will do is make the easy way easier, it won't make the uphill climb any better."

"Reverend Davies will tell you the downhill path is easy for everyone," William said with a grin. "It's going uphill that strengthens us."

Helen gave Megan lunch then sat brooding over a cup of tea. The child was unusually silent, as if sensing something in her mother that hadn't been there the day before. They sat quietly, Megan busy with her chalks and Helen watching and checking the minute hand on the clock that seemed to take forever to reach each quarter chime. Everything was normal. An ordinary day, but dread sat her shoulder like a demon. At two, she rose and went to the dairy for the milk pail, Megan on her heels.

"Can I milk Nanny?" Megan asked.

"Not today, pet." Helen gave her an enamelled bowl. "Why don't you fill this with raspberries? Pick only the red ones, as I showed you. And don't eat too many!" she called after Megan as the child ran into the garden separating the house from the field.

The goat was grazing close to the tethering post in the centre of the field. For over a week, Helen set the time back a little each day until it would correspond with the time she'd be doing the milking when she started teaching.

The goat eyed her nervously. It hadn't forgiven her for the first futile attempt at milking before William left. Cautiously, she patted the goat's neck and back, and then Helen dropped to her knees and set the pail under the swollen udder. Milk squirted into the pail until Helen abruptly stopped the rhythmic movement of her hands. The uneasiness was almost overpowering and her back and shoulders prickled as though doused with iced water. She sat back on her heels and looked around.

Everything was the same: the whitewashed farmhouse rose beyond the hedge separating the field from the garden and farmyard; the field itself was empty as it sloped away, the grass cropped in circles here and there where the goat had been tethered during the past week. From the stream at the far end, a flock of meadowlarks rose in swooping confusion from an angry magpie. She followed the flight of larks and saw a black speck away to the west, flying in from the sun. It grew larger as she watched, then the drone of its single engine hung on the air like the buzz of a bee.

It was rare for an aeroplane to fly over their valley, but anyone could identify this one as an enemy aircraft. She'd seen it on a poster taped to Rowlie's shop window—a fighter the Germans sometimes used for reconnaissance. Its purpose over that part of Wales mystified her; it wasn't as if there were any docks or industries except for the woollen mills. This was one of the safe places to which they evacuated city children.

Helen watched the fighter cross the valley and then it banked and flew back, dropping lower. Upsetting the milk pail, she scrambled to her feet as the aircraft circled the field. It was low enough for her to see the swastika painted on the engine cover and the cold snubs of its guns.

For a second, Helen thought of running to the house for cover, but the tracer bullets could mow her down before she had time to cross the field and she would be leading them to where tall rows of raspberry canes hid Megan. Then Megan was running into the field, shouting with excitement at seeing the plane, her chin stained blood red by the fruit she had eaten.

"Go back, Megan! Get back to the house!" Helen shouted, but Megan didn't know the danger. She wasn't aware of anything being wrong as she ran to Helen's side.

Helen pushed the child behind her; shielding her from the aeroplane while she revolved to face it as it circled the field. She could see the pilot clearly—the dark jacket and the close-fitting leather cap and goggles.

In the midst of her fear, she wondered if it was a premonition of this that caused her earlier uneasiness, and one thought sprang to mind—how ironic if William should return from the war to find his wife and daughter cut down by enemy bullets.

Three times the fighter circled the field, then the pilot waved as if in farewell and the engine's throb changed pitch as the aircraft lifted away, speeding toward Moelfre.

Helen gathered Megan in her arms and ran for the house. As she reached the yard, Big

Bertha boomed from Moelfre's heights. The sound echoed like thunder from the hills and Megan clamped her hands over her ears.

The gun boomed again, and then a third time, its roar ricocheting from hill to hill until it seemed the ground beneath her feet vibrated. Even as the sound rolled around her, Helen heard an explosion and knew Big Bertha's gunners had found their mark. She put Megan down and dropped to her knees in the dust.

It was then she saw Dilys coming across the yard. She was two hours early and she was carrying her postbag.

♥

D. A. I.

Rhys was the only one seated at the massive dining table that left scant room around it for the sixteen chairs to clear the walls. A lopsided arrangement of pink roses eager to drop their petals at the first breath of air graced the pristine white starched cloth.

As he picked his way through the rabbit pie, peas and chips, Rhys was uncomfortably aware of the mounted deer's head glaring at him from the far wall. Of one thing, he was sure; no one could eat venison at that table without choking.

The only other guest at the Red Lion was a young airman in the village to meet his sweetheart's family. He'd gone out in a flurry of Brilliantine and polished buttons just as Rhys arrived back from his tour of the valley.

"Keep it quiet when you come in tonight," Rhys growled when they passed on the stairs. The man hadn't come in until after midnight the night before and his banging about in the next room woke Rhys from a deep sleep. It took him an hour to drop off again, an hour when he sat at the window studying the moonlit valley.

It was odd how things looked different at night. Varying shades of grey, the landscape had been in darkness because any of the villagers still up were observing the blackout law. It was peaceful, too, no sounds other than the hoot of an owl and the gurgling of the stream at the side of the. In the hour he spent looking out, mist formed along the flow, rising here and there where an overhanging branch attracted it. Had he not watched the columns grow, or if he were a more fanciful man, Rhys might well believe the stream bank populated by ghosts.

The door to the kitchen opened and the landlord entered with a generous wedge of blackberry pie sweetened with honey. "Will it be tea or coffee tonight, Mr Pritchard?" he asked.

"Neither, Mr Stock," Rhys picked up his pastry fork. "I think a pint of half-and-half is in order."

"Will I bring it in here? The saloon bar won't be open until seven."

"I'll join you in the taproom," said Rhys. The utilitarian taproom would never be his choice for an evening of relaxation but, in his line of work, eavesdropping on the locals had its advantages. He'd surveyed the area that day and the time had come to infiltrate the front line.

"Whenever you're ready . . ." Elias withdrew taking what was left of Rhys' main course. "He's a strange one, is our Mr Pritchard," he said to Gladys, handing her the dishes for washing.

"Have you found out what he's doing here?" Gladys hadn't had the opportunity to question Rhys because he'd arrived late the night before and gone out right after breakfast.

"Not yet," Elias answered. "He'll be in the bar later. Happen we can loosen his tongue then."

"It'll be our last chance," Gladys pointed out. "He's leaving in the morning. Going back to Cardiff, I expect."

"Helen-the-School is from Cardiff way. You don't suppose he's here to see her, do you?"

Gladys shook her head. "She'd have mentioned it at choir practice last night."

"I suppose . . ." Elias pushed through to the taproom when the outer door opened and two of his regulars came in. "'evening, Bogo. 'evening Ianto. The usual?"

"Unless you feel like treating us to something stronger." Bogo walked up to the bar and Ianto took himself to his usual corner next to the fireplace. "There's a nip in the air tonight."

Ianto filled his pipe. "Fog is what Mam Derw says."

"There was a mist last night." Rhys walked from the dining room into the bar. He nodded in acknowledgement of Bogo.

Elias set Bogo's and Ianto's drinks on the bar. "A half-and-half you said, Mr Pritchard?"

"That's right." Rhys eyed Bogo. "Do you farm around these parts?"

"Not me," said Bogo. "Foreman at Dyffryn Mill, I am, and Ianto over there is a retired postman. Just visiting are you?"

"Taking a bit of a holiday, you might say," answered Rhys.

"Why don't you join Bogo and Ianto by the fire?" Elias suggested. "I'll bring your drink over."

Nothing could suit Rhys better. He followed Bogo to where Ianto sat with a lighted spill held to the bowl of his pipe. He nodded as Bogo introduced them.

Puffing on his pipe to get it started, Ianto flicked the spill against the fender to douse it and moved the stem of the pipe to the corner of his mouth. He squinted up at Rhys. "Heard you say there was a mist last night, Mr Pritchard."

"Yes," said Rhys. "It was all around the river. If I hadn't known better, I'd have said there were ghosts down there."

"There might have been," Ianto said as Elias placed Rhys' beer on the table. "There might have been at that."

Rhys eyed the man over the rim of his glass. Ianto wasn't joking; he was serious about the ghosts. "Don't tell me the village is haunted."

"Oh, aye," said Ianto. "There's ghosts all over the place. Always a couple flitting about Saint Barnabas churchyard across the square, and there's another one down by Henllan Bridge."

"And don't forget Ladi Wen," said Bogo. "All over the place that one is. Follows you about, see," he explained to Rhys. "Body of a man, and the head of a horse. All white it is and, if you look at it, you won't live out the night. Comes after you on the road, it does, trying to get you to look over your shoulder."

Rhys was about to ask how they knew what it looked like if you couldn't look at it without dying, when Ianto broke in.

"And there're the druids Mam Derw sees rising up from the well every Hallows Eve."

"And the newest one," prompted Elias.

"Which one?" asked Bogo. "The ghost of the German pilot I shot down over Moelfre?"

Elias nodded. "Mam Derw says he's wandering about up there, not able to understand when she speaks to him."

"People have actually seen and spoken to these ghosts?" Rhys asked.

"Oh, aye," said Ianto. "You ask Bogo there. He's seen one, haven't you, Bogo? Why don't you tell Mr Pritchard about the ghost on the hill?"

Rhys saw Bogo squirm in his chair. "On which hill did you see the ghost?"

Ianto answered. "Corpse Hill, it was, on the road leading up to the mountain. Bogo saw it up by the stile when he was going home from here one night."

"So did you!" Bogo retorted.

"You saw it too?" Rhys studied Ianto.

"Oh, aye, I saw it all right. Most of us did. It was a new one for the valley."

"A new one . . ." Rhys sat back to ponder that.

"There are a lot of ghosts around here," said Elias. "We didn't want another one cluttering up the place so we had a meeting to see what we could do about our new visitor."

Rhys eyed the three of them in turn, trying to hide his disbelief. "You called a meeting to discuss a ghost?"

"Scaring Bogo and the women, it was," said Ianto, "and those who live beyond Corpse Hill took to using the forest road even though it's a longer way around."

"And they took the risk of stepping on a viper in the dark," Elias contributed.

"Vipers?" Rhys remembered his day of tramping through the fields and shivered.

"There are pit vipers in these parts," said Elias, noting the blanching of Rhys' face. "Whatever the experts tell you, you have to be careful where you step on Moelfre's slopes unless you've bought a charm from Mam Derw."

"Who is this Mam Derw you keep mentioning?" Rhys asked.

"You haven't met her yet?" Ianto asked and watched Rhys shake his head. "You're in for a treat then."

"She's just an old crone," said Elias. "People in these parts think she's a witch." He rose when Gladys shouted for him from the kitchen. "Is there anything I can get you gents before I go?"

"I'll get these." Rhys leapt to his feet and gathered the empty glasses. He carried them to the bar. "Neither of those men are farmers, are they?" he asked Elias in a low voice.

"Not unless keeping a few chickens counts," said Elias. "Mind, Ianto's a fair hand with scything when it comes to harvesting in places too steep for a harvester."

Rhys carried the beer back to the corner by the fire and waved aside their thanks. "You say everybody saw this ghost on the hill?"

"Bogo there wet his pants to prove it," Ianto said with a grin.

"That's a lie, Ianto Evans!" Bogo shouted.

"Cow it was," said Ianto evenly. "A white cow."

"A cow . . ."

"The Horned One." Ianto could control himself no longer. He exploded with laughter that turned into wheezing coughs and had him leaning toward the fire, ready to spit.

"Shut up!" growled Bogo. To Rhys he said: "It was one of Toby Rice's white cows."

"This Rice, he keeps a herd of white cows, does he?" Rhys asked.

"I don't know how many white ones he's got," said Bogo, shooting Ianto a sour look as the man recovered and sat back in his chair, "but he keeps one or two down in the miller's barn and lets them out to graze after dark."

"Why?" Rhys asked, leaning forward.

"It's safer, see." Bogo took a gulp of his beer. "With Wilfred Mathias poking his nose in everywhere, a lot of farmers keep their animals in strange places so they don't have to declare them."

"Wilfred Mathias." Rhys was careful not to make the repeating of the name into a question.

"The D.A.I. The District Agricultural Inspector," Bogo explained.

"Not anymore," said Ianto. "I hear he's been moved to a desk job in Carmarthen. Got too old, I expect."

"That's news to me." The edge to Bogo's voice showed he hadn't forgiven Ianto for what passed between them earlier.

Ianto shrugged. "That's what I heard, any road. Davy-Pen-Farm told me."

"Davy-Pen-Farm?" Rhys asked.

"Owns the farm up by the mountain," Bogo explained, only to have Ianto go one better.

"Owns half the valley, if you ask me."

"Makes it easy to find places to hide the animals he doesn't want the D.A.I. to know about," Bogo said sourly.

"Why's that?" Rhys liked the way the conversation was going. It was rare to find two such as these who would goad each other into telling him all he wanted to know.

"Well, there's gullies and things up on the mountain," explained Ianto.

Bogo leapt in. "And there's a cave up there too. Keeps the animals nice and dry."

"*Diawl*, aye. Nearly as dry as Morgan Ellis' lamb." Ianto leaned forward and tapped his pipe against the hearth to empty it and Bogo took advantage of the pause.

"Kept a lamb in one of the crypts in Penboyr churchyard, Morgan did."

"Dry as a bone in there." Ianto wheezed and laughed at his own joke, and Rhys smiled politely. "Dry as a bone." Ianto doubled over in another coughing fit.

"But Mari Jenkins nearly gave the game away," said Bogo. "Up there to put flowers on Tom's grave she was, and heard the lamb bleating. Ma . . . ma . . . it went, and Mari thought it was Tom calling her. Nearly died of shock, she did."

"In the crypt . . ." Rhys grinned at Bogo. "A clever place to hide an animal."

"They hide them all over the place."

"Like in the church or in the school?"

"That's about the only two places they haven't hidden them."

"Back bedroom." Ianto recovered from his fit of coughing and sipped his beer. "Aled Thomas thought he'd found a good hiding place to put two of his new litter of pigs."

"Put them in the back bedroom when he heard Wilfred's car coming. Then Millie, his wife, found out," Bogo added.

"Screamed blue murder, Millie did, because Aled never bothered to pick up the mats from the floor before he pushed the pigs in and they messed all over them." Ianto took another gulp of beer.

"Poor woman," Rhys murmured.

"Poor Aled," said Ianto. "Millie told him she wasn't going to wash the mats and he'd have to do it."

"He did it all right," said Bogo. "We found out about it because he put the mats in the mill pound. Well, all the muck carried down to the wheel, didn't it, and everybody in the mill was complaining and saying we'd been sent dirty fleeces. Olwen was in the sorting room and she knew the fleeces were clean. We had to find out where the dirt was coming from so we followed the pound up the hill, thinking to find a dead sheep lying in it like the time a viper bit a ewe and it fell in. When we got close to Aled's farm, we saw Millie's mats in the pound. There were big holes in the corners where Aled drove in iron spikes to keep the mats from floating away."

"You have to give him credit though," said Rhys. "I wouldn't have thought of hiding pigs in a bedroom."

"The best I heard tell was the farmer over on the other side of Henllan. Put a pig in his little girl's doll's pram, he did." Ianto informed Rhys. "Everything went all right until he went to give the pig back to the sow. Screamed so hard, his daughter did, that it brought Wilfred back to see what the matter was." Ianto looked up when the door opened and Rowlie appeared.

"Are you ready, Mr Evans?"

"Right with you." Ianto drained his glass and struggling to his feet. "Time for the off."

"So early?" Rhys' dismay was genuine.

"If I go now, Rowlie'll give me a ride home in the grocery van. Goes up to see his old mother every night, he does, and she lives just down the road from me."

Bogo rose when Ianto left. "And I'm into the saloon for a game of darts. You're welcome to join us, Mr Pritchard."

Rhys studied the three men on the other side of the serving hatch. They had the look of farmers about them. "I'm not much for darts," he said, "but I'll join you for a drink and a chat if you'll have me."

"Did you find out any more about Mr Pritchard?" Gladys asked later as she and Elias washed glasses.

"Not much," said Elias. "Davy Thomas saw him wandering up by Penboyr this morning, and Dilys saw him over by Home Farm after lunch when she was delivering the post."

"But they're at opposite ends of the valley!"

"Not only that, Joroway ran into him up at Helen and William's place."

"What would he be doing up there?"

Elias shrugged. "Joroway was in the house having a cup of tea. He saw Pritchard walk past so he followed him. He was in the barn where Helen keeps her pottery wheel when Joroway caught up to him. He didn't seem a bit embarrassed about being caught there, Joroway said, and he asked where the animals were. You know Joroway, he doesn't say much at the best of times, and all he told Pritchard was he'd better ask the owners because he was just the hired hand."

"I wonder what he wants." Gladys put away the last of the glasses.

"It's a mystery to me," said Elias, "but he seemed friendly enough to the regulars. Talked to all of them, he did."

The next morning after breakfast, as Rhys paid his bill and then made for the door with his suitcase, Elias found out who their guest was.

"You'll look us up again if you're ever in these parts, won't you?" Elias held the door open.

"Oh, I'll be back in a couple of days, Mr Stock, but I'll be boarding with Miss Richards at Rose Cottage. You see, I'm taking over from Wilfred Mathias as District Agricultural Inspector."

♥

THE HARVESTING

A keen edge to the breeze darting around Moelfre stole the camouflage from Big Bertha and mocked the gunners as they cursed their way down the slope to rescue the net from the whinberry bushes.

On the breeze went. It bullied the wheat field into waving a greeting, and rattled the lych gate at Penboyr before pitting itself against the sturdy bell tower that proved a worthy and silent opponent. On again, it whistled through the hedge of woven branches to where Eirlys was digging potatoes. It tugged at her braided hair, rushed at a corner of her coarse apron and batted it against her face to demand her attention.

Eirlys straightened and leaned on the fork while she listened. In the distance was the sound of an engine. Holding back the wisps of grey hair blown into her eyes, she studied the hedge bordering the road that curved up past

Moelfre. Here and there, where the weaving of the branches was less dense, she saw the glint of dark metal as a car made its way down the hill.

"Gran! Hurry!" Davy shouted as he ran around the corner of a barn.

Gran . . . When had she been magically transformed from being his Mam to being his Gran? It must have been when he came back from Canada with Dewi and she'd been too excited to notice. She dropped the fork and ran to the house.

Davy waited at the gate as the car drew closer and slowed for the bend. A black Morris with an Agricultural Government sticker on the windscreen, he watched it pass, and then he called to Eirlys: "That's him. That's Rhys Pritchard. Do it quick now!"

With the bundle in her arms, Eirlys ran from the house, through the orchard to the wash line at the top of the slope. Angling the pole so she could reach the line, she pegged the red tablecloth and hoisted it high as Davy joined her. Together they waited their attention on the Ellis farm across the fields.

"This isn't going to work any longer," said Davy. "It was all right when Wilfred Mathias was the D.A.I. because he didn't live in the valley, but this new one will be staying in Rose Cottage."

"Bronwen Richards. The traitor!"

"You can't blame her, she had no choice. The only one in the village with room who isn't a farmer or related to a farmer."

"Who told them?"

"We did. House rates, census, ration books—the Government knows all about us."

"There it is." Eirlys pointed across the fields to where an answering square of red fluttered on a wash line. From there, other warnings would peg across the valley ahead of the Government Inspector.

"I think I'll take a ride into the village." Davy headed toward the house.

Eirlys went with him, half-running to keep up with his long strides. She was tall for a woman, but Davy was taller. "On your bike?" she asked hopefully.

"On Cyclone." He stepped into the kitchen and reached for the enamel washbowl. "I have to bring Midnight back from Plas Gwyn and he'll follow better if there's a mare to lead him."

Eirlys watched while he stripped to the waist. "You're getting dressed up?"

"Can't have Major Braithwaite think I'm a common labourer, can I? Not after he paid the stud fee for Midnight."

"I still say you give the horses funny names. What's the new foal called? Five?"

"It's short for Five-Minutes-To-Midnight. They're the names of bucking horses, Gran."

197

"*Duw mawr*! They're not going to do that, are they?"

"Not these ones, they're thoroughbreds." Midnight's stud fees paid for the new barn, and Cyclone's foal out of Midnight would bring a good price. Sluiced, his hair damp and rumpled from the towelling, Davy crossed to the door leading from the kitchen to the back stairway. "If there's anything you want from the village, better make a list for me or I'm sure to forget something."

"Especially if you stop for a drink with the major," Eirlys commented. "Where's Edwin?"

"He's cutting hay in the bottom field," Davy called down the stairs. With Dewi away in the war, Edwin had come as a servant. Not strong but willing, he eased Davy's workload, and for that he was thankful.

It was time to ease up. Since Meg's death, Davy had done nothing but work from early morning to after dark and he'd done most of what he'd set out to do. He returned from Canada after six years and saw Pen Farm with fresh eyes. Big it was with fields ranging around Moelfre and Penboyr and bordering common grazing land where few people ran their livestock alongside his, but the farmhouse was run down, the roof leaking like a sieve and the slates of the kitchen floor as even as a hayfield scythed by an inexperienced hand. He put those things to rights in the first six months, and with his own hands raised the walls and roof of the bathroom annexed next to the kitchen. Meg chose the white fixtures gathering dust because the plumbing wasn't connected.

His father was good at rotating crops and the fields had always been productive, but animal husbandry was something the old man would allow no special interest. Soon after his father's death, Davy nearly bankrupted the farm to buy Tarw and the bull improved the herd to the extent that six churns waited for the milk lorry every morning. Tarw's stud fees brought in hardly any money, but Davy traded the bull's services for the labour to work his fields at harvesting. Wheeler-dealer his brother Aled called him, but Aled had no cause to complain when his own farm benefitted from Davy's methods.

Cravat knotted about his throat and held in place with the riding-whip pin he bought after Midnight won his first ribbon, Davy picked up the silver-backed brushes, a wedding present from Meg. His hair was as black as it always had been, and thick. Neither of his grandfathers had gone bald, nor his father, but already his sideburns had turned silver as the brushes in his hands. Distinguished looking, Miss Braithwaite called it, pointing him out to her cousin from London at the Hunt last New Year's: "The distinguished gentleman riding the black stallion." *Diawl* What would she say if she saw him mucking out a barn in his corduroys and the flannel shirt with no collar? Would she say then: "Oh, David, I do so admire a man with a good seat." Shocked his mother had been until he explained what Miss Braithwaite meant and for months after she kept on at Dewi to keep his seat still in church.

He eased into the Harris Tweed jacket. Folderols, his mother called his polished riding boots and cavalry-twill breeches, but the Harris Tweed made good sense. Sturdy it was. Never mind that it fitted like a glove across the breadth of his shoulders. Vanity Aled called it until he went with Davy to a horse show and stood out like a moulting duck in his Sunday suit.

"Well, did you decide what you want?" he asked when he returned the kitchen.

"I've got balaclavas to hand in at Rose Cottage and I want more wool. Tell Bronwen I don't want black again; it hurts my eyes." Eirlys studied Davy when he crossed to the mantelpiece and took down the letter he'd written to Dewi the night before. "Not courting Miss Braithwaite, are you?"

"She must be twenty years older than me; sixty if she's a day." He pocketed the letter and took the brown-paper parcel from her hands. "And where would I find a girl who'd put up with you?"

"I'm not getting any younger, Davy, and I could do with a bit of help around here."

In the doorway, he paused to grin at her. "If I bring a girl up here, it will be for something other than doing the cooking and cleaning."

"David Thomas!" Her shocked cry followed him across the yard to the stables. "And no flibbertigibbets, mind!"

Flibbertigibbet. Like Meg whose ways had been strange to Gran. "You eat the leaves off beetroot in Canada? Here we throw them to the pigs."

Bow River whickered softly and he paused to rub her nose. "Not today, girl. You're too close to dropping that foal to have my weight on your back."

Cyclone was watching for him, eyes liquid dark in the white of her face. Beside her, Five pushed his head through the bars of the stall. Davy ran a hand over the velvet blackness. "When I show you, you'll be wearing a red blanket like your namesake." He drew the bar and led Cyclone out, slapping the foal back when it tried to follow.

The saddle he used was western, with the horn and high cantle he used when he rode in Alberta. He tightened the cinch and the mare trembled, anxious to be out and away. He'd run her the day before with the foal at their heels, but it was too cold to leave them out overnight as Meg's father would have done. But the cold in Canada was different, drier than here where heavy dew and mist could easily change into hoar frost.

He led Cyclone out and looked up at the mountain. "Always watching, aren't you," he said. "Biggest thing around these parts, but I wish I could show you the Rockies. They'd soon cut you down to size."

He leapt onto the saddle and heeled Cyclone across the yard to where his mother was chewing her lip.

"Why don't you take the bike?" she asked.

"I'm safer on Cyclone. There're no wheels to puncture and no nuts and bolts to work loose or a chain to break."

"Is the saddle on tight?"

He laughed. "If it isn't, they'll be carrying me home on a gate tonight."

He took to the fields, galloping the mare along the edges of the crops ready for harvesting, knowing if he looked back he'd see Gran standing beside the red cloth pegged to the line. She didn't trust the thoroughbreds, not in the way she trusted the plodding shire they used for the plough and hay wagon. She wanted him to stick to the ponies that still gave a fast turnover for little effort or expense, but he knew the time of the workhorse was over. After the war, machines would do the horse work. Machines like the Morris lying idle in his barn for want of petrol. He cranked it up occasionally, coughing as it belched blue smoke and scattered the chickens but, for the most part, it hulked under its tarpaulin like a broody hen.

He headed Cyclone across Toby Rice's stubbled fields, making for the Forest Road so as to avoid Corpse Hill. The steepness there raised sparks from the horse's shoes and Cyclone slipped the last time he went that way, grazing a velvet flank as she tossed him onto the hedge. He couldn't risk it today, not with calls to make.

And the visit to the post office.

Dilys had been a widow now for two years; two years when he held himself in an agony of impatience. Two years when he'd known exactly the pain she was going through. It would have been worse for her. He at least had Dewi.

Davy dismounted next to the Morris parked outside Rose Cottage and looped Cyclone's reins over a fence post half buried in fragrant pink rambler. "Easy, girl." He stroked her shoulder as she shied away from the car's fumes. With the parcel in his hand, he squeezed around the Morris and entered the gate.

Bronwen came to the door at his knock, her face dimpling when she saw him.

"My mother asked me to bring these." He held out the package. "She wants more wool. Anything but black."

"Come in while I fetch it." Bronwen stepped aside as Davy entered, and then she closed the door. "Nippy out there today isn't it?"

"Summer's coming to an end." He followed her into the kitchen.

Rhys Pritchard was sitting at the table with a cup of tea in his hand. Bronwen introduced them and Davy nodded in acknowledgement while Bronwen opened the package.

"Oh, your mother does nice work. Seems a pity to send these to the Front, doesn't it?"

"Our soldiers need them, Miss Richards," Rhys Pritchard said.

Miss Richards. Davy watched her bustling about looking for the wool his mother wanted. She'd never married, yet she was pretty enough and some men liked an armful. Fatty Richards he'd called her in school, sitting behind her and tying her pigtails together around a rung in her chair. Fatty Richards he practised his kissing on in the back playground before he went after Luned Ellis, the girl he really wanted to kiss.

"How's your father today?" he asked when he heard the man cough somewhere overhead.

"Fair to middling," Bronwen answered, her head buried in the sideboard while she rummaged about in the packets of wool. She emerged and puffed to her feet, red faced. "I don't seem to have anything but black, but Mrs Davies went to the supply depot today with the finished things and she'll be bringing back more wool. If there's any grey or khaki, I'll send it up with Dilys-the-Post tomorrow."

At the sound of her name, heat infused the back of his neck under the cravat. "Fair enough." He nodded to Rhys and made for the door.

"Will you stay for a cup of tea?" Bronwen asked, scuttling to the door ahead of him.

"Another time," he answered. "I have a lot of calls to make."

Davy swung into the saddle, aware of Rhys Pritchard standing at the gate. He heeled Cyclone into fluid movement with a sense of pride. If the man were any judge of horseflesh, he'd know he was looking at the finest mare this side of the Severn.

When he reached the river, Davy dismounted and allowed Cyclone to dip her mouth in the water. He then led her over the bridge and across the square to the post office, and checked that his cravat and pin were in place. As he tethered the mare to the iron railings, Megan Williams ran out. Davy lifted her so she could stroke Cyclone's nose, then he put her down, took a deep breath, and walked into the post office.

Dilys was serving Helen at the counter. She looked up when Davy entered and her cheeks reddened. She hadn't talked to him since the night two years earlier when she made a fool of herself by blubbering on his shoulder. She'd seen him of course. Riding her bike with the postbag in the basket, she'd see him in a distant field ploughing or harvesting; at church, from the pew behind her, his deep base accompanied his mother's tremulous soprano; and when the Hunt gathered outside the Red Lion on New Year's Day, he was one of the three wearing the scarlet. She'd seen him, but not to talk to, and he'd never come into the post office in the two years she'd worked there.

The sight of Dilys doing the job he'd suggested to her pleased Davy into smiling despite his nervousness. He greeted Helen: "How are you today, Mrs Williams?" There was no news of William or he'd have heard through the village grapevine and he decided not to ask what he already knew.

"Fine, Mr Thomas." Helen pushed the postal order back under the grid. "I wanted a one-and nine penny. What's wrong with you today, Dilys?" She turned to Davy. "How is Dewi?"

"He's fine. Somewhere in the Channel when I last heard."

Flustered, Dilys fumbled for the Order Helen wanted. She risked a glance at Davy. He knew she was flustered, and he must have known he was the reason. She wondered if the embarrassment of two years ago was going to disconcert her every time she saw him. Dammit! He was laughing at her! She'd never before known a man who could laugh only with his eyes.

On the other side of the grid, Helen was staring at her, lips curved into a smile. Now Helen was laughing at her! Dilys pushed the one-and-nine penny Order out and gathered back the coins.

"Mam! Come and see the horsey!" Megan shouted as she ran in.

"Was she out there with a horse?" An edge of panic crept into Helen's voice.

"No need to worry," Davy reassured her. "Cyclone's gentle as a lamb. You'll have to bring Megan up to see the new foal one of these days."

"She'd like that." Helen folded the Postal Order into her handbag and Megan dragged her to the door.

Davy stepped up to the counter and passed Dewi's letter under the grid. "It's his eighteenth birthday next week. Do you think this will get to him in time?"

"I'll make sure it goes out tonight." Dilys took the letter and dropped it into the priority bag where went all the Forces mail. "Is there anything else?" She allowed her gaze to glance against his. Dammit! He was still laughing at her.

With a surge of something akin to satisfaction or pleasure, Davy saw she was as disconcerted as he was. Hadn't it been that way when he met Meg, with the two of them sitting on bales of hay eating a boxed lunch and not saying a word? He hadn't expected to feel the same with Dilys, though, not a girl he'd known all his life.

"Is there anything else?"

Her voice broke across his thoughts. He cleared his throat. "A couple of stamps." He passed a shilling under the grid and she slid the stamps and change back. "The . . . er . . . the invitation is there for you, too, if you'd like to come up and see the foal."

"I saw it yesterday when I was out on deliveries. It was running after you and you were riding the white horse." When his face tightened and his eyes lost their smile, she realized her answer must have seemed like a snub.

Davy's jaw tightened. As evenly as he could, he said: "Well, I'd better be going . . ."

Dilys watched him leave. Dammit! She'd missed her chance to apologize and clear the air. Somehow, the words wouldn't form and, if she blurted it out, she could end up more embarrassed than ever. She decided she should stop being silly and write him a letter.

Dear Mr Thomas,

I'm sorry I blubbered all over you and never gave you back your handkerchief. Truth is, I threw it in the hedge so that Mam wouldn't find it in the wash and ask questions.

Yours sincerely,
Dilys Ellis, Postmistress

Dammit! That was even sillier, and what if his Mam opened the letter?

With a practised eye, Davy took note of the leaning fences, the overgrown hedges and the uneven tracks the harvester left in the stubbled field. Without a manager, Plas Gwyn estate was falling into disrepair under a pall of apathy. Rodney Lewis was somewhere in France at the wheel of a tank and replacing him was something the major hadn't been able to do.

White hair bristled like a dandelion seed head, Major Braithwaite was in the exercise yard next to the kennels with a pack of hounds milling around his feet. "David!" he called when he saw Davy. "Come and look at the newest pair."

Davy tethered Cyclone and entered the yard with half of the pack sniffing around his heels.

"Damned fine bloodlines, what?" The Major patted his newest acquisitions.

Davy nodded in agreement, not knowing enough about dogs to argue. Dogs weren't things he raptured over. If they did their job like his sheepdogs Carlo and Cai and didn't bark too much, it was all he asked of them.

"I've a mind to try these out with the pack next Saturday, if you'll do the honours as huntsman."

Davy shook his head. "I've got two fields of wheat and one of hay to get in. It might be better if you waited until all the fields in the valley have been stubbled."

"Just so," Major Braithwaite agreed, "but I can't wait to run them. Come into the house and I'll show you their pedigrees."

"I can't be too long," Davy cautioned, remembering his last visit to Plas Gwyn when Cyclone had to find their way home, "I have to check the harvester for tomorrow."

"You have time for a spot of refreshment, surely?" The major paused to run a hand down Cyclone's foreleg. "Damned fine mare, what? Good bloodlines, eh? Nothing but the best for you, eh, David?"

"David!" From the columned portico, Priscilla Braithwaite trilled a greeting. "Come in! Come in!" With a puppy cuddled in her arms, she led the way into the drawing room ignoring the muck and mud Davy and her brother were tracking across her fine carpets. "Now. What shall it be?" she asked when Davy lowered himself gingerly onto one of the gilt and velvet chairs he always expected to collapse under his weight. "Gin? Brandy? A drop of port, I think. You pour, Dickie, while David and I have a chat."

"Always the same when you go to Plas Gwyn, isn't it," Eirlys snapped. "You can't take the drink, Davy. Never could."

"No, Mam." Davy winced at the sound of his own voice echoing in his head.

Eirlys halted on her trip across the kitchen with two plates in her hands. "You called me *Mam*!"

"Slip of the tongue." He winced again when she slammed a plate onto the table in front of him.

He eased out of the jacket and draped it with deliberate care over the back of the chair before manoeuvring unsteadily to the sink. He turned on the tap and stuck his head underneath, groaning. Dripping water, he came upright. "I'm going to have a lie down," he said in a monotone. "Put my supper in the oven. I'll eat it later."

"You don't put salad and cold ham in the oven," Eirlys said.

His answer was another groan as he groped his way up the stairs to collapse across the bed and the room whirled about him. Almost immediately, he fell into a deep sleep.

Dilys wondered why she'd brought her bike. She could freewheel all the way home after it was true, but pushing it up the hill was hard work. Government issue sit-up-and-beg, she inherited the bike from Ianto Maesgwyn along with a wire basket over the front wheel big enough to carry a month's shopping.

Come to that she wondered why she was going up to Pen Farm at all. True, she had a concrete reason—the wool Bronwen Richards asked her to deliver—but she could have waited until the next day and dropped it off on her rounds. Sure as eggs, she was going to forget her carefully rehearsed speech of apology the minute she laid eyes on Davy Thomas, and then he'd be laughing at her again. And why was she so worried about what he thought of her anyway?

She propped the bicycle against the cement platform where the milk churns sat ready for morning collection and took the package from the basket. Giving her speech a final rehearsal, she failed to notice the black ball of agitated feathers streaking across the yard until Blackie flew at her face.

"Dammit!" she screamed, and lashed out with the package. Then she threw the parcel of wool at the cockerel and fled toward the house. A sharp beak pecked at her legs as she leapt for the door and banged on it. "Mr Thomas! Mrs Thomas! Help!"

The door opened and Eirlys erupted with a broom in her hand. "Away now, Blackie. Off you go."

The cockerel stood off, ruffled its feathers and spread its wings, beady eyes on Dilys as Eirlys asked: "What are you doing up here, Dilys Ellis?"

"Miss Richards—" Dilys backed a step into the house when Blackie started scratching the dust like a bull pawing the ground ready to charge. "The parcel out there is the wool Miss Richards asked me to bring up."

Eirlys went out to get the wool and Blackie hopped alongside, raising little puffs of dust with his wing tips as he crooned low in his throat. "Yes, Blackie, you're a good boy," she said. "Good boy, Blackie." She picked up the package, dusted it off, and walked back to the house. In the doorway, Dilys stood white faced and shaken. "You'd better come in for a cup of tea, girl."

Dilys followed Eirlys into the kitchen, pausing to check what damage Blackie had done to her slacks.

"Are you all right?" Eirlys asked.

"Just a few pulled threads." And there would be bruises, she didn't doubt.

There was no sign of Davy. She couldn't ask if he was at home because Eirlys was bound to ask what she wanted with him, and Dilys would have to tell her. Then she'd have to tell her what she'd been doing in the field in the middle of the night with a man not her husband.

As she sat down, Dilys saw Davy's jacket hanging over the back of the chair and the plate on the table left untouched. So he was home and he was so anxious not to see her he'd got up in the middle of his supper and gone to hide. Well, if that's what he wanted, she'd make him wait as long as she could.

"Why don't I help you wind this wool, Mrs Thomas?" she suggested.

"Well . . ."

"You finish your supper while I drink my tea, then we'll change these skeins into balls. What do you say?"

"It would save a lot of time . . ."

"There we go then." Dilys sipped her tea and looked around. *The kitchen was just as large as she remembered when she'd come here as a child.*

"Is your mother well?" Eirlys asked politely as she took the last bite and poured herself a cup of tea.

"Yes, thank you." *The furniture was dull. Good, solid oak and well dusted, it hadn't had a polish in years.*

"Keep you busy at the post office, do they?" *What was this one doing looking around her kitchen?*

"Some days more than others." *The sideboard would look nice if it had a polishing and a vase of flowers sitting on top.*

"There was a cold wind this morning." *Anybody'd think she was going to make an offer to buy the place, the way she was sizing everything up.*

"Autumn is coming early this year, they say." *The willow-patterned china on the dresser had a yellow film except for two or three cups and saucers used for visitors.*

"I was hoping for an Indian summer." *The way this one was looking at the china, Eirlys decided she'd better take count of the pieces later.*

"Mam Derw says not." *The brass plaques and candlesticks on the mantelpiece needed a good going over with Brasso.*

"Well, she would know." *She'd better count the brass too. And what was she up to now, trying to see into the parlour?*

"I expect." *The place needed a woman's touch — a woman who wasn't always busy in the fields doing a man's job.* Dilys saw Eirlys was watching her scrutiny of the kitchen. *Rude to stare*, a reprimand from childhood made her look away. "Shall we start then?" She reached for the package and untied the string.

"At least it isn't black," Eirlys said, lifting out a skein of khaki-coloured wool. "Will you wind, or shall I?"

"You'd better. I'm a slow winder." Dilys spread her arms; the skein looped over her hands, and studied Eirlys. She was thinner than Dilys remembered.

"Do you knit?" Eirlys studied Dilys. *All that red hair! Never could keep it tidy, could Mari, and now Dilys cut it short like a man's. Shingled, they called it.*

"I drop too many stitches." *The weather-beaten skin was drawn tight on the bones of Eirlys' face, and there were hollows under her eyes that hadn't been there at Easter.*

Flibbertigibbet! Couldn't even knit. Probably couldn't cook either. Eirlys wound in silence until the last length left Dilys' hands. "That's one done."

215

"Why don't you start knitting with that one while I wind the rest?" That would keep Davy hopping.

"Can you do it by yourself?"

"Do it all the time for Mam." Dilys reached for the second skein. She moved her chair out from the table and spread her knees. Draping the skein around them, she started to wind.

Eirlys brought her knitting needles and sat down. *Hussy, Dilys was, dressed in trousers like a man and doing a man's job. What was the world coming to?*

They sat in silence except for the clicking of knitting needles until Dilys finished winding the second skein and started on the third. "Don't you ever listen to the wireless, Mrs Thomas?"

"Davy's the only one who can switch it on." *One of these days, she'd get him to show her again what to do with the knobs.*

"Oh?" *What a sod! He didn't even let his mother listen to the wireless.*

At nine, with seven balls of wool on the table, Dilys rose to leave and Eirlys breathed a sigh of relief. "Blackie'll still be out there," she said. "I'd better walk you to the gate."

Once Dilys was safely out of the yard, Eirlys closed and fastened the gate with a loop of wire, then she went back to the house, muttering to herself: "Flibbertigibbet!"

Dilys watched Eirlys cross the yard as she turned her bike around. By now, Davy

Thomas would be in the kitchen wolfing down his supper. Serve him right if the lettuce was limp and the ham turned green. She gave the pedals a whirl to start her down the hill.

She was going fast, anger making her reckless as she angled the bike around the bends, leaning into them precariously. She was heading toward the last bend before home when a black mass came around the corner in the middle of the road. Going too fast to brake before she hit the car, Dilys wrenched the wheel toward a gateway in the hedge praying Edwin had left it open after cutting hay that day.

With a quick prayer of thanks, she hurtled through the gap and flipped head first into a bale of hay. Stunned, she was aware of a wheel spinning next to her and the prick of a thistle under her back.

"Are you all right?"

Dilys blinked, attempting to make sense of the words and bring into focus the man bending over her. She tried to sit up but he pressed her back onto the thistle.

"Lie still for a moment. You took a bad tumble."

She laid back, the man's hand on her shoulder. "Who—?"

"Who am I? Rhys Pritchard, the new District Agricultural Inspector. You're the Postmistress, aren't you? No—don't try to move," he said when she tried to lift herself off the thistle. "Are you badly hurt?"

"Right now all I can feel is a thistle sticking into my back. And you're not helping!"

"Oh." He helped her to sit up and wrapped his jacket around her shoulders. "I'm very sorry about this, but you shouldn't have been coming down the hill at such a pace."

"And you should have had your headlights on." She massaged her shoulder, working at the stiffness.

"The blackout," he explained. "If I'd shown lights while travelling uphill, they would have shone into the sky."

"Then you should have tooted your horn as you came around the bend!"

"But—" He couldn't tell her why his movements had to go undetected by the blare of a car horn. "Look. If there's any damage to the bike, I'll pay."

"Damn right! That's government property."

"I'm more concerned about you. Are you badly hurt?" With a handkerchief, he dabbed at a scratch on her face.

She snatched the handkerchief from him and held it to the place on her cheek that was stinging. "Am I bleeding?"

"A bit, yes." He adjusted the jacket around her shoulders. "Where else are you hurt?"

"All over," she complained. "I don't know how I'll do my rounds tomorrow. I'll be hobbling and aching worse than old Ianto Maesgwyn used to."

"If there's anything I can do . . ."

"Short of driving me around for the next few days, you can help me up." Gingerly, she got to her feet and he steadied her as she swayed. "Dammit! I don't think I can walk." Her knees gave way despite her determination to stand.

"I've got you." Rhys swung her into his arms. "I'll come back for the bike later; first I'm going to drive you home. Where do you live?"

"Car—" *Cartref,* she wanted to say but couldn't finish the word. Everything spun. One minute the moon was steady in the sky, and then there were three waltzing around the clouds. Her head felt heavy, like the time she played one of the Three Kings in Primary and wore the wooden crown her father made and painted gold. She let her head drop onto his shoulder. "We three kings of O-o-rient are," she sang.

"Oh, God!" Rhys cried in panic. He struggled to open the back door of the Morris and then eased her inside. "Look—whatever your name is . . ."

"King Alha— Alhaza— Bringing gifts we come from af-f-a-a-r," Dilys sang drunkenly. "Where am I?"

"You're in the back seat of my car. If you'll tell me where you live . . ."

Dilys slid sideways as the lights went out.

Rhys ran to the boot and rummaged for the flask of tea Bronwen prepared for him, and then he eased in beside Dilys. As she began to come round, he helped her to sit up and held the cup to her lips. "Slowly now. It's hot."

Dilys drained the cup and focussed on his face. "Who are you?"

"Rhys Pritchard. An accident . . ."

"I remember." The handkerchief was still balled in her fist. She raised it to her cheek. "Am I still bleeding?"

"Just a bit." He took the empty cup from her and screwed it onto the flask. "I don't know where you live or even what your name is."

"Dilys Ellis. I live down the road at Cartref."

"I'll turn the car around and take you home, and then I'll come back for the bike."

"No, dammit! If Mam saw you!" And heard she'd been in the back seat of the car with him . . !

"But you're hurt. I insist you let me see you safely home."

"I'll be all right." She clambered out of the car and steadied herself against it as he got out on the far side and ran around to her.

"Wait here. I'll get the bike," he said. "Can you hang on?"

"I'm all right!" she snapped.

"Nevertheless . . ." He ran to the bike and brought it back. "It seems to have come through without a scratch," he said as he wheeled it onto the road.

"That's more than can be said for me," Dilys pressed the handkerchief to her cheek.

"I'm sorry. The last thing a pretty girl wants is a scratched face." Wheeling the bike with one hand, he wrapped an arm around her waist. "Raise any objections you like, I'm seeing you home."

"All right," said Dilys, glad of his supporting arm, "but no farther than the garden hedge."

"Agreed, but I'll wait until I've seen you enter the house."

Pushing the bike, Dilys limped toward the gate. As she walked up the path, she tossed Rhys' handkerchief into the hedge and braced herself for her mother's questions.

"Will you look at that!" Aled stood on the hay wagon, stacking the stooks Davy and Edwin forked up to him. He pointed across the field to the gate opposite the farmyard entrance. "She's got him trained like a puppy on a leash."

"Who's that?" Davy leaned against the pitchfork and wiped the sweat from his brow with a forearm.

"Dilys-the-Post," Aled answered. "Millie said she'd seen her in the D.A.I.'s car yesterday."

"Rhys Pritchard?"

"Got him driving her on her rounds, and it's him runs to every house with the post."

"Never!" said Davy.

"It's right, Mr Thomas," Edwin confirmed, "and he drives her to and from work every day. I've seen him."

"Good for her," said Aled. "While she's got him running around after her like a tomcat in heat, he's not nosing about our barns."

"Don't know what she sees in him," Davy muttered, jabbing the pitchfork into another stook.

"That's what I said to Millie," Aled said, "but she reckons he's not bad looking for a Government Inspector."

"He'll be bald on top by the time he's forty," Davy retorted. "Let's get on, there's another field to cut tomorrow."

"Was Dilys up here?" Davy asked as he sat down to supper.

"When? Today or Wednesday night?" Eirlys asked.

"She was here Wednesday night?"

"Brought up the wool and helped me to wind it. Here 'til nine o'clock she was."

"Why didn't you call me?"

"And you sleeping like a dead man with a drunk on you worse than Bogo Griffiths?"

"I only had three drinks! You could have woken me."

"What for? To wind wool? Anyway, if the fuss she made when Blackie went after her didn't wake you—"

"Blackie went for her? Why didn't you tell me? Was she hurt?"

"Pulled some threads in them trousers she wears." Eirlys watched him get up from the table and cross to the sink to run water into the washbowl. "Are you going out?"

"Yes," was the clipped reply. "Where are the clothing coupons?"

"What do you need them for?"

"If Blackie tore her clothes, she'll need coupons to buy more. Damn! Why didn't you tell me before?"

Davy freewheeled around the bend above Cartref and saw the Morris parked outside. He skidded to a halt and walked the last few paces as Rhys Pritchard came out of the gate. Without a word, they stared at each, and then Rhys went to his car and Mari came to the gate.

"Is Dilys home, Mrs Jenkins?" Davy asked when Rhys drove off down the hill.

"Yes, but she's gone to bed. Not feeling very well, she isn't, after what happened the other night."

"Oh." Then it was worse than his mother made out. Blackie must have hurt Dilys bad for her to take to her bed this early and have that man drive her around. "I brought her these." He held out the strip of clothing coupons.

"For Dilys? Well, well . . . Lot of presents she's getting these days." Mari held up a box of chocolates tied around with a yellow ribbon. "Mr Pritchard just now brought this. Don't know where he found chocolates in wartime but I expect he's got connections, him working for the Government and all."

Compared with the box of chocolates, the strip of coupons looked shoddy. "Well, tell Dilys I hope she'll be better soon, and tell her I'm sorry about what happened. I only just heard about it." He pushed the bike back up the hill, walking like a man carrying Moelfre on his back.

In church the following Sunday, Davy sat in his customary place in the pew behind Dilys. She wore a wide-brimmed hat trimmed with the yellow ribbon from the box of chocolates. When the service was over, he rushed outside to wait for her as the vicar came to the doorway to greet his congregation.

"How is Dewi doing?" Reverend Davies asked.

"He's fine, Vicar. Trained on radar, he is now." Davy stepped to one side as others began to leave the church, then he saw Dilys come out with Bethan Stock and Rachel Griffiths.

"Dilys?"

She turned with a puzzled look on her face. "Oh, hello, Mr Thomas."

"Oh, Dilys!" In dismay, he studied the scratches on her face and half raised his hand as if to touch his fingers to her cheek. "I'm sorry. How are you feeling?"

"I'm all right." Her eyes met his for a second before she blushed and looked toward the gates. "Oh, there's Rhys." She began to walk away, and then she paused and looked back. "Thanks for the coupons, Mr Thomas, but there was no need." Then she was gone, running down the path to Rhys Pritchard.

"Are you all right, Mr Thomas? You're looking very pale."

Before him, Bethan Stock's face swam into focus. He nodded.

"David! How nice!" Priscilla Braithwaite claimed his arm. "You must join us for lunch. Dickie laid in a new stock he wants you to sample."

Davy sighed and allowed her to lead between the gravestones as he watched Dilys and Rhys drive off in the Morris.

Years had passed since Davy attended one of the dances held in the village hall. He escorted Eirlys to plays and pantomimes there over the years, but he'd forgotten how different the auditorium looked with the chairs cleared away and piled precariously on the stage behind the band brought in from Newcastle Emlyn.

As a dance floor, Davy thought it had no equal. Thank God. Sloping its whole length, the front section of the floor was made of oak boards worn smooth over the years, but the back section was a resilient slab of concrete where they held the dance lessons when he was a boy. Impervious to the studded boots the farm boys wore and dusted with French chalk, it could be lethal.

Siona Maesgwyn started the lessons after taking a course at the Ivy Bush in Carmarthen where she was a chambermaid before she married Ianto. Penny a week for children and tuppence for adults, every Thursday night they trooped into the hall, past where Ianto stood with his hand on the phonograph ready to wind it up. The boys would form a line on one side of the hall daring each other to be the first to cross the floor, studded boots on the concrete warning the girls some brave body was heading to where they stood in giggling groups.

Bronwen was always the wallflower unless Siona bullied a boy into asking her to dance, or she'd call for a Paul Jones: "Girls in the middle walk anti-clockwise; boys on the outside walk clockwise. When the music stops, dance with the person facing you." There'd be a bottleneck opposite Luned, the boys slowing down and hoping the music would stop when they stood before her, but there was always a gap in the circle opposite Bronwen and, when the music stopped, they'd push a boy forward from where he cowered without a partner on the far side of the circle. Like the pool beneath the waterfall where black eels bit unwary paddlers, they avoided Bronwen, not because she was fat and had to be pushed up the slope but because she was heavy and could pull her partner around, swinging him into twirls that left him giddy.

The intricacies of the foxtrot feather and the quickstep fishtail were beyond most of them and, every once in a while one of them, concentrating hard on what his feet were doing, would forget which way was anticlockwise and change directions, confusing everybody.

At the end-of-the-year dance they were exposed to the public and put through their paces. With the front half of the hall cleared of chairs as well the whole glorious slope and scope sent them into paralysed panic and they spent the first hour huddled in a corner at the back of the hall on familiar concrete. There were always plenty of volunteers to go in before the dance to spread French chalk on the floor. Better than tobogganing, it was, and when the rest of the dancers turned up there'd be skid marks all over the place.

Not all of the first hour was spent in self-conscious huddling. At any given time, a couple could be seen skittering down the slope on one side of the floor to short step across the width of the hall as they approached the bottleneck at the bottom of the uphill slope.

There were bets on Old Ned's ability to push his partner up the slope one more time, and bets on whether Bronwen would slip out of Ianto Maesgwyn's hands during the next tango dip.

As then, the mothers and older women sat on chairs lining the walls, some of them with knitting in their hands as though the dance floor was a Welsh form of the guillotine, and a crowd of children milled in the centre of the floor, giggling as they imitated the circling dancers. Lifting his attention from them, Davy saw Dilys with Rhys Pritchard. The man was a good dancer, he'd give him that, but he was holding Dilys a bit closer than was called for in a Samba.

Davy waited for the next waltz and invited Bronwen-the-wallflower onto the floor, practising his rusty steps on her just as he once practised his kissing. He waited with a group of men while the band played five different dances, and when the waltz came around again he approached Bethan Stock who was standing close by.

"I'm not very good at the waltz, Mr Thomas," she warned.

"Neither am I," he said, drawing her onto the floor as Dilys and Rhys whirled by. "Home for the weekend, are you?" he asked, remembering Bethan was an ambulance driver in Swansea these days.

"Couldn't miss the Harvest Dance, could I," she said. "But it's back to camp first thing tomorrow morning."

"The war won't last forever," he said and watched Dilys smile up at Rhys.

"No, but it's funny how it changes everything, isn't it? Ann Jones told me tonight she's getting engaged to one of the guards out at the prisoner-of-war camp at Henllan. And Rachel is dating a Yank." Bethan's grip tightened on his arm as if to draw his attention back to her. "Got your eye on her, haven't you."

Davy tore his gaze from Dilys and studied Bethan. "What?"

"I've been watching you. Can't keep your eyes off her, can you."

"What are you talking about?"

"Dilys. I think I knew which way the wind was blowing when I saw you talking to her outside Saint Barnabas that time. And from the look on your face when she went off with Pritchard, I'd say you were ready to kill."

"Bethan Stock!" Twenty, if she was a day, she was talking to him as if they were the same age group.

"Don't act coy. I told you war changes everything and these days I say what I feel because there might not be a tomorrow. I don't beat about the bush, but it's what you're doing, Mr Thomas, and now that slimy little toad is stealing her from under your nose."

"Rhys Pritchard?"

"Who else? He's asked her to go home with him to Cardiff for Christmas. I wouldn't be surprised if she didn't come back wearing an engagement ring. Aw!" Bethan yelped when Davy's hand clenched on hers. "So you're not dead after all."

He eyed her in astonishment. "Is that what you think I am?"

"You should see your face!" She laughed. "You think I'm meddling. Well, so I am, and I'm going to meddle some more. Can't stand the bloke, but I'm going to get him away from Dilys for the next dance. Then it's up to you."

He gave her a conspiratorial grin. "Make it a waltz," he said when the music stopped.

"Righto. But you'd better be ready."

Keeping track of the sequence of dances, Davy saw Bethan pull a uniformed Twm-the-Organ onto the floor. Except for the tango, when Bethan and Twm took a rest, they stuck close to Dilys and Rhys Pritchard through three dances.

Before he knew what was happening, the band was striking up a waltz and Bethan was pulling Rhys Pritchard away from Dilys. Davy pushed his way toward Dilys in time to see Twm-the-Organ ask her to dance. He tapped Twm on the shoulder. "Sorry, boyo, this is my dance."

Faced with the older man, Twm stepped back and went to stand beside Ianto.

"I thought he was going to hit me," he commented.

"You don't mind, do you?" Davy watched Dilys' face redden as they moved onto the packed floor. In the golden sprinkle of freckles, the scratches left paler streaks.

Now what was he to say? Ahead, Bogo manoeuvred Bronwen into the corner to execute a double whirl. He grinned at the look of surprise on the man's face when the pivotal weight of his partner swung him around for the third time. Slightly dizzy, Bogo came out of the corner, heading straight for them.

Davy changed directions, manoeuvring Dilys out of harm's way, his arm instinctively tightened around her as he braced himself for the impact.

Dilys looked up at him with a question in her eyes. Dammit! She thought. He was laughing at her again. This time she had to make her apologies and put an end to it. "I'm sorry about—"

Bogo and Bronwen slammed into Davy's back and bounced away.

"Oh! Sorry-e-e-e!" Bogo's voice rose to a wail as Bronwen whirled him on.

"What did you say?" Davy asked Dilys.

"I said I was sorry."

"What about? If you stepped on my toe, I didn't feel it."

"No, dammit! About crying all over you that night. Dat always said it was the most embarrassing thing in the world to have a

231

woman cry all over you, and that's what I did and I'm sorry about it. And now you can stop laughing at me all the time."

"When have I ever laughed at you?"

"All the time since that night."

"I'm sorry if it looked that way. I wasn't embarrassed. Are you sorry you cried?"

"No, only that you were there to see it."

"And who better? I'd been through what you were going through."

She looked up. There was no laughter in his eyes now. Aware of the silence around them, she realized the music had stopped and everyone was looking at them while she stood there with Davy's arms around her. And he hadn't loosened his hold since just before Bogo danced into them. She freed herself and stepped away, her cheeks red, as the band struck up the next tune.

"A quickstep!" Davy said in dismay.

"We'd better sit this one out. I was watching you—you only dance when there's a waltz."

A warm glow filled Davy at her words. "I didn't see you watching me."

Dammit! Now he had that amused look in his eyes again. "Well, I was. You're taller than everybody else is so it's hard not to see what you're doing in a crowd. Bethan must have said something to shock you. She always was a minx."

"But with a good heart." Bethan danced by with Rhys, grinning over his shoulder as she winked at Davy to remind him of their conspiracy.

Dilys saw the wink and it made her angry. So what if Bethan and Davy had something going between them, it didn't affect her. Unwillingly, she recognized much of her anger resulted from jealousy and she had no right to feel that way. The silence between them was uncomfortable and begged to be filled with words. "Is your back all right where Bogo ran into us?"

"He hit the same spot Midnight did when he nudged me into the muck pile yesterday."

She chuckled. "That's the peril of being a farmer, I suppose."

"One of them. Bow River had her foal. You should come up to see it."

With her luck, it would probably nudge her into the muck pile and then he'd be laughing about it for months. "I might come up if it's safe."

Now she wouldn't come up because of Blackie. Damn him! "I'm sorry Blackie went for you. He shouldn't have been out."

Puzzled by the shift of topic, she said: "Blackie?"

"If I didn't think he'd be such a tough old bird, I'd have him for Sunday dinner."

"Knowing Blackie, he'd get right off the plate and bite you back."

"That'd be a sight!" He laughed; glad some form of camaraderie was entering their conversation. "Especially if Gran puts those frilly paper things on his legs."

They both laughed, Dilys doubling over, one hand clutching Davy's arm to steady herself.

Disentangling himself from Bethan as they drew level with Dilys and Davy, Rhys bore down on them, his face black with anger. "Come on!" He grabbed Dilys by the arm and dragged her onto the dance floor.

"What the—!" Davy started after them, but a hand on his arm held him back.

"Don't worry, she won't let him get away with that," said Bethan, keeping a tight hold of him. "He's been hopping mad ever since the two of you stood with your arms around each other and the music had stopped."

"He can't treat her like that!"

"No, but it was a shock for him, see. Didn't know he had competition until then, did he?"

"I'm going to have a word with him!" Davy tried to free himself from Bethan's clutches.

"You're not going to do anything except sit here by me," she said, pulling him to a couple of empty chairs. "The worst thing you can do now is interfere. Dilys won't thank you for it. Fights her own battles, she does."

He sat down and studied her. "When did you get to be so wise, Bethan Stock?"

"Learn a lot about human nature you do, when you grow up in a pub. You see and hear everything there. And I'll tell you something else. That's where Rhys Pritchard found out where you farmers hide your animals when you don't want him to know about them."

Davy's fists clenched. "Who's been talking to him?"

"Everybody. He spent a couple of nights at the Red Lion before anybody knew who he was."

"The sneaky little—!"

"Why d'you think nobody likes him? It isn't because of his job. Wilfred Mathias had the same job and most people liked him."

"How can Dilys like him? Why would she—?"

"Don't know much about women, do you?" Bethan got to her feet. "Now, here's a Military Two-Step and you can't tell me you don't know how to do it."

Davy allowed her to pull him onto the floor. His mind on other things, he did passably well as she guided him through the dance: "Heel, toe — one, two, three. Turn!"

Breathless, they ended the dance next to the door as Twm-the-Organ and Ifor Ellis came in smelling of the cider they'd swigged from a flagon hidden outside.

"There's a row!" said Twm. "Hell of a temper, she's got."

"Who's that?" asked Bethan.

"Dilys-the-Post," answered Ifor. "She was out there giving that Pritchard bloke a comeuppance."

"Was?" asked Davy. "Has she gone?"

"Gone off crying," said Twm.

Bethan nudged Davy. "Do something!"

In two strides, Davy was at the door, brushing aside Bogo's apology for barrelling into him earlier. There was no sign of Dilys or Rhys Pritchard, and the Morris parked next to him earlier was gone. They must have made up their quarrel and Rhys had taken Dilys home.

Davy went to his own car and started it up. There seemed no point in staying at the dance now Dilys had left. Gran had questioned his reason for wasting precious petrol coupons on a trip into the village, and he'd given his reason as the need to keep the engine oiled.

With shielded headlights, he was on the flat stretch below Corpse Hill when he saw Dilys ahead. He honked the horn and started to slow down when he drew level.

She halted and swung around, skirts swirling, and screamed, "Go away and leave me alone, you sod!"

He stopped the car and got out. "Dilys?"

"Oh, it's you. I'm sorry . . . When I heard a car, I thought . . ."

"Get in and I'll drive you home." When she hesitated, he said: "You don't want to walk up the hill in those strappy sandals, do you?"

She moved toward the car and he opened the passenger's door. "You've been crying."

"Yes. Now shut up about it!" She swung into the car and gathered her skirts away from the door as he closed it.

Getting behind the wheel, Davy said, "You shouldn't waste tears on Rhys Pritchard. He isn't worth it."

"I'm not crying because of him! I'm crying because I'm in a temper." She rummaged around in her beaded evening bag for a handkerchief and Davy placed his in her hand.

He watched her dry her eyes. "He's not the man for you, Dilys."

"How would you know?" she snapped.

"Because I know you."

"You don't know Rhys."

"No, but I know the job he does. It takes a certain type of man to do a job like that, and he does it very well."

She sniffled and looked out of the window. "Why aren't we moving?"

"Perhaps I ran out of petrol . . ."

She looked at him. "You? Davy Thomas who checks everything twice? Davy Thomas-the-Careful? The stick-in-the-mu—" She stopped short. Because she was angry with Rhys was no reason to take it out on the man who offered her a lift home.

"Dead inside, you were going to add?" he said, remembering Bethan's words. He leaned toward Dilys and cupped her face in his hands. "How well do you think you know me?" He touched his lips to hers, tasting the salt of her tears. Tears for another man. He released her, let out the clutch, and the gears grated in protest.

The car started forward and Dilys was too surprised to move.

Not a word passed between them as Davy set the Morris at Corpse Hill. Within minutes, he was pulling up outside Cartref. "Good night, Dilys." In spite of the way he felt, his voice was deliberately calm and controlled.

And final, Dilys thought. Well, what did she expect? What did she hope? That he'd grab her and kiss her again? Was that what she was hoping for? Waiting for? She got out and slammed the door, hearing the Morris pull away as she creaked open the gate. Half way up the path, she realized she still had Davy's handkerchief in her hand. She tossed it into the hedge a second before her mother opened the front door.

There was very little moonlight, but Morgan Ellis kept to the hedges while he made for Penboyr. He avoided the centre of the field where someone might see him. Who knew when Rhys Pritchard would be out and about? He didn't always come by car, knowing the sound of its engine gave them warning, and he wasn't above creeping around their farms in the dark, setting the dogs to barking.

It had been different with Wilfred Mathias. They could always hear him coming and the animals would be hidden away before he got anywhere near the farmyard. Not that they needed the car to warn them when Wilfred was about; the red banners would flutter across the valley ahead of him, or messengers would hurtle from one farm to another on bikes that could fly when they had to. It was a game then, and they counted it fair play when Wilfred caught one of them, but it wasn't a game any more, not now Rhys Pritchard had come.

It wasn't that the farmers weren't aware of how the country needed everything they could produce but they were crippling themselves with the rock-bottom prices the Government paid. Where was the harm in keeping back one pig from a litter of ten? No harm when the pig went to pay the mortgage or put food in the bellies of the farmers' families. How could a man work his fields with an empty belly? There had to be give and take, but those at their desks knew nothing of the sweat that went into running a farm. Pushing a pen must be a lot easier than pushing a plough.

Cheating the government, Rhys Pritchard called it. Treason, he said, sitting down to a dinner of roast beef he'd brought Bronwen to cook. Spam was good enough for the soldiers at the Front but the Districts Agricultural Inspector had roast beef.

They could count on Wilfred to turn a blind eye if it looked as if a farmer was going under, but Wilfred was a farmer's son. This man Pritchard was a city boy used to desks and red tape.

Toby Rice spent a night in jail, and Aled, until Davy-Pen -Farm put up the bail for both. Rhys Pritchard knew who got them out and he knew who was paying the fines for the farmers looking at going broke if they paid for themselves. Like him.

Morgan tossed the bale of hay over then unfastened the latch on the lych gate. He'd oiled the hinges to keep them from squeaking but the latch could bang like a shotgun if he wasn't careful. Taking his time, he closed the gate quietly and then hefted the bale of hay onto his shoulder and picked his way between the gravestones to the crypt.

He didn't know whose crypt it was. The name carved into the stone had long since been obliterated by the harsh weather Moelfre threw at Penboyr. Some said it belonged to the family that used to live in Plas Gwyn before Major Braithwaite came. The date could still be made out—1689. Well, after all these years, those resting in the boxes around the walls didn't bother the calves any, and if the cow shit offended them it was a shame. Better that than see his family thrown off their land.

It wasn't the first time he'd hidden animals in the crypt. Last time it had been a lamb. Mari Jenkins nearly gave the game away. She came up to put flowers on her husband's grave and heard the lamb going *maa-maa* . She thought it was her husband calling her. She was missing all day and they'd been out half the night searching for her, thinking she'd fallen somewhere and broken her leg. Reverend Davies found her hiding under the cloth on the altar, praying to God to tell her husband not to call her yet because she wasn't ready to go.

This time, he'd hidden two calves. On the Black Market, they'd bring in enough to keep the farm going and make up for the crop of potatoes he'd lost to the blight. Morgan spread the bale of hay and checked the calves. Goods ones they were, thanks to Davy's bull. Even the servicing of the two cows had to be done in secret because Rhys Pritchard was keeping a record of Tarw's betrothals so he knew where and when a calf was due. Davy'd caught onto that fast. No record was kept and no money changed hands, but he owed Davy two day's labour at harvest.

Morgan picked up the bucket and turned to go for water. In the square of moonlight stood Rhys Pritchard.

Christmas fled in half-hearted celebration with many of the tables supporting empty places for the men away fighting for their country, and for one or two thrown in prison as the result of Rhys Pritchard's zealous snooping.

"And it's going to get worse," said Aled, looking around at the dozen or so farmers gathered in his kitchen. "With the sprinkling of snow, all he's got to do is follow our tracks to where we've hidden the new lambs."

"There was no snow on the ground when I went to the crypt," Morgan pointed out. "How did he know I'd put two calves in there?"

"And how did he know Toby'd put a calf down in the miller's barn?" asked Aled. He looked at Davy. "Do you think Dilys-the-Post is telling him?"

"Dilys wouldn't do that," Davy said firmly.

"No, she wouldn't," Morgan echoed.

"Well, she's been seeing him for months," said Millie. "And they got engaged at Christmas."

"She wouldn't tell him anything!" The hard edge in Davy's voice was not entirely due to their speculation about Dilys. "And neither would Bronwen, just in case any of you are thinking that."

"No need to shout," grumbled Toby. "We've got to think of a way to outwit him."

"Isn't it why we're all here?" asked Morgan. "Apart from the vendetta he's got going against Davy here, he's after all of us. I've got ten ewes due to lamb any day. I'll need to hold two of those lambs to break even this year."

"I need to keep one of mine," said Aled.

"And I need two," said Toby. "What about you, Davy?"

"Major Braithwaite lost two last week when one of the hounds got out. I'm keeping one back for him." He looked around at those who hadn't spoken. "Does everyone here need to hide a lamb?" He waited until they'd nodded confirmation then said: "I have a plan that might keep Rhys Pritchard out of our way for a few days. It's why I asked Mam Derw to this meeting."

Millie glanced at the only other woman present. Mam Derw was huddled in the rocking chair by the fire, her eyes closed. "I think she's gone to sleep."

"I'm not asleep," Mam Derw croaked. "But I don't know why Davy Thomas dragged me up here in the middle of the night."

"All I need from you is when to expect the next heavy fall of snow," said Davy.

"Oh?" She twisted in the chair to look at him. "And what do I get out of it?"

"Call it doing your bit for the war effort," said Toby with a grin.

She ignored him and looked at each of the others in turn. "Well?"

"There'll be enough lamb from all of us to keep you fed for a while," said Davy.

"And a fleece for my mattress? These old bones need something soft."

"A fleece! That's too much," said Toby. "Isn't it, boys?"

Davy shrugged. "It's that or have every lamb accounted for. It's up to you."

"Do we have to have her help?" Aled asked.

"Not if there's one of us can forecast the weather days ahead," said Davy.

"We're sunk then," said Morgan. "Between us we'll have to give her what she wants. Now tell us what your plan is, Davy."

"I need two or three men who are strong and can ride."

Rhys smiled as he followed the tracks. Down in the valley there was barely a sprinkling of white, but up here on the mountain, the snow was deeper. He'd had a hunch the heavy snowfall of the day before would lead him to a cache of illicit animals. At this time of the year, it would be lambs, and where better to hide lambs than on the mountain?

He'd caught most of them, one by one. Watching from behind a tree or hedge, and once from behind a gravestone, he waited until they came to tend the hidden animals then he pounced and caught them red handed. A few he hadn't caught. Not Major Braithwaite whose wire fences were too high for him to climb without causing damage to the man's property; and not Helen Williams whose labourer tried to tell him there were no animals beyond the goat and a few chickens; and not Davy Thomas. Until now.

Davy had been cleverer than most. Even the cave on the mountain was empty although it showed evidence they'd kept animals there. However, Davy Thomas hadn't used the cave in months and the trap Rhys set for him was undisturbed.

Rhys wasted precious weeks watching Davy Thomas. He even followed him down the valley to the Teifi one morning, watching as he swam in the river. In addition, he followed him out of breath when he exercised his horses, leading Rhys into all the gorges and gullies in and around the mountain. However, he had him at last. He knew he would, sooner or later.

Rhys dropped behind a clump of gorse and studied the dilapidated cottage on the slope below. Abandoned for years by the look of it, from where he crouched he could see the low thatched roof was patched here and there with galvanized sheets. Someone had boarded up the windows from the inside and fastened the new and sturdy door with a shiny padlock. Seeing no sign of movement, he slithered down the slope toward it.

Outside the cottage door, men, sheep and horses had milled about, but leading away there were only horse tracks. They told their own story—someone herded sheep into the cottage and they were still there. He crept closer and set his ear against the door, listening for sounds from within. He heard a rustling in the straw, and then a heavy weight thumped against the inside of the sturdy boards.

For three days and parts of three nights, Rhys kept watch on the cottage. He'd seen no sign of Davy Thomas or anyone else near the place, but there were new tracks in the snow so someone had been there to feed the animals still inside. On the fourth day, duty forced him to spend the daylight hours at the farms around Newcastle Emlyn, but he was back by night, investigating the ground around the cottage by flashlight. The fifth day was spent sitting in the rocks above the cottage as the wind whistled around him, then a letter from his superiors questioning the lack of reports from his district forced him into action.

Constable Owens was less than helpful, as Rhys expected.

"Look!" Rhys argued. "I have the authority to search all farmland and buildings. All I need is for you to accompany me and witness the cutting of a padlock."

"I can't stand by while you damage private property," Constable Owens said. "You'll need a higher authority than mine to do that."

The authority in question, Major Braithwaite, was more amenable. "Cutting a padlock, you say. I suppose I can authorize it, what? When do you want it done?"

"Today." Rhys had wasted enough time on Davy Thomas and revenge would not be any sweeter for the waiting. Then, too, there was always a chance someone would warn Davy and he'd take the ewes and lambs away before Rhys could open the door and prove they were there and unregistered.

"Today . . ." Major Braithwaite rubbed a hand over his bristly thatch of hair. "I have the veterinary coming to see one of the bitches due to whelp—"

"This is a Government matter, Major Braithwaite. Top priority. A matter of treason."

"Oh, my!" cried Priscilla. "Treason!"

"Well . . ." The major looked at his sister, "Can you handle the veterinary on your own, Prissy?"

"Of course I can, if Mr Pritchard thinks this matter so urgent. But you must let me know where you're going, Dickie, in case the vet needs you."

"Just so." The major eyed Rhys. "Where is this place? Whose farm?"

"It's up on the mountain, bordering common land. Part of Pen Farm property."

"David's place?" Priscilla flopped weakly onto a gilded chair. "David is being accused of treason?"

"That's a bit strong, what?" the Major commented.

"When a man fails to aid his country in time of war, I'd call it treason." Rhys headed for the door. "Shall we go, Major?"

"Oh, Dickie, that dreadful man!" cried Priscilla when Rhys went out to the car. "Whatever can we do to help David?"

"Nothing. There isn't time to warn him, and if the evidence is where he says it is . . ."

"Would David be so careless?"

"He's nobody's fool, but neither is Pritchard. I've met his type before. He's a trouble shooter, sent in when Mathias didn't report enough farmers."

"I'm going to telephone the post office. If there's someone there with a car, they could get to Pen Farm ahead of you and warn David."

"Good idea," said the Major. "You do that and I'll find some way of delaying Pritchard in the village."

However, Rhys wouldn't be delayed and drove through the village as fast as he dared. They sped across the humpbacked bridge by the square and Constable Owens, sitting in the back seat, uttered an oath as he bounced against the roof and his helmet collapsed about his ears.

"I'll 'ave you for speeding if you don't slow down," he muttered.

Half way up Corpse Hill, shifting the Morris into low gear, Rhys saw a woman pushing a bike, not realizing it was Dilys until he was past. Farther on, when he sped past Cartref, he saw Davy Thomas walking a string of horses down the road.

"Slow down!" Constable Owens shouted. "In the country, you're supposed to slow down when you pass livestock."

"I'll remember that," said Rhys in a clipped voice. He had half a mind to turn the car around in the next gateway and go back, so sure was he that Dilys and Davy Thomas had arranged a tryst, but sweeter was the revenge that lay on the mountain. He gunned the Morris, careless of the ruts and boulders on the road, and scattered gravel as he screamed the car to a halt beside the track leading to the abandoned cottage.

"Bloody hell!" said Constable Owens as he got out of the car and examined the damage done to his helmet. "Drive like a maniac, you do."

"I quite agree," said Major Braithwaite, visibly shaken by his ordeal in the front seat. "And it would have been a nice gesture to allow David to accompany us."

"When I have shown you the evidence, I shall personally conduct Mr Thomas here." Rhys led the way to the cottage, pointing out the sheep and horse tracks. "I would deduce that he, and possibly others, herded pregnant ewes into the cottage where he hoped they would lamb without my knowledge."

"By *he* you mean David Thomas of Pen Farm?" Constable Owens asked, scribbling in his notebook.

"Put that away, man," said Major Braithwaite. "There's no need to take notes."

"Habit," said the Constable, sliding the pencil inside and fastening the notebook with a length of knicker elastic tied into a frayed knot.

"You see," said Rhys, pointing out the tracks around the cottage. "Ewes were brought here, but there are only horse tracks leading away." He moved toward the door, wire cutters in hand.

"Just a minute, Mr Pritchard," said Constable Owens. "Have you checked the lock to see if it's open?"

"Of course I have," said Rhys as he applied the cutters.

"Breaking and entering," muttered the Constable.

"Quiet, man," said Major Braithwaite.

Rhys almost gave a whoop of triumph when the lock fell apart. He glanced at the two men standing a few paces away. "Now, gentlemen—the evidence!"

He threw the door wide and prepared to step inside. From the darkness, a deeper darkness hurtled toward him. He had time to raise his arms to protect his face before a weight threw him off balance and claws ripped at his hand.

"Oh hell! It's Blackie!" shouted Constable Owens. "Run, Major!"

They had a few yards start on Blackie. A younger man, the constable made it up an oak to safety, and then he reached down to help the major clamber up as Blackie pecked at the man's boots.

"What in devil's name is that?" asked the major, studying Blackie's widespread wings as he strutted about under their branch.

"It's Pen Farm's cockerel. Better than a guard dog, it is. Had a go at nearly everybody in the village at one time or another."

"It could fly up here if it had a mind to. Where's your gun, Owens?"

"Gun? This isn't America. I don't carry a gun. You can have my truncheon, if you think it'll do any good."

"Where's Pritchard gone?"

"Must be inside the cottage. The door's closed any road."

"Pritchard!" called the major. "Come out of there!"

"No!" came the reply. "Fetch the police!"

"I'm here!" Constable Owens shouted from his branch.

The major studied Blackie. "How long is that thing going to wander about down there?"

"I don't know much about cockerels, Major."

"Look, it's moving back to the cottage. Give me your truncheon. I'm going to try to get to the car."

"Well, it's up to you," Constable Owens straightened a leg so he could pull the truncheon out of his side pocket, "but I'd be careful."

"It's only a cockerel, man!" One eye on Blackie, the major eased out of the tree and dropped to the ground. On tiptoe, he took a few paces then froze. The cockerel was facing him and ruffling its feathers. It pawed the ground like a bull and then charged, wings

251

held out stiffly on either side like a wind-blown cloak as it ran over the snow.

"It's coming back, Major!" The warning was unnecessary for the major was already running to the tree.

"Help me up, Owens!" the major shouted and dropped the truncheon as he leapt for the nearest branch. Panting, he climbed as high as he dared without the branches giving under his weight. "That's a black devil straight from hell."

"And you lost my truncheon," Constable Owens pointed out.

"It's not lost, it's down there." The major braced himself against the tree trunk and looked down. "What's it doing to your truncheon, Owens?"

"Same thing as last time," was the morose answer. "That's the second truncheon I've lost this year."

"What's it doing now, a victory dance?"

"I don't know, Major, but I'm not moving while it's down there." Constable Owens took a bag of mints from his pocket and stood on his branch to offer one up to the major. "We could be in for a long wait. There isn't a house anywhere nearer than Pen Farm and it's beyond shouting distance. They can't even see us from there."

"That thing's got to sleep sometime, doesn't it?"

"Don't know much about cockerels," said Constable Owens. "Ducks is what I keep.

Ducks is safe. I had six little ducklings in an incubator until yesterday."

"What happened yesterday?" Major Braithwaite asked politely but without any real interest. "Did a fox get them?"

"No, sir. It was my little girl. She let them out and they went running about in the slush and got mud all over themselves. So she washed them."

"And they drowned."

"No, sir. To dry them she pegged them on the wash line by their webs. The Missus looked everywhere for them, then we saw them this morning. Frozen stiff they were."

Major Braithwaite's body shook as he tried to suppress his laughter and the oak trembled as if in sympathy.

"Don't shake the tree, Major! You'll have Blackie up here to investigate."

"Where is he now? I can't see him."

"He's flown to the roof of the cottage," Constable Owens informed him.

"What's he doing up there?"

"I can't be sure but I think he's going to go down the chimney."

"Don't be silly, man!"

"Well, you look and see for yourself then."

The major craned his neck to look over a branch and saw Blackie's curved tail feathers disappear inside the square brick of the chimney. "I never would have believed it!" he said, as a shower of sticks and leaves exploded from the chimney. "What's he doing?"

"Must have found a bird's nest blocking the chimney," said the Constable. Then he shouted: "Mr Pritchard! You'd better come out now."

"No!" came the emphatic cry from inside the cottage. An eruption of a cloud of ash from the chimney preceded a series of cries and shouts. "Help! Somebody, help!"

The sounds of scuffling came from inside the cottage as Major Braithwaite and Constable Owens climbed out of the tree. They ran to the door and everything went quiet.

"Mr Pritchard!" Constable Owens shouted. "Are you in there?"

"Of course I'm in here!"

"Why don't you come out?" called the major.

"Because that—that thing is guarding the door. I can't get near it."

"Open the door, Owens," said the Major, picking up the splintered remains of the truncheon.

"Not me," said Constable Owens. "I think we'd be better off getting Davy Thomas."

"You fetch him, Major," Rhys called. "Constable Owens—do you still have your notebook?"

"Yes, sir."

"Right. I'm going to have the law on him for this. These are the charges. Write them down. Number one: Preventing a District Agricultural Inspector from discharging his duties in accordance with wartime law."

"Preventing a D.A.I. . . . Beg pardon, sir, but who are we laying these charges against?"

"David Thomas of course."

"Oh." Sounding out the words as he wrote them, Constable Owens wrote: "Allegedly pre—"

"Allegedly? What do you mean allegedly?" shouted Rhys.

"Well, sir, he's innocent until proven guilty."

"He's right, Pritchard," said the major. "You don't know David Thomas is involved."

"It's his land, and the constable identified the cockerel as belonging to Pen Farm."

"That may be so," said the major, "but what exactly was your duty regarding the cockerel?"

"Never mind!" snapped Rhys. "Number two: Failure to restrain a dangerous animal, resulting in an attack upon my person by said animal."

"With respect, Pritchard, the animal was restrained until you let it loose."

"But it attacked me!" shouted Rhys. "Write it down, Constable."

Still sounding out the words, Constable Owens wrote: "Attack on person of D.A.I. by cockerel."

"Animal, you fool!" shouted Rhys.

"No, sir. Strictly speaking, a cockerel is a bird. I'll put bird then, shall I?"

"Whatever it is, it has sharp claws," said Rhys.

"That's why I stick to ducks," Constable Owens mumbled to himself.

"What?" Rhys shouted.

"Ducks, sir. No trouble is ducks. No claws and no—" He was interrupted by the sounds of renewed outbreaks of scuffling inside the cottage.

"Come on," said the major. "We'd better find David and let him out of there."

Davy hadn't expected to meet Dilys coming up the hill. It was too early for her to be going home from work and it was the wrong time of day for the normal delivery of post. His initial joy at seeing her turned to dread. Dewi! The thought sprang unwillingly to mind. She was bringing him a telegram about Dewi. He dismounted and waited, leaning against Midnight for support, his hand clenched on the lead rope.

"I was coming to your place," she said, when she reached him. "I have a message from—" She noted the tension in his hand and the drawn look on his face. "It isn't about Dewi," she said quickly and saw his shoulders sag with relief. "Oh, Davy!" She covered his hand with her own. "I wouldn't blurt out news like that."

"How else do you deliver bad news?"

"Not like that." She took her hand away when he failed to respond to her touch. "This isn't about Dewi, but it's bad news all the same, and I think I'm too late bringing it even though I left right away."

"Go on."

"It's from Miss Braithwaite. She telephoned and asked for someone to get a message to you urgent, only there wasn't anybody around with a car. Even Rowlie is out on deliveries so I couldn't ask him."

"What's the message?"

"Rhys got Major Braithwaite to authorize forced entry to your old cottage and they've got the bobby with them. They passed me as I was coming up Corpse Hill."

"I saw them."

"But you didn't know where they were going. If you leave the ponies with me, you can ride across the fields and be there soon after they do. I'll go and tell Aled to come up to help."

"No need. There's nothing there Rhys Pritchard can't see."

"Miss Braithwaite said he was so sure. He was accusing you of all sorts of things."

"I know. He's been hounding me ever since the Harvest Dance, but he won't find anything."

"Nothing at all?" She studied him, disbelief in her eyes. Then she realized it was possible he didn't trust her.

"I've got one lamb, but Bogo's got in the wheelhouse at Dyffryn."

"Is it safe there?"

"You tell me." He watched her blush.

"Bethan told me how Rhys has been harassing you. Vendetta, she called it."

"Bethan's home?"

"You didn't know?" Dilys was surprised. She would have thought . . . If they had something going between them . . . "She was shot. Well, not really shot but tracer bullets followed her ambulance down a street in Swansea and some chips of stone and glass cut her hands and arms. She's all right, but I'm sure she'd like your company." Dilys manoeuvred the bike around. "I'd better get back. I left in such a hurry I don't remember if I locked the post office door."

"And if you can call the police station in Newcastle Emlyn to tell them where they can find Owens and Pritchard . . .

"Righto."

"Dilys?" She paused, one foot on a pedal ready to push off. "Rhys is your friend. Why did you bring me the warning?"

"I'm part of the valley. I'm not a farmer, but I was married to a farmer's son. What affects you, affects all of us."

"I see. One more thing—I never congratulated you on your engagement."

She laughed; a harsh sound that carried back to him as she sped down the hill.

Davy parked the Morris outside the Red Lion and went around to the back door. A favourite entry and exit point of after-hours drinkers, he remembered delivering Dewi there for Bethan's birthday parties before Dewi reached the handful of years when it became shameful to play with girls.

Bethan lifted the latch at his knock, her hands and arms bandaged to the elbows. "Davy Thomas, as I live and breathe. Come in."

She crossed the kitchen to turn down the volume on the wireless as he entered. With Vera Lynn subdued he could hear muffled conversations from the bar.

"What happened to you? Did your father catch you with your hands in the till?"

"Something like that," she said with a laugh. "Half a brick wall decided it wanted a ride in my ambulance. What have you been up to?"

"Not as much as you, by the look of you."

"This?" Bethan held up hands bandaged to shapeless wads. "The bandages come off in a week then I'll be back to camp. I'm more interested in what you've been doing. Whatever it is, Dilys broke off her engagement."

"When? I saw her today and she didn't say anything."

"She told me last Monday. Said she couldn't stomach what he was doing to the farmers around here. I think what did it was the fine Rhys made Morgan Ellis pay. After all, Morgan was Alun's father. Whatever, she found out Rhys Pritchard's a slimy little toad, as I've said all along."

Davy felt light headed, as if he'd sampled Elias' brew. He grinned. "That's a relief."

"Now don't go thinking you can tarry or somebody else will snap her up."

"I've got to catch her on the rebound, you mean?"

"Not much of a rebound from what I hear. She says it was after Christmas dinner, with all his family and the aunts and uncles gathered around, that he presented her with the ring. I don't think she'd have taken it if it weren't for making him look bad in front of everybody. And, of course, Mari was all for it."

"I don't know if you should be telling me what she probably said to you in confidence."

"Don't be silly! I consider myself one of her best friends, and what are best friends for if not to further a romance?"

"And I suppose you've been talking to her about me?"

"Not a word. She thinks we've got something going. She's eaten up with curiosity and a bit of jealousy, I think, but I didn't put her right because I thought it might do her some good to think she had competition. Mind you, best friend or not, if I thought I stood a chance against her I'd give her a run for her money."

"Bethan Stock! I'm old enough to be your father!"

"But you're much better looking. There's a touch of the Errol Flynn's about you, and you're a nice man, Davy Thomas."

"Careful, you mean? Stick-in-the-mud and dead inside?"

Bethan laughed. "Well, I was wrong about that, wasn't I? And I heard Luned and a couple of others talking about you the other night. Bit of a heart breaker you were, and all the girls fighting over you before you went off to Canada."

"I was only a boy!"

"And a silly one, like all the others I expect. You're a man now with a lot to offer, but I'm telling you—Dilys won't hang about much longer."

The door to the bar opened and Elias entered the kitchen in a surge of noise. "I thought I heard voices. How are you, Davy?"

"Fine. And you?"

"Can't complain. Can I get you a drink from the bar?"

"Not for me. I only dropped in for a few minutes to see how Bethan was doing. I didn't hear about her accident until this afternoon."

"How's Dewi these days? Must be getting quite a man now."

"He's not as wise as your Bethan, I don't suppose, but so far he's kept out of trouble. A picture of his ship came at Christmas. It's bigger than I expected." Davy got to his feet. "I've got to get going, but I'm driving into Carmarthen tomorrow, Bethan. If you want to come—if you'll let her come, Elias."

"Doesn't matter what he says," said Bethan, ignoring her father's grimace. "What time?"

"About ten in the morning." At the door, he nodded to Bethan. "And I'll take note of what you said."

"Don't forget. And—good luck, Davy."

"You mustn't go around calling him Davy," Elias said when they were alone. "It isn't respectful for you to use his first name until you're a lot older, my girl."

As Davy approached the gate at Cartref, he saw Mari on her knees beside the hedge.

"You look busy, Mrs Jenkins."

"It's all these leaves," said Mari. "There's daffodils under here somewhere, but if I don't clear these leaves the buds will rot before the flowers can open."

"Is Dilys home?"

"Gone over to see Helen-the-School, she has," said Mari, busy with the hand fork.

"Well! Now there's a thing! That's the third handkerchief I've found in the last half hour. Where do you think they're all coming from?"

"Perhaps you've got a handkerchief tree growing in there."

"What?" She looked up. "Oh, you're joking me, Mr Thomas. Did you want to see Dilys urgent?"

"It can wait until the next time she's up with the post." Deflated, he walked away.

"I'll tell her you called," Mari shouted after him as she studied the handkerchiefs she'd found.

From the Post Office window, Dilys saw the Morris pull up outside the Red Lion, then Bethan came out and Davy ran around to open the car door for her. She should feel happy for Bethan, but she didn't. In an odd way, she felt as if Bethan had stolen something from her.

"What's the matter?" Helen looked up from the form she was filling out.

"I was just thinking . . . There's Davy Thomas, for the second time this week, going out for the day and leaving the farm work to his mother."

"Hardly," said Helen. "Edwin is there full time and Joroway goes up two days a week. And Mrs Thomas has Olwen up to help her twice a week now the mill has laid off the women."

"I didn't know. You could say I've been out of touch with what's going on."

"Do you miss Rhys at all?"

"No. I'm glad he moved to Newcastle Emlyn."

"I don't suppose he could take the teasing any longer. A crowd of children were in the playground one day, imitating cockerels when he walked by."

"Bronwen said they were outside Rose Cottage three nights in a row, all shouting cock-a-doodle-doo." Dilys laughed. "What a bloke. Bought me a box of chocolates and a pair of nylons and thought he owned me."

"Rachel says the same about the Yanks."

"No Yanks for me. I'm sticking to the men in the valley from now on."

"Anyone in particular?" Helen put the form into an envelope and passed it under the grid.

Dilys hesitated. "I'm not sure. But I think I'm too late anyway."

"Why? Is he married?"

"He isn't married, but— Helen, I love you like a sister, but this is something I've got to work out for myself."

"Is he a decent man?"

"He's probably the best respected man in the valley. Now don't try and wheedle any more out of me."

Pulling on her gloves, Helen strolled toward to the door. She opened it then said,

"It's Davy Thomas, isn't it?" She smiled knowingly and left Dilys with a red face.

Skulking behind the milk churns as she watched the house, Dilys felt like a criminal. Just after eleven o'clock, Eirlys came out with a basket in her hands. Dilys gauged the other woman's speed, and then she wheeled the bike out to meet her.

"Good morning, Mrs Thomas. Is that for the men in the top field?"

"And where else would I be going with sandwiches and a bottle of tea?" Eirlys snapped.

"I'll be passing the gate. Why don't I take it up?"

For a moment, Eirlys hesitated and Dilys held her breath, then: "I suppose it would give me more time for baking . . . All right." She handed the basket to Dilys. "Make sure and tell Davy to bring the basket back tonight."

"I will." Dilys hung the basket from the handlebars and kept on up the hill. It had been easier than she thought.

"Flibbertigibbet!" Eirlys muttered as she went back to the house.

Dilys propped the bike against the gate to the field and took out the picnic basket hidden under the postbag, then she lifted the other basket from the handlebars.

Joroway and Edwin were on her side of the field with the plough. She gave them Eirlys' basket before making her way to where Davy was seeding at the far side.

As the horse reached the hedge at the end of a row, Davy turned it around. It was then he saw Dilys picking her way across the ploughed ridges. His first thought was for Dewi, but he saw Dilys had left the postbag by the gate. There was no yellow telegram in her hands, only a basket covered with a blue cloth.

"What brings you up here?" he asked.

She shrugged, stopped a pace away from him and set the basket down. "I feel like Mohammed coming to the mountain." She pointed to the basket. "I brought a picnic."

For a long moment, they stared at each other, and then Davy gestured to the basket. "If you were to auction it . . ."

"What would you bid, Davy?"

Heedless of Joroway and Edwin watching, Davy stepped forward and took Dilys in his arms. "I'd bid every penny I have in the world."

♥

DRAGON OF WAR

In the stillness of predawn, Dewi hunched into the rocky niche at Moelfre's feet. The crevice fitted him less well than when he was a boy, but it afforded some shelter from the winds that would strafe the heights at dawn to raise a dull ache in his ears.

At that hour all was silent, even the owls had gone to roost, and below the valley slept beneath a mantle of mist, concealed from a world where guns blasted night into hellish day.

Memories woke him from a sweat-drenched sleep earlier, the horror creeping back to toss him this way and that like an angry sea. And the phantom pain drove him from his bed, nerves jangling, to wage war against his wakefulness, to embark on a quest for exhaustion that always led to the mountain.

Perhaps it was foolish to continue to climb so late into December, foolish to try it now at any time of the year. The hill road was treacherous when black ice quilted the surface and caught the unwary. Where he once raced up the hill, legs pumping and lungs near bursting, today he came slowly, puffing like an old man. After falling twice, he took to rimed fields, leaving man tracks around the flock of sheep as he kept a sharp look out for the ram. Time was when he pitted himself against it, imagining it was Jesse Owens at his heels and the field Berlin's Olympic arena as he raced across to vault over the five-barred gate just as the ram butted into it.

Today he came cautiously, vulnerable if the ram should challenge him and leaning heavily on the hawthorn cane that had been his grandfather's. As a boy, he'd laughed at the old man who limped with one leg permanently twisted after falling from a dray.

Dot-down-carry-one, he'd called him, taking the name from an arithmetic lesson when they learned to add pounds, shillings and pence: If the penny column comes to more than twelve, put a dot down and carry one. The other children copied him; calling his grandfather by the cruel name.

"God pays back," Gran said. "Don't make fun because God pays back."

Dewi had laughed at her. Full of prophetic clichés she'd always been. "Pride goeth before a fall." "God helps those who help themselves." And the oddest one of all: "Three tries for a Welshman."

"That's wrong, Gran," he argued once with the omnipotence of his twelve years. "It's supposed to be if at first you don't succeed, try, try again."

She faced to him, the tall angular figure he inherited dominating the kitchen. "No, Dewi. If you don't succeed after three tries, God never meant you to do it. Remember now—three tries for a Welshman."

Would he have remembered?

Dewi watched a rabbit scoot under a snow-laden clump of gorse. It moved like a shadow, blending with the background, and when it paused, he couldn't be sure it was there. No more than he could be sure of what happened that night when Gran stood in a pool of light aboard the doomed Chieftain. It smacked of the unnatural; of sailor superstition, he wouldn't willingly acknowledge: a woman on board a warship was bad luck.

In the stillness of predawn, the ocean was grey and empty, as if HMS Chieftain was the last thing afloat. They barely moved fast enough to push water away from the prow, but speed in those waters and at night could be deadly. Three battleships and a supply ship had gone down there during the past week, victims of German U-boats and moored mines. Travelling ahead of the convoy, the mines they swept for could be detected, but their sophisticated equipment couldn't save a ship travelling at high speed because the danger would register on their scanners milliseconds before the hull made contact with death.

Dewi lit a cigarette, shielding the flare of the match with his hands, and leaned against the rail. Still shaken, he couldn't be sure if what happened hadn't been a trick of a mind hovering between sleep and wakefulness.

In the darkness amidships he'd been jarred awake in the swaying hammock, knowing by the snores of the men around him that it wasn't time to change watch, yet not knowing what woke him. As he lay there, he became aware of a dull glow playing across the bulkhead, a light where there shouldn't have been a light. Turning towards it, he blinked at the figure standing there. "Gran?"

Within the glow, she was unmistakable. Grey hair drawn tight into a braided bun, she wore the coarse apron she used for her work about the farm. "Three tries, Dewi," she said. "Three tries." Then she was gone.

He had seen her, yet she couldn't have been there. Gran had been in the kitchen at Pen Farm, sinking into the final sleep in the rocking chair by the fire.

She spoke of him that night, his father said; interrupting the wedding plans his father and Dilys were making to talk about him.

"Dewi was the first one of us Thomas's to go to Grammar School."

"Dewi won a silver cup when he was nine for reciting at the Eisteddfod."

"Dewi would have run for Wales at the Empire Games if the war hadn't come."

Dewi. Dewi. Dewi.

And her call had roused him from sleep.

Dewi flicked the butt of his cigarette into the undulating greyness and heard a low warning growl from the guard on the bridge. This was his least favourite watch; one when he fought to stay awake as the flickering radar screen lulled his brain with the mesmeric swing of its searching arm orbiting on a captive course. A stolen break away from his post, five minutes when Third Engineer Watkins kept an eye open for any blips on the radar and sonar screens.

An Alert shrilled across all decks and Dewi ran back to the radio room. A quick glance showed him the radar screen was blank. He leapt into the chair in front of the sonar. "Why the hell did you press the Alert?" he asked, cutting the alarm as Watkins answered.

"I thought I was supposed to." Watkins' voice had a belligerent edge.

"Get out of here!" Dewi reached for the radio and signalled the bridge. The roster told him First Officer Grey was taking the watch. "Number One? There's something down there, sir," Dewi informed him, keeping an eye on the blip. "It isn't moving and I can't detect any sound waves."

"Is it a U-boat with its engines cut?" Grey's disembodied voice asked.

"Perhaps it hoped we'd pass over without detecting it, sir."

"But we found her, eh?" Grey sounded jubilant. "Jolly good."

"It looks as though it might be sitting on the bottom, sir." As he spoke, Captain Cranshaw entered the bridge. Dewi waited while Grey told Cranshaw the reason for the Alert, then he heard the First Officer suggest *Full Ahead* to get them out of range.

"Blithering idiot!" Cranshaw's voice boomed from the radio. "Full Speed Ahead could put us into a minefield."

"But, sir—" Above Grey's protest, Cranshaw ordered All Engines Stop.

"We're sitting ducks," Dewi muttered to himself. But Cranshaw was probably right. At that angle, any torpedoes fired from the sub would have to take a circuitous route to reach Chieftain, and they might be able to manoeuvre out of danger.

"Who's on duty in the radio room?" Cranshaw asked casually, as if asking who was up to bat.

"Thomas, Radio Officer Second Class, sir," Dewi answered.

"The Welshman, sir," Grey said.

"Damn! Where's the senior officer?" Cranshaw asked.

"Don't know, sir," Dewi lied. Muldoon would be in his berth, curled up with an illicit bottle of gin for company, oblivious to the Alert that shrilled through the ship. The Captain ordered a seaman to fetch Muldoon.

For a moment there was silence but for the wash of the ocean against Chieftain's hull. Then the Captain Cranshaw spoke: "Signal the submerged craft," he ordered. "You do know how to signal, seaman?"

"Yes, sir." Dewi bit back his anger. He knew the signal procedure as well as Muldoon, but there had never been reason to use it. He transmitted the signal as Muldoon lurched in bleary eyed.

"What did you send?" Muldoon asked, dropping into the second chair.

"I sent *Identify Yourself,* sir."

"Has there been a reply?"

"No, sir." Dewy leaned to one side while Muldoon prepared to signal the bridge.

"Captain?"

"Is that you, Muldoon? Thank God." The relief in Cranshaw's voice was evident. "Now—what do you make of the submerged craft?"

"Impossible to say, sir." Muldoon flicked the screen with a fingernail. "There's no movement from her and we can't detect any engine or propeller noise." He paused. "There was no answering signal."

"Try her again. With all due respect to young Thomas, he might have fouled up."

"I did not—!" Dewi began to protest.

"Quiet!" Muldoon pushed Dewi to one side as he checked the controls. Duplicating Dewi earlier action, he signalled the submerged craft: *Identify Yourself.*

"Any reply?" Captain Cranshaw walked into the radio room with the gun he rarely wore strapped to his waist. Ignoring Dewi, he went to stand behind Muldoon, his eyes on the sonar.

"We should give them a few more seconds, sir," Muldoon suggested.

"And with every second, the torpedoes they might have fired could be aiming at our hull."

"Sir?" Muldoon twisted around to look up at the captain. "Do you think it's a Jerry down there?"

"Why else hasn't she responded to our signal?" Cranshaw ordered Muldoon to open the radio link with the bridge. "Number One? Position the depth charges and hold them at the ready. We've had no response to two tries at making contact."

Two tries. Dewi saw a red glow spread across the drab walls like the glow of sunrise washing across Moelfre, and he heard Gran's voice: *Three tries . . .* "You don't know it's a Jerry, sir. Not for sure," he said in a half shout, quailing when the two men stared at him. "We must signal her again."

Cranshaw's scathing glance took him in from head to toe as if searching for gold braid on Dewi's uniform. Without comment, he turned back to the radio. "Number One? On my —"

"No!" Dewi darted forward. He pushed Cranshaw away from the radio and wrenched the gun from the captain's holster. Cranshaw recovered his balance and rounded on Dewi, his face purple with rage and disbelief. Then he saw the gun in Dewi's hand and stepped back. Dewi closed the radio link with the bridge and used the gun to motion to Muldoon. "Signal them a third time."

"Put the gun down, Thomas." Muldoon rose to his feet.

"Stay back!" Dewi released the safety catch when Muldoon took a step toward him. The hand holding the gun trembled. He brought his other hand and sandwiched the gun between his palms to steady it.

"This is mutiny, Mister." Cranshaw raised his hands above his head and took another step away from Dewi until his back was pressed against the scanner. "We dare not wait before we release the depth charges. Put the gun down."

"Put the gun down, Dewi," his father said quietly.

For a moment, fleeting rebellion gave Dewi the courage to disobey.

"Dewi!" His father's voice was low, holding a threat of a whipping as Dewi bent over the sawhorse at the back of the house. "Put the gun down."

The habit of a lifetime took control of Dewi's hands. He took the shotgun barrel from his mouth and laid the gun on the table.

He couldn't remember his father holding him before that day. An arm around his shoulder, a brief hug, yes, and a lingering handclasp when he boarded the troop train in Carmarthen three years earlier. In addition, he'd never before seen his father cry.

"Put the gun down," Muldoon repeated.

Dewi levelled the gun and motioned Muldoon back to the radio. "Signal the sub again. Be careful," he added as Muldoon sat down. "If you signal the bridge, I'll fire." When Muldoon hesitated, he barked the order again: "Signal her!"

"Do it, man!" Cranshaw ordered. As Muldoon carried out the order, Cranshaw said to Dewi. "This will get you a court martial, Mister."

"How do you know it's a Jerry, sir?" Dewi asked in defence of his action.

"If it was one of ours, it would have returned identification." Cranshaw jerked toward the radio when the bridge signalled, then he halted and glanced at Dewi.

"Move away." Dewi circled warily, his eyes on the two senior officers while he edged to the radio. He flicked the receiver but held a hand over the transmitter.

"Captain? Something rather odd." Grey's voice showed a trace of excitement for all that he tried to sound professional. "You must come up on deck, sir."

Cranshaw took an involuntary step toward the door then halted when Dewi traced his movements with the gun.

"My God!" cried Muldoon; able to see the scanner now Cranshaw had moved away. "They've launched a torpedo!"

Dewi swung around to look at the screen, his mouth open in disbelief, and Cranshaw seized his chance. He leapt at Dewi and wrested the gun from his hand. Wedging him against the bulkhead, he pressed the muzzle to Dewi's ribs. "Bloody spy! I'll make damn sure you're the first to die!" he breathed in Dewi's ear.

"It can't be a torpedo; it's following an abnormal path," said Muldoon. "It's moving too slowly . . . I think they jettisoned something."

Even as Muldoon spoke, Grey signalled. "Sir? There are things bobbing to the surface."

"Ask him what they are," Cranshaw ordered, retaining his grip on Dewi.

Muldoon relayed the question and Grey answered. "We're just training the searchlights on them now. One of them looks like—rather like a tin of Ovaltine."

"Blithering idiot!" Cranshaw manhandled Dewi toward the door. "On deck, Mister. Any tricks and I'll use this." With the gun, he prodded Dewi ahead of him.

The sailors crowding the rails failed to notice the gun Cranshaw held to Dewi's back. They studied the sea around the searchlights and vied with each other to identify the debris rising to the surface.

"There's the paper off a loaf of Hovis," one of them said.

"I've got a pack of Woodbines over here," another cried. "And here comes the front cover of Punch."

"They probably heard our signal but couldn't respond," Muldoon suggested.

"That's a navy hat," a voice called from the stern. "HMS Cor . . . Cordelia."

"The Cordelia was reported missing," Muldoon reminded the Captain and pushed through to stand next to Dewi at the rail. He peered over the side. "What the hell's that?"

They looked to where Muldoon pointed and studied the green and red square of cloth unfolding as it rose to undulate on top of the waves. Dewi's knees buckled when he recognized it, and he sagged against the rail.

"It's Taffy's flag, sir," Watkins said from beside Muldoon. "It's the bloody Red Dragon of Wales!"

"I knew the Cordelia's Captain, sir," Muldoon said quietly. "He was a career man from some Godforsaken place in Wales with a name I could never pronounce. It must be his flag."

Amid the cheer that ran the length of the ship, Cranshaw turned to Dewi. "Is that right, Mister? Is that your flag?"

Dewi nodded. "It's the Dragon of War, sir."

"How did you know?"

Dewi couldn't answer. Who'd believe Gran had been amidships?

"We could . . . I could have ordered . . ." Cranshaw released Dewi and leaned weakly against the rail, beads of sweat forming on his brow. "In God's name, if they couldn't signal why didn't they jettison earlier?" In the glow of the searchlights, Cranshaw eyed Dewi as he holstered his gun. "We'll say no more about what happened in the radio room. It's forgotten. Is that understood?"

"It's forgotten, Dewi. Is that understood?" His father's fist hit the table and rattled the supper plates Gran put on the table. "You can serve your country by doing what you know best. You're a farmer. What do you know about guns except for shooting rabbits on a Saturday morning?"

"They need wireless operators. I know about them. Haven't I repaired enough of them here on this table?" Dewi argued.

"Wirelesses! From what I hear, wireless operators are like Captains; they go down with their ships. You'll be stuck at your post sending an S.O.S. while everybody else jumps into the lifeboats."

"If that is what I must do—"

"Well, you won't! You forget it, Dewi. You're only sixteen. I'll go to the recruitment office and tell them how you altered your birth certificate."

"Davy! No!" Gran rarely opposed his father, but she argued with him then. "You can't stop Dewi doing what he wants to do any more than I could stop you going to Canada."

"This is different!" his father shouted. "He's still a child. I won't have him risk his life when he doesn't have to. I won't risk losing him."

"It's a risk we must take, Davy," Gran said. "If he goes there's a chance he won't come back. But if you force him to stay, we'll lose him for sure."

Back in the radio room, the sub's blip registered on sonar, but the radar scanner drew Dewi's attention. Not believing what he'd seen, he waited as the arm took a swing with what seemed like agonizing slowness until it reached the point where it confirmed what he thought was there. He leaned forward and pressed the Alert, temporarily blinded by the sudden darkness as someone doused the searchlights.

It was a matter of seconds before Cranshaw signalled from the bridge and Muldoon appeared at Dewi's back.

"Radar detects five enemy craft—three battleships and two frigates—heading in our direction, bearing zero-zero-five. Travelling at twenty-two knots." Dewi informed them both.

"Did you say enemy craft? How do you know?" Muldoon asked. "It's too dark out there to identify them at this distance."

"Radar doesn't recognize dark or light, sir," Dewi said quietly, remembering that radar was a new device and one on which Muldoon hadn't been trained yet because there hadn't been the opportunity to release him from his duties aboard Chieftain. To the Captain, he said. "Convoy speed has increased to twenty-four knots, sir."

"They'll have seen our searchlights when they came over the horizon," said Muldoon. He inclined his head at the sonar blip. "What do we do about her? She must be disabled. Let her know we're under attack," he ordered Dewi as he signalled the bridge for orders.

Cranshaw's reply was slow in coming. "Our duty is to provide protection for other vessels, be they above or below the surface. We stand and fight."

"Bloody twit!" Muldoon spat, his hand over the transmitter.

"He's right, sir," Dewi said. "If we move away, Jerry will detect the Cordelia." In front of him the radar screen was aglow with blips. "It's our convoy! They're just clearing the horizon."

Muldoon checked the screen. "But farther away than Jerry. We're caught in the middle. Signal them that Jerry's headed for us," Muldoon ordered. "I'll be on the bridge for a couple of minutes."

Dewi did a quick calculation. The convoys would not yet have been picked up on each other's screens. The Friendlies were holding a steady speed, unaware of the danger racing toward Chieftain from the other horizon. "Piggy in the middle," he muttered as he tapped out a transmission informing the Friendlies of the German convoy's position, and ended with: *HMS Chieftain at stand-off above HMS Cordelia submerged and disabled. Assist.*

With satisfaction, Dewi watched the Friendlies gather speed, going from a cruising sixteen knots to a galloping twenty knots and rising. Five smaller blips detached themselves from the convoy and sped ahead. Dewi clocked them at twenty-nine knots and rising, while the enemy frigates were descending on Chieftain at the rate of thirty-one knots.

As the reply tapped in from the Friendlies, Chieftain's engines juddered to life and threw Dewi away from the transmitter. He recovered and slipped back into his chair when Muldoon hurried in.

"We're going to use evasive tactics until reinforcements arrive," he said, lowering himself into a chair alongside Dewi's. "Cranshaw will save our ammunition until we are at closer range. Prepare yourself for choppy seas, Boy Wonder."

Dewi braced himself in his chair and watched the screens. The Friendlies would be visible to the naked eye by now; black specks against a rising sun.

Dewi blinked as the sun's first rays crept around the mountain and the wind sheared across the niche where he huddled. Beneath him, the frost-encrusted branches of the oaks caught the light and led it down into the valley. The sprinkling of snow clinging to Moelfre's crags was pink tinged and he could almost hear Gran say, "Red sky morning, shepherd's warning."

Across the upper slope, he knew the tracks he'd made were probably erratic—a normal footprint with a heel embedded deeper than the toe; a print of even inflexibility; and a round hole where the cane bit into the snow for balance. Dot-down-carry-one. God pays back.

When exactly had payment come? As adrenalin pumped fear and courage to a mind racing with split-second decisions and actions, in calmer times they couldn't recount the sequence of events accurately. When had Chieftain's armoured hull shattered like an eggshell, scattering shrapnel that took his leg from the knee down? Was it before his last desperate *me-de* to the Friendlies? Had his last signal been a whisper lost beneath the screams of a dying ship? Did he only imagine the foreshortened, snub-nosed grey eels speeding like shadows past the limping ship toward the enemy frigates?

Some of them survived. Cranshaw had; and Watkins, blinded by a burst of steam from a fractured valve on the engines he tended. Floating amid the Cordelia's jettisoned debris and the remnants of the valiant Chieftain, they were dragged to safety. Dewi remembered little of those hours except for one man, a shipmate with a blood-spattered face holding him to a shattered spar. "Count your blessings, Taffy."

It had taken a long time to accept the cost and count is blessings. His father forced him up here the first time, leaving him in the dray when he went in search of a strayed lamb. It was springtime and the warm winds whirled about him insistently, refusing to let him ignore them as they forced him to look outward from his bitterness.

He came again on his own. Falling, he dragged himself on his stomach across the whinberry bushes, his sobs chasing away the death coils he would have reached for as eagerly as he once gathered grass snakes to race across the pigsty wall. But he came back and came back again; cursing when the whinberries trapped the limb he could not accept as his own. "The attachment drags through the bushes like a croquet mallet," he complained to his father.

Dewi hauled himself upright into the wind and reached for the hawthorn cane. Cautiously, he retraced his steps down the upper slope to where the sea of whinberries lay blanketed beneath the snow. Behind him, the marks his cane made on the uphill journey weren't visible, only footsteps equally balanced and marching steadily ahead.

♥

SUNDAY SERMON

Saint Barnabas would be cold that morning, Reverend Davies thought, as he added a cable-knit vest to the clothes his wife had laid out.

The third Sunday of the month, the early-morning service would be conducted in English to accommodate those of his parishioners who couldn't speak Welsh. Some of his flock couldn't speak English but, occasionally, especially at harvest time, they came to the English service to free the rest of the day for the fields.

Not that Reverend Davies was supposed to know about their toil on this day of rest, but only a fool wouldn't question their reason for attending a service in a language they didn't understand. Though the words were strange to them, when he allowed his voice to thunder to the vaulted roof, rattling the stained-glass windows, they understood the sentiment. And *Amen* was the same in both languages.

And the hymn singing . . . No more than three or four voices would join the organ for the first verse but, by the time they reached the middle of the second verse, they'd forget in which language the service was conducted and the hymn would come at him in Welsh and English, with Tom Evans' Welsh tenor accompanying Miss Braithwaite's English soprano in perfect harmony.

He wondered what the singing would be like today, with half his congregation speaking neither Welsh nor English. One of the hymns he'd chosen was by a German composer. He hoped the melody would, for one brief interlude, have the prisoners believe they were in a church in their homeland.

But would they? Would the Church-of-England-in-Wales service mimic theirs in any way? And did he care if it did not? He didn't fool himself that they chose his Church above the Baptist and Methodist Chapels because of his great oratorical skill; it was simply that he was the only preacher in the five valleys who conducted a service in English. Although the Germans understood very little English, the guards told him, it was a vast improvement on their ability to understand Welsh.

Reverend Davies had agonized over his sermon for that morning. None of the themes dare touch upon areas that might antagonize the strange mixture of British and German ex-soldiers who would fill the oak pews. The Resurrection was what he finally settled on. It was an Easter sermon, unsuited to the July heat. After thirty years of ministry, he had never before prepared for Church without a thunderous ending for a sermon. That day's sermon trailed into nothingness. The story of the Resurrection was complete, but he hadn't found a parallel with which he usually ended his sermons. If all else failed, he would show Christ's ascension as a symbol of hope paralleling a hope for peace now the war was at an end. However, it lacked the personal touch he always looked for.

He had to trust in the One who guided his pen. Perhaps the blood and thunder ending was out of place this time. Perhaps the Germans would be offended by it and, not understanding the words fully, take it as an attack upon themselves. And perhaps his familiar flock would be too agitated to notice his sermon ended without the customary hell fire.

Perhaps the fault lay within him, in the barely acknowledged resentment at finding enemy soldiers taking their places in his church. If God could forgive them, so must he. He must welcome the strangers and see them only as Christians, not as Nazis.

As he descended the stairs, Margaret was ready with the starched surplice. She laid it over his arm, folding it so it wouldn't crease.

"You won't forget we're expected at Plas Gwyn for dinner?"

"I won't forget." He touched his hand to her cheek. "Will you forget to fidget?"

"Away with you!" She moved toward the dining room then paused in the doorway to watch him leave. "Is it finished?"

"And when have I ever not finished a sermon before Sunday?"

Lord, forgive me, he prayed silently as he left the Rectory, *it wasn't a real lie, was it?*

What else could he have said? If Margaret knew the ending hadn't come to him, she would spend the whole of the service sitting in the front pew shredding her handkerchief. It was a secret best kept between himself and the Lord.

Nevertheless, he would miss the hell-fire ending. From his lofty perch in the pulpit, he would lull them, his voice well-modulated, and hypnotic. Then, when Miss Braithwaite popped a mint humbug into her mouth under cover of a lace handkerchief, and Bogo Griffiths' chin sank onto his chest, mouth open preparatory to a grunting snore, Reverend Davies' voice would suddenly thunder. Miss Braithwaite would swallow the mint and Bogo Griffiths would jump to his feet, startled and unaware of where he was. Pulled back onto the pew by his wife, Eira, Bogo would stare at the vicar in wide-eyed bewilderment as the Reverend Davies slammed his fist on the pulpit and ranted. But he got their attention. They would remember the wrath of God would descend on them if they transgressed during the coming week.

There were times when Reverend Davies told the Lord he would have been well suited as an actor. That morning would prove or disprove that belief and he had better give the performance of his life. Whatever he felt in his heart, outwardly he must have all believe that from his pulpit, he saw nothing but Christians come to hear the word of God.

He must forget Dilys Ellis beating her fists against his chest while she railed against a God who took Alun from her before he'd seen his unborn child. And he must forget too that her outburst of anger brought an end to the life within her.

He must forget little Megan Williams coming shyly after Sunday school to ask if he'd speak to Jesus. "Ask Him if He's seen my daddy. He'll be wearing an R.A.F. uniform and a leather jacket."

And Dewi Thomas, the finest runner the five valleys ever produced, he must forget him just as Dewi must forget his dreams of Olympic medals as he strapped on the artificial leg he'd won.

He must forget . . . Forget the thousands of innocents fallen beneath the jackboots. Forget and see only brothers in Christ.

The church was as chilly as he had expected, rays from the barely risen sun filtering through the east windows in a myriad of red and gold lights to give the illusion of warmth. Margaret and Helen had taken special care with the flowers weighting the altar, and Reverend Davies knelt to pray wreathed in the heady fragrance of roses and wild honeysuckle.

"Lord, let me be as forgiving as You. Let me welcome these strangers among us." He prayed silently for a while longer, and then he rose and went into the vestry to mull over possible endings to his sermon.

From the top of the high stone wall marking the boundary between the churchyard and the village square, tenaciously rooted ferns shed dew onto the villagers massed beside the tall wrought-iron gates.

Eira Griffiths, shivering in the thin warmth of her Sunday best, stepped away from the wall and asked of no one in particular: "Do you think they'll come?"

"They'll come." Aled Thomas pocketed his hands and eyed the Red Lion across the square. What wouldn't he give for a tot of rum; he could taste its syrupy burning in his mouth and the warmth of it coursing through him.

Beside him, the boys scuffled over a pile of stones they'd gathered. One was his own boy, bad tempered because the war was over and he hadn't been old enough to join up.

Made a hero of his cousin, Dewi, Johnny did, marvelling over his tin leg. And he'd listen for hours to Rodney Lewis tell how he chased Germans all over France in his tank. He even made a fuss over Bethan Red Lion, just because she drove an ambulance in Swansea during the air raids.

What about the others—the real heroes—men like himself who kept the wheels oiled by producing the crops and meat that went to feed the soldiers? Where was the praise for they who had to steal from themselves to feed their families and be fined or jailed if the Government Inspector caught them? Now they were expected to feed the enemy soldiers kept in prison camps like the one at Henllan while they waited for repatriation. Better for all if they lined them up against a wall and shot them instead of bringing them into the village for a church service.

"Rat-tat-tat-tat-tat!"

The sound exploded at his side and Johnny pointed a piece of wood at the girls standing by the wall. "Line them up and shoot them down!" the boy shouted, repeating what he'd heard his father say often enough.

"Johnny!" Aled uttered a threat as Megan Williams broke away from the wall and ran shrieking for her mother's skirts.

Johnny dropped the wood and went back to the pile of stone, his face sullen.

"Hope they won't be late." Morgan Ellis ground the stub of a cigarette under his heel. "I want to cut the top field while the weather holds."

Aled nodded. "The BBC said rain tonight, so me and Johnny have to lift the hay in the bottom meadow or it's mouldy it'll be."

"They can't be much longer." Eira edged closer to Bogo, touching her arm to the warmth of his and regretting not wearing a cardigan under her linen suit.

Except for the boys adding to their pile of stones, they waited in silence, a massed defence of villagers with their eyes glued to the road to Henllan that stretched like a grey ribbon past the village hall and the newsagents and finally crept behind the wall of the woollen mill.

Then their herald hurtled out of the shadows on his bicycle. "They're coming! They're coming!" he shouted, coat flapping and one trouser turn up fighting against the cycle clip, dangerously close to the chain as the rider pedalled on.

A murmur passed through the crowd and they shifted uneasily, then they stiffened as a dark mass marched into sight.

"Jesus Christ!"
"Good God!"
"Bloody hell!"

The melding of blasphemies assailed Reverend Davies as he made his way along the path between stone angels to the gates. His ears reddened at the onslaught, and then the breath caught in his throat when he looked along the road to Henllan.

With half a dozen British troops to make sure none of them strayed from the road, three abreast the Germans came in columns of some twenty men, marching in flawless unity. Had he not been so aware of his vestments, the Reverend Davies might have added to the bleating of blasphemy rising from his flock. He shivered.

Half way along the straight stretch of road leading to the square, the Germans broke stride. And a good thing too, the vicar thought, otherwise the Bus Stop sign, bent drunkenly by revellers after the last church social, might swing around and rattle against the telephone box as it did during thunderstorms.

Reverend Davies saw Helen Williams pull Megan away from the crowd. She turned toward the road leading to her farm and the vicar stepped into her path.

"Why don't you and Megan go inside, Mrs Williams?" He held the gate open. He saw anger, pain and loneliness in her eyes, and a fleeting rebellion before she looked away. "Take your mother in, Megan. There's a good girl." He turned back to the crowd.

The village men stood shoulder to shoulder, their women cowering against their backs. To one side, Johnny bent to gather a handful of stones from the pile at his feet.

"Johnny!" The vicar voiced a low warning and the villagers jumped nervously, unaware until then that he stood behind them.

"'Morning, Vicar." Aled reddened and reached for the boy, but Johnny was running to meet the man hobbling over the humpbacked bridge.

"Time to go in, I think," Reverend Davies said quietly.

One by one, they shuffled through the gates, leaving him alone to meet the strangers.

He tucked his hands under the wide sleeves of his vestments, gripping his forearms in an effort to control his anger. What was the point of greeting the Germans? How could he tell which, if any, spoke a language he could understand? Their visit to Saint Barnabas was a waste if none of them could understand the word of God in English well enough to follow a sermon. He nodded coldly in acknowledgement of the prisoners and, as they passed, he sensed their apprehension. Outnumbered and unarmed, more than one eyed the pile of ammunition the boys gathered.

"*Bore da*, Vicar." Dewi limped closer. "Sorry I'm late."

"Take your time, Dewi." He waited until Dewi, with Johnny at his side, made his way through the gates, then he scattered the pile of stones with his foot.

He moved without haste so as not to crowd the man and boy moving slowly along the path ahead of him. Dewi was silent, but

Johnny was chattering and clamouring for the attention of his hero.

"Everybody's mad about it," Johnny was saying. "Even Mam Derw, although she never goes to church or chapel. Heathens, the Germans are, everybody's saying. Not Christians, like us."

"If they come from Germany, they're Christians," Dewi said.

"How can they be?" Johnny asked. "They don't speak Welsh or English!"

"Neither did Christ," Dewi reminded him.

Reverend Davies halted in mid stride, watched the last of his congregation enter the Church, and then turned onto the path leading to the vestry, walking slowly in deep thought. Dear God. If Your Son came among us this day, we would deny Him even as Mary denied Him in the garden of Resurrection because He would use a language other than our own. At last, he had his parallel.

Back straight, hands relaxed inside the wide sleeves of his gown, Reverend Davies walked briskly toward the vestry door, the starched surplice fluttering at his back.

♥

P L Crompton

MARI'S MONDAY

Mari's voice exploded with exasperation, "Drat!" Every Monday there was something: If it didn't rain, it blew clouds of dust onto the line of clean washing. She ran into the garden and leapt for the flapping ends of a sheet.

"Drat it all!" With wash-reddened hands, she beat at the specks of dust, smearing them across the wet linen. She'd blued the sheets and all, giving them an edge of brilliant white she could hang out with pride every Monday. Now look at them—no better than Her's down the road.

"*Ach a fi!*" Gypsy to hang such dirty clothes on the line; grey they were, no better than before she put them in water. "Cleanliness is next to Godliness," Mari's mother used to say. Well, them that hung dirty washing on the line didn't go to church of a

Sunday either, not even now when Mr Churchill said to pray for the boys not come home after the war.

Not that Mari had any sons that went as soldiers. A sad thing when the Women's Institute got together over their knitting and boasted about what their sons had done in the war. The closest Mari came to joining in was to talk of Alun, her daughter' first husband. Even then, she couldn't say much because Alun had fallen off the troopship at Swansea docks at the beginning of the war. Funny thing, Mari thought, when a man going to fight for his country was killed before he ever got to where the fighting is.

Still, it was better than Her down the road. They said her boy, Edwin, ate soap before going for his medical. Made his heart beat too fast, they said, and the doctors wouldn't let him go for a soldier. Went as a servant to Pen Farm, Edwin did, and Davy's own boy went for a sailor.

Mari unpegged the sheet from the line and was about to start on the other when she heard a truck coming down the road. More prisoners of war to put in the camp at Henllan, she guessed, there to wait for the time when the government repatriated them. Why did they have to send so many to this corner of Wales? Rigid as the pole propping up the centre of the wash line, she waited as the truck drove by.

Two rows of faces turned her way, the hunched shoulders covered in an array of uniforms, none of them the British Tommy's except for the two sitting at the back.

Mari bundled the sheet before her. She clutched the neck of her blouse tight about her throat, and then she ran back to the house. Behind her she heard their laughter. Heathens, they were, all of them. Some said they didn't have a choice; had to do what Hitler said. Well, some of them could have eaten soap like the boy of Her down the road.

Mari dumped the streaked sheet into the laundry basket at the side of the fireplace. Pouring a cup of tea, she sat at the table and dribbled milk into her cup. The sooner sugar came off rationing, the better she'd enjoy her tea.

There were Germans all over the place now. Let out of the camp they were, especially on Sundays. Came to tea with the people in the village they did. "Hmph," muttered Mari. It was nice to know some people had the rations to spare, and it was nice to know they were so forgiving.

"The war is over," Dilys was always telling her.

Well, so it might be, but there was no call to go taking enemy soldiers into your own home.

Mari finished her tea and went out to fetch the second sheet from the line. Bundling it in her arms, she walked to the gate to look out over the valley. The prisoner-of-war camp was over a mile away but from here, half way up the mountain road, she could see the fir trees flanking the Teifi that ran past the camp.

She saw the servant boy coming down the road from Pen Farm and her back stiffened. Considering a return to the house a form of defeat, she waited for him to pass by and gave her attention to the rose growing at the side of the gate. It hadn't done well for a couple of years and the next winter might see the end of it.

"Needs a good mulch and the hedge cut back. Roots are taking all the goodness from the soil, see."

Affronted, Mari looked up. How dare this son of Her down the road address Mari!

"I could come over on Saturday and do it for you, Mrs Jenkins." Edwin dropped his gaze in face of her stony stare. "Came to tell you the bull is out," he said before making his way back up the hill.

Tarw was out! Mari cast a swift glance past the house to where her back garden bordered onto Pen Farm's fields. Bellowing and running around, Tarw was a nasty old thing, especially when the children came up from the village to throw stones at it. Made a ruckus they did and they'd broken the glass on a cold frame last year when a stone aimed at Tarw came over Mari's hedge instead.

Well, the hedge was a lot taller this year but left unchecked it had grown too close to the rose. The boy could be right, Mari admitted grudgingly. Perhaps it was taking all the goodness out of the soil.

"What it mean?" a voice asked close to her ear.

Startled, Mari jumped and swung around. Her eyes widened when she saw the young man standing by the gate, pointing to the word carved into it. She answered before she could stop herself: "It means *home.*"

He was from the prisoner-of-war camp, she could tell by the uniform he wore, but he hardly looked old enough to be called a soldier.

"Home . . ." He studied the carving. "How you say?"

"*Car-tref,*" Mari said slowly. "The *f* in Welsh sounds like *v.*"

Now there's a thing, Mari thought. With washing still to do, she was standing there teaching Welsh to the first foreigner she'd ever spoken to. Of course, she'd met foreigners before, like them who came to Plas Gwyn from London every summer, and then there was Her down the road. From Cardiff way she was, like the nice man who had wanted to marry Dilys before she married Davy Thomas.

"*Car-tref* . . ." The word rolled from his tongue. "Home." He nodded to himself then eyed Mari in a way that made her nervous and caused her to clutch the bundled sheet tighter.

Mari judged the distance between the gate and the house, wondering if her game ankle would allow her to cover it fast enough for her to slam herself inside before he caught her. He reached toward her and Mari froze.

"My *mutter* . . . She have this . . ." He touched the brooch at Mari's throat. "I show."

He reached inside his jacket and Mari cringed against the rose, her feet rooted to the spot. He could have a gun or a knife ready to kill her, and there she was, no more able to move than the telegraph pole across the road.

"See?" He held out a tattered photograph.

Better to humour him, Mari thought, and took the photograph. The woman was grey haired like Mari, and the house at her back was white washed like Mari's but with an ivy growing from beside the door to fan out around the windows like the tines of a fork. "Nice." She handed the photograph back and managed a strained smile.

"I not know . . ." He glanced from the photograph to the house, no doubt seeing the similarity, Mari supposed, and she was surprised to see tears in his eyes. "I from Berlin . . ." He shrugged. "I not know if home—"

They'd flattened Berlin, the droning bombers converging on Hitler's city like flies to a cowpat. Flattened this man's home, perhaps. Well, it was their own fault; they started the war after all.

Mari backed away from the gate, her eyes on the man, watching his every move. He looked sad, as though her reluctance to talk saddened him. He doffed the peaked cap and mumbled something Mari didn't understand before he continued along the road to Pen Farm.

Mari ran to the house and locked herself in. "Oh, dear! Oh, dear me!" She dumped the sheets in the basket and poured a cup of cold tea with a trembling hand. What was the world coming to that German soldiers could walk up to her gate in broad daylight!

The cup had been empty in her hand for some time before a commotion at the gate drew Mari's attention. She ran to the window and saw the servant boy helping the German soldier up the path. She went to the door, intending to tell them to leave.

"Where are you going?" she demanded; her attempt to block their entry as futile as her earlier battle against the dust cloud.

"Tarw got him when he was crossing the pasture." The servant boy—the son of Her down the road—laid the German on the rug before the empty fireplace. "He's hurt bad."

"Then take him to a doctor. Why bring him here?" she asked. The soldier was bleeding heavily and now looked unconscious.

"He kept saying *Cartref*." The boy loosened the soldier's collar. "I thought you knew him."

"Hmph!" Know a German soldier, indeed!

"Mrs Jenkins?"

Mari saw Davy Thomas in the doorway. Her mouth fell open. Never, not since the night he'd come to tell her he was marrying Dilys and she screamed at him, had Davy set foot in her house. "Come in," she said coldly.

Davy crossed to where the servant boy knelt beside the soldier. "How bad is he hurt, Edwin?"

"Very bad. I'd better go for the doctor." Edwin started to rise.

"I'll go." Davy placed a restraining hand on Edwin's shoulder. "I can go faster." Davy left in a hurry, ignoring Mari.

Wasn't right. Davy shouldn't be running around while this young strip sat in the comfort of her kitchen. She pursed her lips, ready to give him a comeuppance, and saw him take a bottle of pills from his pocket and put one under his tongue.

"What's that you're eating?" she demanded to know.

Edwin drew his attention from the soldier and looked at her with a question in his eyes.

"Them pills." Mari pointed to the bottle in his hand.

"For this." He thumped his chest and put the bottle back in his pocket.

So the boy had a bad heart after all. Mari moved closer. "Will he live?" She inclined her head at the man who was fast turning her multi-coloured rug into an all over shade of red.

The boy shrugged. "Tarw doesn't let up once he's got his horns into a man. Don't know what the German was doing in the field; can't have understood the signs. Gored him twice before I got to them."

"You stopped Tarw?" Mari looked at the boy with new respect.

"Knows me, does Tarw. When it's windy like today he takes to being frisky, but he's gentle as a lamb really."

"Hmph!" Mari commented. "Can't we do something to help this man until the doctor comes?"

"If we could stop the bleeding . . ."

"We'd have to cut his jacket . . ."

"It's all ripped by Tarw anyway." The boy glanced up at her. "I'll do it if you give me some scissors."

Mari fetched her sewing basket from the parlour and handed him the scissors. He was gentle even though the soldier was past feeling any pain for the moment, but he couldn't wield the scissors very well. Awkwardly, Mari dropped to her knees and took the scissors.

Now there's a thing, Mari thought in wonder. Her and the boy of Her down the road, kneeling on the rag rug either side of German soldier cutting his uniform to bits. "Well! Well!" said Mari in astonishment.

With the jacket cut away, they could see where Tarw's horns had pierced the man's shoulder and arm. "Lucky it wasn't a bit lower or he'd have gored him in the heart," said

Mari, forgetting that a few minutes earlier she'd wished death to all German soldiers.

"If we had something to pack in the wounds . . ." The boy cast about and saw the dust-streaked sheet lying on top of the basket. He reached for it.

"No!" Mari spoke sharply and a hard look entered the boy's eyes. "That one's dirty," she explained. "I'll get a clean one."

Mari ran up the stairs to the airing cupboard and took out the nearest sheet. Back in the kitchen, she saw the boy had wadded his grey handkerchief into one of the wounds. She knelt beside the soldier and took the handkerchief away, throwing it in the laundry basket. Snipping an edge of the clean sheet with the scissors, she was half way through tearing off a strip when she realized it was her best linen. "Drat!" She stopped mid strip.

"Let me do it." Edwin took the sheet from her and Mari sat on her heels watching the son of Her down the road shredding Mari's best linen. She sighed and helped him pack the strips against the soldier's wounds.

Mari was beside herself. She'd never had so many people in her kitchen all at one time since Tom died.

Such a commotion! The doctor pushing Edwin to one side as he knelt next to the soldier, and then two orderlies from the camp moving the man from the rug onto the stretcher. Lost a lot of blood, the doctor said, but he'll be as good as new in a few weeks.

The soldier came to when they carried him from the house. He smiled shakily at Mari and reached for her hand. "*Car-tref,*" he said in his funny accent.

Surprised at herself, Mari felt tears in her eyes. Looked a bit like Tom when she'd first met him, he did. Tom had fair hair and blue eyes, too. She nodded and squeezed his hand as she returned his smile. "When you're better, you'll have to come to tea on Sundays."

Mari followed the stretcher to the door and watched them down the path before she went to look at the rug. There were too many memories sewn up in it to just throw it away. In one corner was a strip of pink ribbon taken from the box of chocolates Tom gave her when Dilys was born, and next to it was a splash of green from the crepe-de-chine dress Dilys once had. In the other corner was what was left of Mari's last pair of silk stockings bought before the Depression. Her life was in the rug, but half of it was now soaked in a German soldier's blood.

"There's a terrible mess here, Mrs Jenkins." Edwin was gathering the blood-soaked strips that had been her best sheet. "What shall I do with this?"

Mari sank to her knees. Suddenly she felt very tired. "I don't know . . ." She heard her voice crack, then tears filled her eyes. She dashed them away with an angry hand and smiled at the boy. "Don't worry, Edwin," she said. "It will come out in the wash. Everything comes out in the wash.

♥

A SMALL SACRIFICE

Sleep eluded Helen. Careful not to wake Megan, she gave up her search for oblivion and went downstairs to make a pot of tea. The clock on the mantelpiece chimed the hour as she poured boiling water into the teapot, and the last clap of thunder came from farther south beyond Moelfre.

Helen went to the foot of the stairs and listened. Megan was terrified of thunder. She woke screaming at midnight and Helen had gone to her, squeezing into the single bed with her daughter. The storm was moving away and the thunder was too distant to wake the child.

Helen took her cup to the window to watch the rain. For three days, it rained and thundered with the children in her class huddled nervously in the middle of the room. All except Johnny Thomas. He'd laughed at the others. Standing in the window to watch the lightning, of the thunderclaps he said: "It's only God throwing boxes down the stairs."

The other children laughed hysterically, breaking the tension, and Helen faced the blackboard to hide her smile, unable to reprimand Johnny.

The storm brought down the power and telephone lines, leaving the valley cut off from the outside world. Even the GPO van couldn't get through with the post. Some buses were able to make it, but even they were off schedule and unreliable as bridges gave way to the onrush of water.

The farmyard was awash, a mud trap stretching to the solitary oak towering over the gate, an offering to the gods.

Mam Derw told her that. "You take note," said the old crone. "All the houses hereabouts have trees grown taller than the houses, and in the fields where the cows and sheep graze you'll find a tree standing on its own. Our offering to the gods so they'll leave our homes and animals alone."

Their oak had survived yet again, an offering denied. A sacrifice not asked of her.

At two, the rain stopped and the clouds cleared. A bright moon emerged, reflecting soft light on the glistening landscape. It was as though the storms were sent to wash the land clean of war. Helen shook her head as if to clear her mind of the fanciful thought and decided a lack of sleep made her light headed.

She turned back to the room. It was chilly and the air held a dampness that clung like a white bloom to everything. She lit the lamps then cleaned the cold ashes from the grate and lit the fire. All hope of sleep gone, in her nightdress she brought out the cloths and the tin of Mansion Rose Polish. Systematically, she set about polishing the furniture and the linoleum surrounding the square of carpet.

At four, she brewed a fresh pot of tea and sank into the rocking chair to drink it. The rose bouquet of the room enfolded her, reminding her of the pink rambler cascading over the wall inside the gate. It had budded early. If enough buds survived the storm, she'd fill the room with them as soon as it was light enough to go outside.

Sipping her tea, she went through the agenda for that day.

It was to be a victory celebration, the first carnival since before the war. There was little for her to do except line up the children for the fancy-dress parade. Bronwen had seen to the choirs; Bette and Dilys organized the food; and Tom Evans choreographed the dancing that reminded Helen of the Morris dancing she'd seen on a visit to Cornwall. The vicar was running the Bran Tub; Elias Stock would man the lemonade stall; and Joroway would help Davy Thomas with the pony rides. She forgot who was running the Coconut Shy and the Darts Booth.

There had been talk of postponing the carnival because of the storms that rolled in from the coast one after the other, but Mam Derw promised them good weather and the plans went ahead. Perhaps the old witch was right because from her window she could see the first rays of dawn outlining the hills to the east.

She attended the planning meetings with little heart, feeling no reason to celebrate but owing it to Megan to make the day a festival she would remember. It was Megan's first carnival; her first chance to dress in the national costume Bette unearthed from her attic. Helen smiled. Megan thought the tall-crowned hat a witch's hat until Bette showed her pictures of women wearing them.

Helen wouldn't bother going if it weren't for Megan. Without William, there was nothing to celebrate. *Missing in action* . . . The words still cut her like a whip.

"There's always hope," Dilys told her.

But how could she hope? Nearly six hundred bombers were lost during the night raids on Hamburg, that much she had gleaned since the day when Dilys brought her the telegram.

"But you don't know his bomber went on those raids," Dilys pointed out.

"I know," Helen said. "I know . . ."

By the time Megan rose for breakfast, Helen had black-leaded the grate and polished the fender with Brasso. Cooling on the table was a fresh batch of Welsh cakes made with the last of the hoarded sugar and the currants she and Megan picked and dried the year before.

"Are we having visitors, Mam?" Megan asked, eyeing the cakes and the bowl of roses on the piano next to her father's photograph.

"No," Helen answered. Until then, she hadn't questioned her need to have the house shine. She had done the same thing before Megan was born, spending the night making the house a shining welcome for the newest member of the family. Who was she preparing to welcome now? "People might drop in on their way to the carnival," she said, as much in explanation to herself as to Megan.

"Can we go up Moelfre this morning?" Megan asked as they washed the breakfast dishes. "I want to see Big Bertha before they take her away."

"It," corrected Helen. "Big Bertha is a gun. But they won't be taking her—it—away just yet."

"But they might. They were talking about it at school yesterday. Everybody else has seen her, but I haven't."

"We can go another day," Helen suggested. It was years since she'd climbed Moelfre and the place brought back memories to make her heart ache.

315

The mountain was the first place William showed her when she came to visit the village before they were married. They got off the bus close to Moelfre because it was quicker to walk into the village along the Penboyr road than to sit on the bus that waited half an hour at the edge of the moors for the connecting bus from New Quay.

She'd worn high heels, anxious to impress her future in-laws, and the walk down the hill had been murder on shoes and ankles. She walked barefoot for some of the way, and William carried her over the roughest parts, laughing at the picture they made.

"I've heard of carrying a bride over the threshold," he said, "but this is ridiculous."

They climbed Moelfre the day before he went away, trudging through the mud so he could carry away one last memory of his valley. Perhaps he knew it would be the last time he'd see it.

It was all very well for people to tell her they hadn't confirmed his death; that he was only missing in action. In her heart, she knew she'd never see William again. But her mind kept throwing up memories to generate hope and confusion.

Mam Derw had questioned her, hobbling into the house with a pack of Tarot cards to spread across Helen's table. "The cards don't say he's dead, girlie."

The word *girlie* goaded Helen into saying what she thought of what William called

Mam Derw's mumbo jumbo. "I know he's dead! Before that day when the telegram came, I knew he was alive. But that morning, and after that . . ." No, she couldn't elaborate on the feeling, not even to herself, except to say in some way there was an empty place in her being that had always been William.

"Heard of this before, I have," Mam Derw said. "When there's a loss of memory, the link between people is lost. That's why you think he's dead. But I'm telling you William is alive. Now, you've got a nice little nanny out there. Partial to a drop of goat's milk, I am."

Witch woman; seeking to tell her what she thought Helen wanted to hear, and all for a bottle of milk. But she triggered a hope quickly dashed after a day spent in the public library at Carmarthen researching psychic phenomena. There was nothing written to confirm what Mam Derw reputedly heard.

"We could take some of the cakes with us and cat them up there," Megan said, breaking across Helen's thoughts.

"We'd have to take sandwiches—" Too late, Helen realized she'd spoken in a way that allowed Megan an opening for persuasion. "It's impossible, Megan. We have to be in the village by one-thirty for the parade."

"It isn't far if we walk down past Penboyr."

Where William carried her that first day. "We still have jobs to do around here."

"No, we haven't. I heard you outside earlier, feeding the chickens and gathering the eggs." The tone of Megan's voice changed. "Please, Mam?" she wheedled. "We can leave right away and have a picnic."

Helen sighed. Since William left, it was getting harder and harder to say no to Megan. "All right. But you'd better stay out of the mud."

Megan helped pack the basket, an over-abundance of Welsh cakes leaving little room for the sandwiches and the bottle of raspberry-leaf tea.

"Not so many cakes, Megan," Helen said quietly. "You know I won't eat the ones with currants in, only your fa—" She passed her two of the cakes rolled out and cut from a separate and plain batch of dough. She'd never liked currants, but on the first visit to William's parents, Bette proudly set a platter of Welsh cakes stuffed with currants on the table. Surreptitiously, Helen picked out the currants and put them in her pocket where William found them later.

Helen smiled when she thought of the elderly woman sitting across from them in the train compartment on the journey back to Cardiff. What had she thought when William kept digging his hand into Helen's pocket to retrieve a currant? A treasured moment to share with Megan when she was older; a way of showing her who her father had been. But there was no way of sharing with William the joy of watching Megan grow; of telling him Megan's reaction to the newspaper headline: D-day Landings at Normandy. "Mam! Mam!" she'd cried. "The man who wrote this had a stutter."

"I'll take some extra cakes for Granda Jo." Megan piled more cakes on top of the sandwiches.

"We're not going through the village so we won't see Granda Jo."

Granda Jo. How delighted Joroway had been when Megan first called him that. Rowlie was put out at first, unhappy to be sharing his only grandchild with an odd-job man, but Joroway was more than an odd-job man who came to take care of the heavier work around the small farm; he had become one of Helen's family, filling in for the grandparents Megan hadn't seen since the beginning of the war. Helen had thought about taking Megan to Cardiff to see them, but travel was restricted and she could not risk taking her into a city threatened by bombings. Perhaps now the war was over, they would go. First for a visit, and then—

Could she leave the valley? It was odd how she had come into her own in the years William was away. Before, she had been William's wife or Bette and Rowlie's daughter-in-law. Now she was Helen-the-School, moving from her nondescript wifely niche into a person in her own right. "Helen-the-School will help you write that letter to the Council."

"Helen-the-School will tell you if the bank is charging too much interest." "Helen-the-School will know about this, about that." "Ask Helen-the-School." And ask her they did, about everything from train timetables to politics. They demanded her presence at the Women's Institute meetings; appointed her liaison for the evacuees in the district; and she helped the vicar's wife with the flower arrangements at Saint Barnabas. Little by little, no doubt with the intent of keeping her occupied so she didn't dwell on William's loss, they embroiled her in the village's activities. It would be hard to move away; to go back to where she grew up; to where she wasn't Helen-the-School.

They left soon after ten with Megan dressed in national costume, her red cloak a bright splash against greenery dark and dripping after the rain. Helen watched her pick her way across the muddy yard in her black patent shoes. Rowlie had cut buckles from cardboard, painted them silver, and Helen had tied them to the straps of Megan's shoes. She thought about calling her back and making her wear her Wellingtons because the buckles were bound to be damaged on the trek to Moelfre, then she decided against it. The buckles were only make-believe, like the victory celebration and people pretending everything was right with the world.

Helen pulled the door to behind her. She never locked it now, day or night, in case William came home. "You're an inconsistent fool, Helen Williams!" she told herself as she crossed the yard. "You know William isn't coming back."

Megan was waiting on the rough road barely more than a cart track. "Look," she said as Helen made her way around a pool of water by the gate. "See what the storm did to our tree."

Trailing across the road, one end still attached to the trunk by a fold of bark, a branch lay bedraggled in the mud. Helen picked her way to it then grabbed a handful of thin branches and dragged the whole parallel with the hedge.

Her sacrifice. Her small sacrifice. Couldn't the thunder god have taken the whole tree and given back William? Suddenly angry, she took the basket from Megan. "Come on!"

An hour later, while they struggled up the hill, Helen regretted having given in to Megan. The going had been slow on the rough road, but once they left it to cut through the forest, it became almost impossible. Slipping and sliding on the path, they took to the storm-lashed way between the trees, trampling the drooping carpet of bluebells beneath branches dripping yesterday's raindrops on their heads.

It was her fault. It was her decision to go that way even though it wasn't much shorter than going through the village. But she had wanted to avoid the village and those who would question her sanity for going up to the mountain so soon after it had rained.

Climbing Moelfre was something Helen had never shared with Megan. Always, it was with William. They'd brought Megan once, soon after she was born, and William held the babe up so she could see the valley stretched beneath them.

"In the old days," William said, "according to Mam Derw, they used to worship Moelfre. They'd bring their new-borns up here to show the mountain."

And some new-borns were sacrificed to the mountain. Helen shivered.

Her arms filled with bluebells, Megan dropped onto one of the rocks that grew among the flowers. "Can we have our picnic here, Mam? I'm hungry."

"It's too cold here in the shade. Let's wait until we get farther up." Farther up, beyond where the whinberry bushes carpeted the lower slopes and hid those long-ago sacrifices. The berries would still be flowers, but by August, women and children would fill the slopes, scrambling around with stained fingers and pails of berries. They'd be singing and calling to one another, the vibrations chasing away any vipers coiled beneath the ground-hugging branches. The villagers were never bitten, only the visitors attracted by the blue abundance, picking in greedy silence, believing the naturalists who wrote that poisonous snakes were extinct in Britain.

"It's Moelfre," said Mam Derw when a viper bit a tourist. "Claiming his sacrifices, he is."

"I'm tired," Megan said when they emerged from the trees into full sunlight. "Can we take the bus back?"

Helen checked her watch. "We can catch the twelve-fifteen if it's on time. If it comes. And if we hurry our picnic."

"Let's eat by Big Bertha." Megan started to run ahead. "Come on, Mam, I'll race you."

"Wait! The buckles! You'll ruin them." Not that Helen cared, but Rowlie would be disappointed if they were spoilt after the time he'd spent making them. Helen reached for Megan's hand and they moved cautiously through the whinberries. It was too early for snakes, but the ground beneath the bushes was wet and slippery. Higher up, the land was already dry; the windblown grass as parched looking as if it never rained. Megan freed herself and ran ahead to the ledge where Big Bertha rested.

When Helen reached her, Megan was lifting the camouflage net to peer at the dull metal of the cannon. "When are they going to fire it?"

They had fired it for war; now they would fire it for peace. "At one-thirty," Helen answered. "The gunners will be up soon to get it ready."

"Can we stay to watch?"

"Not if we're to get back in time for the parade." Helen lowered herself onto a boulder and took the food and bottle of tea from the basket.

Megan took her sandwich and explored the gun. "It's beautiful, isn't it, Mam?"

"No gun is beautiful." Certainly not a gun like the one that might have shot down the bomber carrying William. As Megan pestered her with questions, Tom Evans and Bogo Griffiths emerged from the Penboyr road. Relieved, Helen said: "They'll be able to answer you."

"What're you doing up here then, Mrs Williams?" Tom unpacked the firing mechanism he'd removed for safety.

"Megan wanted to see Big Bertha before they took it away."

As Megan dragged Tom and Bogo to the gun, firing question after question at them, Helen packed the basket, laying the bunch of bluebells on top. She moved to a boulder farther down the slope.

The one time they fired the gun was clear in her mind, and she wondered if somewhere in Germany another woman believed her husband was missing in action.

At her feet, a black beetle scrabbled toward the bunch of bluebells and a white butterfly settled on a stalk of grass as brown and dried as a reed. Farther down the slope, a bee buzzed around the whinberry flowers, and before her the valley spread fresh-washed in the sun. Here and there, the hills were dotted with cattle and sheep. The pastoral scene that might have come from Constable's brush, calm and peaceful, no wonder William came here whenever he could. "The mountain heals," he always said, but she hadn't known what he meant until then. She felt drowsy, soul and body at peace.

"Mam! Look!" Megan's excited cries brought Helen out of her trance. "Mr Evans says it's the Gypsies."

"That's a sight, isn't it, Mrs Williams." Bogo called down to her. "With them coming into the valley again, things are getting back to normal, aren't they?"

"I'm going down to see them." Megan was off down the slope.

"Wait!" Helen picked up the basket and scrambled after her. "Be careful of the buckles on your shoes!"

When they reached the road, Helen saw one of the buckles had worked loose. She knelt to tie it back on while Megan watched the caravans come closer.

"There's a baby, Mam. Look at the baby." Megan took some of the bluebells and ran with them to the lead caravan. She reached up and gave them to the woman holding the baby. "What's the baby's name?" she asked, walking alongside the caravan.

"Seth," the woman answered. "Named for his father."

"Megan!" Helen pulled her away. "Be careful or you'll be under the wheels."

"Gift to a Romany brings good luck, lady." The woman smiled.

Helen drew Megan to one side, away from the horses and the wheels, and with Tom and Bogo they watched the caravans roll by. White for the most part, they painted the eaves, doors and window shutters gaily in yellows, reds and greens. Alien to the valley, yet not alien, only different.

"There's the twelve-fifteen bus," Bogo said.

Over the top of the hedge, the red roof of the Western Welsh bus glinting in the sun as it sped on down the main road. "Damn!"

Megan's eyes grow round and she clamped a hand to her mouth. Behind her, Tom and Bogo were chuckling. By nightfall, it would be all around the village that Helen-the-School said a swear word. The vicar was sure to mention it. No, not Reverend Davies, he was too broad-minded, it would be prim-lipped Julius Beckingham.

"Didn't know you wanted to catch the bus, Mrs Williams," said Tom.

"It doesn't matter," Helen said. "We can take the Penboyr road."

"If you get to Pen Farm on time, Davy and Dilys will give you a ride down," Bogo suggested. "They might even let Megan ride one of the ponies they're taking down for the carnival."

Megan jumped up and down with excitement. "Yes! I want to ride a pony! Come on, Mam, we'll have to run." She caught Helen's hand and started pulling her toward the Penboyr road. Then she halted and stared toward the main road. "Who's that, Mam?"

Helen looked to where Megan was pointing. The breath caught in her throat. A kitbag thrown casually over his shoulder, he was thinner, but the rugger-player's stride was unmistakable.

"William!"

♥

EPILOGUE

Once there was a war, but cradled in Moelfre's arms the valley looks untouched.

Here and there, reminders stand in mute evidence like the memorial erected in the square for those from the five valleys who will not be coming home. A miniature church steeple—a finger raised in warning.

As with the things left by the Romans, the valley is assimilating what it inherited. The long arms of Moelfre extend to encompass the prisoner-of-war camp turned into a Secondary Modern School. And high on the mountain, the ammunitions storehouse, without a door after the Gypsies chopped it for firewood, is named Mabel House after Davy-Pen-Farm's prize ewe decided it made an ideal place to have her lambs. Some say Mabel feels at home there because she spent the first three months of her life in a crypt. And on hot summer days, the concrete slab where Big Bertha once rested is home to the non-existent poisonous pit vipers.

Although it is overgrown with ivy so that it blends into the hedgerow, there is talk of pulling down the pillbox at the crossroads beside the Vicarage, to the dismay of courting couples. Bogo is relieved because he is afraid to pass it at night after Mam Derw said the ghost of Bogo's granny was dallying there with the ghost of the German soldier he shot down. They're said to be plotting ways to avenge themselves on him.

Cambrian Mill went electric. Selling their tapestries to make coats, they are now. High fashion, Bethan says it is.

It is doubtful the valley will ever be able to cut itself off from the rest of the world again. The world has touched people in ways they never expected. Some have left to run the race while others brought the race to the valley. Exposed to a world they can no longer ignore, it sets fear in some hearts—a feeling that doom lays on the other side of Moelfre. They watch, reading of events outside their tiny realm and grow ever fearful, and if a murder takes place fifty miles away, they tell each other with foreboding that it's getting nearer, as though murder were a disease that could infect the valley.

Exposure to the outside world has brought the greatest change in the people. In a valley insular for generations, a broadening of the horizons has weakened the old superstitions and prejudices—the old beliefs and old fears. The younger generations will have bigger fears to contend with than Mam Derw.

Yes, the valley looks much the same. It will endure, rooted in a tradition that adapts, assimilates, and accepts—if only after a stubborn digging in of heels—and if the voice rising from the morning mist does not sing the song of a druid, the valley still sings.

One thing that has not changed is the way the newest generation carries the old names, and the search for tags to add on the end is still a rewarding past time.

Also by P L Crompton:

The Last Druid

In Roman-occupied Cambria, a powerful druid does all he can to undermine Roman authority and influence the future.

He claims a young girl as novice because she has the Sight, but her sight opens into the past and she wonders how she can be of help to him. When the answer comes, it is not what she expected.

The Agency

In 2033, governments worldwide are bankrupt. There is no unemployment insurance, no social services or welfare, no pensions, and no health care subsidy. Unemployment sits at close to 60 percent and those with jobs are the new elite.

Sheila Davenport owns a successful employment agency. When other agencies begin to go out of business, she attributes it to their inability to compete. Then she hears a hellish rumour: Sign with Davenport; they'll find you a job even if they have to kill someone.

Other agency owners are murdered and the Davenport Agency comes under police scrutiny. Sheila investigates and uncovers a sinister plot.

Coming soon:

Witch Bay

Police informer, Bethan Davies, leaves London to claim a guesthouse inherited in a sleepy Welsh village. She learns her aunt was murdered, and sets out to find the killer.

The Wizard of Dyfed

A sequel to The Last Druid

The early life of Merlin.

Scarborough Fair

Liz Reid is looking for love in the wrong century.

Disenchanted with the men she meets, Liz discovers a way back to a gentler time, she thinks. She's mistaken for Elizabeth, daughter of a wealthy shipbuilder and meets the man of her dreams. But reality in both time periods forces some unpleasant truths at her. In the past, she is property and the man of her dreams considered unsuitable. In the present, using the time portal risks death or entrapment if it fails, and the more she uses it, the likelier it is to fail.

Worse: somebody else knows about the portal and is stalking Liz on both sides. One woman has already died...